SACRED RAGE

Also by the author:

NOVELS

The Shadow Boxer (2000)
Afterlands (2005)
Every Lost Country (2010)
The Nightingale Won't Let You Sleep (2017)

SHORT STORIES

Flight Paths of the Emperor (1992)
On earth as it is (1995)
The Dead Are More Visible (2012)
Instructions for the Drowning (2023)

POETRY

Stalin's Carnival (1989)
Foreign Ghosts (1989)
The Ecstasy of Skeptics (1994)
The Address Book (2004)
Patient Frame (2010)
The Waking Comes Late (2016)
Selected Poems: 1983–2020 (2021)

NONFICTION

The Admen Move on Lhasa:
Writing & Culture in a Virtual World (1997)
Workbook (2011)
Reaching Mithymna (2020)
The Virtues of Disillusionment (2020)
Songbook: The Lyrics and Music of Steven Heighton (2024)

CHILDREN'S BOOKS

The Stray and the Strangers (2020)

SACRED RAGE

Selected Stories

STEVEN HEIGHTON

A John Metcalf Book

Biblioasis
Windsor, Ontario

FIRST EDITION
10 9 8 7 6 5 4 3 2 1

Library and Archives Canada Cataloguing in Publication
Title: Sacred rage : selected stories / Steven Heighton ; introduction by John Metcalf.
Names: Heighton, Steven, 1961–2022, author | Metcalf, John, 1938– writer of introduction
Description: "A John Metcalf book."
Identifiers: Canadiana (print) 2025018902X | Canadiana (ebook) 20250189046
ISBN 9781771966498 (softcover) | ISBN 9781771966504 (EPUB)
Subjects: LCGFT: Short stories.
Classification: LCC PS8565.E451 S33 2025 | DDC C813/.54—dc23

Edited by John Metcalf and Ginger Pharand
Copyedited by John Sweet
Text and cover designed by Ingrid Paulson

Canada Council for the Arts Conseil des Arts du Canada

Biblioasis acknowledges the support of the Canada Council for the Arts and funding support from the Ontario Arts Council and the Government of Ontario, including through the Ontario Book Publishing Tax Credit and Ontario Creates.

PRINTED AND BOUND IN CANADA

Contents

INTRODUCTION

The Age of Clowns

THE INDEPENDENT on Sunday (UK) reviewed *The Shadow Boxer* (2000) enthusiastically:

> Steven Heighton's first novel comes out of its corner with both fists swinging... Essentially the story of one man's troubled love affair with literature, *The Shadow Boxer* fizzes with life and energy, its prose a heated mix of lyricism and muscularity. A bravura performance... a post-beat *Bildungsroman* of the sort that isn't written anymore... its adhesion to the old vanities of authenticity and the primacy of experience [make it] nothing less than a full-blooded argument with postmodern trickery. Intense and poetic... has a swaggering, larger-than-life quality.

We may reasonably suspect that some aspects of the novel's principal character, Sevigne Torrins, also represent some aspect of the young Heighton.

Here is the novel's opening sentence:

> At twenty-four, soon after his father's death, Sevigne Torrins went down from the Soo to the city to make it, to make himself a writer, swagger, shine and recite on the ivory stages, find love—all the old dreams.

There, then, is Sevigne the romantic, about to make his entrance, to strut and fret his hour upon the stage.

Before considering Heighton's stories, it will be useful to consider his way of looking at the world and learning something about how he felt about what he was seeing, not through the words of a fictional character but in his own words in his essays and opinion pieces, because those thoughts and feelings are the ground, the bedrock of the stories.

If I had to characterize the dominant tone of his stories, my immediate thought would be: *elegy*. Immediately followed by *requiem,* the musical setting for the Catholic mass for the repose of the souls of the dead.

In a collection of interviews called *Writers Talking,* (John Metcalf and Claire Wilkshire, eds., 2003), Heighton had this to say about the younger Heighton:

> In the early eighties, cultural theorists were not yet talking much about capitalism's increasingly successful co-opting and merchandising of dissent—or of dissent's outwards signs, styles, gestures and lingo. But it was happening. Being an outsider became a "lifestyle choice." Not that there weren't (and aren't) genuine outsiders; it's just that they don't often dress the part. But I was naive enough then to believe in any façade that was enviably attractive and energetically maintained. At university in fact, we were almost all

middle-class kids playing at Rimbaud or Corso or Genet—or in my own case, at something else. Yet almost by accident my shadow boxing with phantom opponents led me into the ring with what I now see as the real enemy of artists: a culture that impersonally pressures everyone to be hip, to be cool, hyper-ironic, self-conscious, plugged in and eternally collegiate, whether in dress or in attitude, speech or range of pop-cultural reference, grasp of the latest technologies, latest buzzwords and styles. In other words: to conform, though in the guise of stylish rebellion.

At the turn of the millennium being a true rebel means being, by postmodern standards, unabashedly uncool—an aesthete, devoted to the old pursuit of truth and beauty in artistic form.

In a rather condescending and faintly hostile "Profile" of Heighton in *Books in Canada* (Vol. XXIV, No. 4, 1995) David Homel wrote:

> Issues of judgement always arise when Heighton talks about writing...Judgement in the Heighton universe is a form of intelligence applied to the world, the act of taking a personal stand, without which there is no art of any kind.
>
> ...The sin of postmodern writing is the sin of hyper-cerebralism, according to Heighton; the tongue may be involved, but not the rest of the body. In life, the result is the separation of the body and the emotions. In literature, it has produced the reigning school of brittle, self-conscious, smart-alec narrators who fill the pages of much current Canadian fiction.
>
> ...Although he's thought of as an "up-and-coming" fiction writer and poet at the age of 33, Heighton has chosen a pretty unpopular path for himself. To make matters worse, he's not afraid to use the M-word. "M" as in moral...

The tone of the "Profile" consistently registers as faintly negative. Since his travels in Asian countries and Australia, Heighton has

> happily come to rest in Kingston, and the place plays an important role in his new collection of stories, *On earth as it is* (believers will recognize the line from the Lord's Prayer, [Matthew 6: 9–13]). Some of the new stories make use of the loneliness of Canadian Shield country, which is as good a place to be a moralist as anywhere else…
>
> To hear Heighton tell it, Kingston is a good place to write because of the surrounding landscape's resistance to human incursions. "By now it's a cliché, I suppose, to say that we do not belong on the land—but it's true! I like the Shield landscape but it scares me; it's so inhospitable, so incurious. I think there's that sense of lostness and not belonging in a story like 'Townsmen' ['Townsmen of a Stiller Town']."

Homel continues:

> The manic humour of this story is a welcome new direction for Heighton, who has a tendency to wax high-lyrical—"my gushiness," he calls it.
>
> "It's true I have a bardic streak, like Walt Whitman or Dylan Thomas," he says. "But since I'm not a genius like they were, I can't get away with it—and even they don't sometimes. So, draft after draft, I have to keep reining myself in. That's where I depend on John Metcalf, my editor. He helps me put the brakes on."

Of which, more later.

In his essay "The Age of Clowns" in his essay collection *The Admen Move on Lhasa* (1997), Heighton builds his argument on the basis of Oswald Spengler's *The Decline of the West.*

Spengler argued that the basic biological pattern—of birth, flowering, and maturity followed by a slow decline into rigidity and death—can be applied to anything that exists in time: a human life, of course, but also the life of a solar system or a planet, a love affair, a career, a five-year sitcom or a Thousand-Year Reich, a revolution or a poker party.

Spengler applied his model primarily to civilizations, and especially the civilization of the West, but he never spoke of an "Age of Clowns"; he wasn't living in the heart of one. It seems to me—as the product and student of such an age—that the lives of civilizations and persons alike pass through a cycle involving an Unconscious Age (or "Age of Heroes," to use Spengler's term), an Age of Integration, an Age of Disintegration, and an Age of Clowns. In individual terms the roughly corresponding terms would be childhood/youth, maturity, old age, then senility and death. In historical terms the Bronze Age and the Dark Ages are Unconscious or "Heroic" times—the ones we glimpse in Homer and Herodotus, in the Old Testament, in *The Battle of Maldon* and *Beowulf.* If the Book of Genesis declares that "There were giants in the earth in those days," the other authors, each in a different manner, are saying the same thing. And though we only glimpse such epochs in a dauntingly mediated way, and we can't help sensing how the dust of time and the will to nostalgia have blurred and elongated the inhabitants into giants roaming the Sinai or contesting "the plains of windy Troy," we still get the impression of a radically foreign sensibility, a deeply different people. Unconscious or at least un*self*conscious, in a way we can hardly conceive. Not giants, but people of an inflated sense of honour, an aggressive ardency, almost unthinkable courage, and a marked lack of irony. This is an age where people live, like children or fervent youths, viscerally—a useful mode when it comes to romance, war, and the writing of unselfconscious bardic poems, but one which also dictates that people's lives are brutal, humourless, Spartan and autocratic. Intensely felt, but nasty and short.

The Age of Integration, in the Classical world, sees the flourishing of Periclean Athens and later, of Augustan Rome. Now irony and a civilized sense of proportion have taken the blade-edge off the Unconscious Age and its savagery, but the irony is still fresh, humane, far from reaching the nihilistic, devitalizing pitch it will finally rise to. This is a time when—as Eliot claimed of a later Age of Integration, in Renaissance Europe—no "dissociation of sensibility" has set in, and people can still "think their feelings and feel their thought." This is a time when art flourishes, and not just for the benefit of an educated elite; Shelley's later boast that poets are "the unacknowledged legislators of the world" did not fully fit the situation in his time, and does not fit ours at all, but embodies a nostalgia for Classical and Renaissance Ages of Integration when poets were still socially important, when the aesthetic was not yet split off from the ethical, the poetic from the political.

An Age of Disintegration gradually sets in. The old borders of the empire buckle and contract. As the sense of communal cohesion and responsibility fails, the priest, the pharaoh, the senator, the president are guided more and more by a self-interest which hastens the process of decay. Still, for artists this is a fertile time. Even as their audience fragments and drifts away, the sense of impending apocalypseand the usefully disorienting pressures of life in limbo—between the old world of integration and the coming dark age—whet their efforts with political urgency and personal passion. But as things fall apart and the centre fails to hold, the Age of Disintegration shades imperceptibly into the cycle's terminal phase, the Age of Clowns, where citizens hide their confusion and pain behind comic masks and snarky punchlines, where the emperor fiddles as Rome burns, where jugglers and dwarves and trained bears dance for rich couples fornicating among the vomitoria as the Visigoths sweep down from the north.

The jesters themselves are a symptom, not a cause, and likeable in their own way, even noble, like those rodeo-clowns who distract the bull from the fallen bronco rider—but their sudden ubiquity and hellbent capering, hand in hand with the Grim Reaper, are signs that the bracing, vital irony of the Age of Integration has cancered into glibness and cynicism, anomie, a claustrophobic and sterile self-consciousness.

Now the culture can produce little important art. There are as many brave creative spirits as ever, but for them the freshness and spontaneity that good art requires, along with the artist's essential self-trust, are fraught commodities, while their faith in the ultimate relevance of art is lost. Or they turn from the very idea of ultimacy because it seems not merely authorial but authoritarian, imperialistic. But when artists stop trying to mean, art begins to wither. Heroic ages and their aftermaths produce largely unselfconscious and visceral works like the Norse sagas and the *Bhagavad Gita;* Ages of Integration give us writers of Classical confidence like the Poets Sappho, Virgil, and Dante, and the dramatists Sophocles, Shakespeare, and Molière; Ages of Disintegration "hurt into poetry" anxious, rootless writers like T.S. Eliot, Gertrude Stein, W.H. Auden, and W.B. Yeats. In the Age of Clowns it's far more difficult for writers to produce anything of deep value, partly because some of the artists themselves are too busy winking at their own reflections, in the ceiling mirrors, during the orgy.

Until the Corporate Hordes and Technogoths batter down the doors and usher in another dark age, or "unconscious civilization," to use John Ralston Saul's term.

If the aesthetic era known as "modernist" can be aligned with the Age of Disintegration, the postmodern era is coeval with the Age of Clowns. When pain without purpose has made the world retreat behind a leering mask and has set the word "love" in quotation marks. When self-consciousness becomes an end in itself, a dead-end, rather than a means to greater self-knowledge. When society's annual and essential self-parody, in time of Carnival, has become a year-round routine of smarmy and heartless street theatre or, on five hundred channels, a round-the-clock round-the-calendar festival of vacuity. When the artist's duty of discerning and expressing human meaning of one kind or another seems obsolete since the vast majority would rather read *People* for the latest update on the clownish Royals. When "virtual" realities crowd out visceral realities and the passionate context of nature and the body. When it becomes impossible to stay earnest and reverent about anything without looking like a dupe or a dangerous fanatic.

•

I know there's no way back to some fresher Age of Integration, and as a child of a different time I could not feel at home there anyway; I know I would find its confidence haughty, its certainties and unities coercive, constraining, its hierarchies oppressive and unfair. But is it futile to dream of a new and fully humane Age of Integration? Is it possible to arrive there without first passing through a new Unconscious Age ruled over by Technogoths, Fundamentalists, feudal Multinationals, or whatever rough beast comes after them? Spengler's view of historical cycles was strictly deterministic and left little or no leeway for rejuvenating intervention—and artists, after all, are no longer legislators of any kind. The repeated upwelling this century of romantic nostalgia for a Heroic Age of Blood and Soil—most notably in fascist Italy, Germany,

Japan, and in Stalinist Russia—along with the recent rise of militant fundamentalism all over the world, does suggest a growing resistance to modern life and to its sensibility, its complexities, its barren abstractions, its clinical self-consciousness. This hankering for creeds and heroes to spring us from the jail of over-consciousness may be a harbinger of the new cycle, a sign that the only road to another Age of Integration must pass through the shadow of the apocalypse and over the scorched earth of another Dark, Unconscious Age.

Perhaps the best that individual artists can do is to try to foster Ages of Integration in their own hearts. An integrated writer may not have the power to overthrow the centralized rule of the cynical and the grasping, but the power to move a few thousand people deeply is something, is much; in a world so fragmented, any gesture that radically connects mind to mind and heart to heart is hugely significant. And surely the first stop for any writer who dreams of reaching the cells and cadres of the fed-up and the disaffected is to shun capitulation to the Disneyesque spirit of the age, to Casper, the friendly Zeitgeist; to refuse to fiddle around in cyberspace while the ghettoes burn; to remain a believer, unafraid of the unfashionably serious engagement with human joy and sorrow that still yields meaning and still seeds in readers the socially vital habit of empathy; to resist not only the virtual realities and cyber-abstractions of post-modernity but also the atavistic impulse to heroic vitalism, that fascist denial of the modern world that seduced and so often stultified Eliot, Pound, D.H. Lawrence, and others.

This important essay was framed by its seemingly comic introduction, which I've moved here to form instead a sombre conclusion.

> Throughout the 1980s a one-mile footrace was held each November down Princess Street in Kingston. The McDonald's Corporation—perhaps in hopes of softening up City Council, which had so far excluded its restaurants from the historical downtown core—had assumed sponsorship, and the race was called the McMile.
>
> The year I entered the McMile—1984—the sponsors and organizers were trying to expand and popularize the event by adding a playful new dimension: runners were now encouraged to compete in costume, and laurels would be awarded not only to the fit and the swift but also to the frolicsome and preposterous.
>
> I arrived at the starting line in nothing more preposterous than running shoes and sweats. Standing there among the yetis and the samurai, the Ronald McDonalds, the romping skeletons and self-propelled condoms, I felt as stiff and lost and stodgy as a neatly groomed Jehovah's Witness who knocks and is let in to some manic frat party.

Readers coming to Heighton's work for the first time should by this point be beginning to get a sense of this man, of his seriousness, his passions. But who was he? Where did he come from? How did he build himself into the important writer he became?

In *Workbook: memos and dispatches on writing* (2011) he wrote of himself and many of his contemporaries:

> A scattered, discontinuous life is the postmodern norm; most of us, raised in generic suburbia, come from nowhere; writers of this drifting cohort seek to root themselves in language.
>
> Each book is a room in the home that the rootless writer, the *deracinado,* seeks to build out of words, images, ideas, and narrative.
>
> *Deracinados*—bred in suburbia, atopia, the generic North American milieu—might as well have been born in cyberspace and raised

in the food court of an international airport. Or an Old Navy outlet. If they're writers, they have one authentic subject: rootlessness. They'll never have the Deep South of Flannery O'Connor, the working class New Jersey of Bruce Springsteen, the midcentury Souwesto of Alice Munro, the seething Victorian London of Dickens. Pretending to have a true place they know in a radical, intimate way can result only in frantic mimicry. Their life is a postmodern patchwork and they have no native soil. They can write only of their exile, create books that will be their one home.

I am a *deracinado.*

How did the Age of Clowns engulf us, and so rapidly? By what process were so many of us left bereft? And here I must stop pretending to any remnants of objectivity. Steve and I were friends for many years. I have edited four of his books. I have struggled to temper his verbal exuberance. So here I want to join him openly in his dissection of the causes of our malaise.

From "The Electrocution of the World" in *The Admen Move on Lhasa* (1997):

> ... it seems second nature in this institutional age to look to institutions and committees to solve our problems. Some problems can be tackled that way, but the growth of one's writing—one's voice—is indivisibly bound up with the growth of the soul, and committees are no help there. The truth is, our excessive insistence on niceness here in Canada is merely facilitating and aggravating a malaise that's increasingly global. The muses and the magic are not just absent here, they're endangered throughout the so-called First World and their disappearance is linked to the accelerating decline in individuality and individual thought. You don't need to be a conspiracy theorist to see that governments and burgeoning multinationals have a vested

interest in leveling out individuality and diversity wherever they find it, and in rendering all of us dull, decent, sedated consumers. Compliant. Nice…

…McLuhan promised us a global village. We're getting a global suburb instead.

Because of its origins in and emphasis on the organic world, with its anarchic and inexhaustibly diverse forms and energies, the poetic imagination is subversive of institutions and standardizing monopolies and always has been. So that we need the muses and the angels now more than ever. When diversity of thought and personality and expression—diversity of soul—are crushed among the bureaucratic, conformative structures of a more and more centralized world, the imagining soul, which feeds on freedom and variety, starves and lapses into silence.

From his essay "Apollo VI and the Flight from Emotion" in *The Admen Move on Lhasa:*

Cool or coyly intellectual work can only contribute to the near-terminal process accelerating around us. A poem packed full of theory, but dead to the world of the senses, is a kind of capitulation, a collaboration with the enemies of the heart. Likewise the icy detached neoformalism currently in vogue with many British and American academic poets, like the worst examples of pat, precious, self-indulgent postmodernism, exemplify what John Metcalf has called "a flight from emotion"—which is to say a further flight from the body, from the ground of our being, from the organic and the authentic. From the earth.

"Flight." Metcalf can hardly be using the word, with the implications our century has layered on to it, by accident. I think by using it he aligns formalist or postmodern intellectualism with the heartless, clinical complexity of the machine, the jetliner, the space shuttle, the Apollo.

In the next century it will be the near-impossible task of writers and other artists to bring at least a few people back down to earth.

From "The Electrocution of the World" in *The Admen Move on Lhasa*:

> The problem with electronic media in terms of writers and their evolving forms is that the media have pushed to the forefront and now lead the Western world's march into terminal abstraction, and the effect of this process is, predictably, to make writers more abstract, more detached from the sensual sources of imaginative power, more mediated—more remote and controlled. For forty years now, and despite its name, television has been eroding our capacity of vision by framing an image of the world that's largely formulaic, stereotyped, flat, and blandly secular. Visual clichés blur the eye just as aural clichés dull the ear—and, as Neil Postman has remarked, watching TV is the one human activity at which it's impossible to get any better. Meanwhile scene-bite video offers an even more fleeting focus on the world, or what little we glance of it, as it infects the eye with a violently accelerated and hostile impatience.
>
> Most of the literary forms evolving today signal a kind of mindless capitulation to this addictive and antihuman trend, an opportunistic pimping to ever shorter attention spans. Most of the new forms symptomize our growing blindness to the world.

In *Temerity and Gall* (2022), an account of my own most recent wanderings through the Funfair, I was myself writing about our malaise:

> I had the sudden perception that the digital world and the proponents of Theory share in some sort of pseudo-intellectual abstractionism that brings to mind the word *cult.* I had the feeling that this abstractionism could be thought of as being not unlike Puritanism, not in the sense of extreme spiritual certainty, not in the sense of an opposition to cakes and ale, but as a fervour, as a denying of the world's messy *thereness,* as *circumventing* its undigitizable and absolute presence, the blister on your heel, the taste of cumin, the coconut smell of gorse in bloom, the world that John Cheever so beautifully evoked and urges us to celebrate "that lies spread out around us like a bewildering and stupendous dream."

All of the foregoing has been tending toward the question Natalee Caple puts to Steve in *The Notebooks: Interviews and New Fiction from Contemporary Writers* edited by Michelle Berry and Natalee Caple (2002).

> NC: You've described the writer as a kind of priest—which seems a bit self-important. Can you elaborate on this? How do you see the social role of the writer in an increasingly democratic but increasingly homogeneous society?
>
> SH: The seeming self-importance may have been more an effect of the tone than of the assertion. My tone was oratorical and sententious. I regret it now. All I was trying to say is that there's a moral dimension to literature—not moralistic, but moral—and that many people now look to literature to provide the staple meanings, small redemptions, epiphanies, metaphors, and significant narratives they might once have sought in the Bible or in a church. This gets back to Romanticism and how, with the rational secularization of life, art became an important repository of the sacred. As for the word "priest"—people balk at all the baggage. I wasn't trying to evoke

> cassocks, hard pews, conventional pieties. My mental image was of a writer passionately trying to convey to a group of listeners something she believes to be crucial and true…

Steve returns to this in "Still Possible to Be Haunted," perhaps the most important essay in *The Admen Move on Lhasa.*

> It's in the context of organized religion that many artists as children first encounter that sense of impenetrable, irreducible mystery which, transposed into art, gives a poem or a sketch or a score its lasting, nagging power.
>
> When I was five years old our family moved from Northern Ontario, where my father had found his first teaching job, to Toronto. And because at that time my Greek-Canadian mother was the only parent keen on organized religion, and there were a number of Greek Orthodox churches in the city, we began, for the first time, to go. My childhood exposure to church, clergy, scripture, and even Sunday school offered an unlimited experience of mind-scrambling mystery. I had seen Byzantine icons before, in the houses of Greek relatives, but never in such lavish abundance, and underlit by tiny, ranked choirs of candles, and hazed, like the upper air of the church itself, by marbled clouds of frankincense. The priest's cassock, hair, huge beard, and high brimless stovepipe hat were all as black as the long grieving-gowns of the widows who could be seen hunched or kneeling in every pew. How their veiled features—like coffined faces under shrouds of ebony mesh—unsettled me. And how the priest himself frightened me, towering past as he ushered the slow, solemn procession up the aisle during the Eucharist and his filigreed censer swung back and forth in a fog of fragrant myrrh like a blazing pendulum in the Book of the Apocalypse. The smell of the incense was sweet and foreign and made me think of funerals. The priest

intoning and repeating phrases in a language I did not know—an old language, my mother would explain in a grave whisper, and one that even she could not translate. I came to learn certain cadences phonetically and to whisper them to myself, as all children repeat and incorporate new words. *Kirie Eleison. Thanatos, thanatos.* And when I grew bored during the long services I would look up and watch sunlit smatterings of incense snaking among rafters, and sometimes as I craned my head back to focus on the ribbed, vaulted ceiling I had the dizzying illusion of peering down into the hull of some vast wooden ship, as when the night sky about you seems like a chasm below, or like an ocean where multitudinous candles flick and bob.

•

I mentioned before how the rich unfamiliarity of the Greek Orthodox Church was, for me, a kind of agitation and inspiration. (Or to use the critical terminology of Russian Formalist Victor Schlovsky, it was a weekly *ostrenenie,* or defamiliarization, a kind of ontological wake-up call.) But I think the mass and the atmosphere of the church had a further helpful effect, as it has for so many writers with religion in their backgrounds—that of instilling a sense of ritual and tradition.

Alyda Faber interviews Heighton in *The Dalhousie Review* (2023):

AF: Throughout your work, you often use religious language like "soul," "blessed," "revelation," "Psalm," "calling," "reverence," and "sacramental." Why is this language important to you?

SF: Because I'm essentially a religious writer. Again, by religious I mean concerned with whatever transcends the limited "I" consciousness (to use jazz musician Kenny Werner's term for the ego).

I guess most people would say "spiritual" here, and they'd urge me to do the same instead of committing career suicide by calling my work religious in a secular age. But "secular art," by my definition, is a contradiction in terms. Okay, some might use that phrase to distinguish the photographs of Diane Arbus or a novel like *Tom Jones* (1749) from devotional Christian poems, paintings of Bible scenes, or Handel's Messiah (1742), but I can't think of any great work of contemporary art that isn't religious in the sense that I mean. At the same time, many or most of the artists in question are atheists, like me, or at least agnostic.

AF: What would you say to your twenty-years-younger self who writes in *The Admen Move on Lhasa,* "art is not only religious, it serves a religious function"?

SH: I'd say you were right. And you were wrong to turn on the idea and disown it just because you were derided for it. I'd say you should revise, improve, and republish "Still Possible to be Haunted"—the essay that develops that point most fully—and make no apologies. You'll be mocked again, though perhaps a bit less this time, not only because this new version will be stronger and define its terms (as I've tried to do above with both "soul" and "religion") but because the world has changed somewhat. These days people—even self-consciously hip humanities profs with their horror of seeming uncool, middle-aged, out of touch with popular culture, insufficiently secular—are more open to the idea that a desire for some kind of spiritual relationship to the world is not only forgivable but a human necessity.

I *loved* that image of the Orthodox church's ribbed and vaulted wooden ceiling as the inverted hull of a vast wooden ship, the ribs its strakes. I loved the child's seeing and inventing. BUT "sunlit smatterings of incense snaking among rafters..."

Holy Smoke, Steve!

Smatterings! and *snaking?*

I feel a prim little cough in my throat, reach for the red pencil.

Which brings me to the topic of editing.

From *An Aesthetic Underground*

Some people are curious about the process of editing. I have always felt editing to be mildly impertinent and arrogant and I only feel that I can do it because I am a writer myself and know that most of the writers I work with have read my fiction and have some regard for it.

Major editing involves rearranging the building blocks of a story, cutting passages, finding a more effective starting place, giving greater weight to pertinent images. This is emotional and intuitive work.

Minor editing, though vastly important, is line-by-line testing and probing. An aspect of this kind of editing more common than readers might suppose is forcing writers to be logical and precise. I edited two books for the Honourable Heward Grafftey, science minister in Joe Clark's brief government, because he was a neighbour and because I liked him. I remember handing him a chapter scored with red ink marking lapses in logic.

"But, well," he sputtered, "I am by training a lawyer."

"Then I'm glad," I replied, "you're not representing *me*."

I once wrote jokingly that the essence of editing was to go through each typescript finding the word *careen* and crossing it out. Writers refuse to accept that the word means "to cause a ship to lean or lie on one side for calking, barnacle removal, or repair."

Sometimes manuscripts beg to be reshaped or rewritten. It often happens that the energy level in a story drops in one or more places. A good editor can feel these lapses or collapses as easily as an electrician can check current with a voltmeter. Conversely the voltmeter can pick up an energy surge; sometimes a paragraph or a couple of pages will stand out from surrounding competence and proclaim themselves and it often turns out that that paragraph or those pages are the emotional core of the story demanding to be taken out and reshaped.

To return to the image of a voltmeter checking current. This is as real to me as sewing on buttons might be for someone else. And, for me, as commonplace. I remember performing tricks once at the Humber School for Writers. A student submitted a story to the class and I rather astonished her by saying, "This story you've totally invented just as you've invented the characters. It's all rather plodding, I'm afraid. The only place in the story where you've connected to any real emotion is in the description of the inside of the sheds in the garden. And those sheds are drawn from your own life and childhood." She agreed that this was true, so I sent her off to think more about sheds.

I am not saying here that the current surges because material is autobiographical or "sincere," or that the "real" is more real than the imagined. It is simply that the real, the sheds came alive in her story because *nouns* were coming into play. She was looking at *things* rather than playing with Lego. Sometimes the voltmeter picks up a sentence or paragraph because the writer is not concentrating sufficiently on the imagined world. When writers wander from the concrete, the particular, the current always drops. As I work on this book, I'm working with an ex–Humber student, Judith McCormack, on a short story collection. One of the stories is called "The Cardinal Humours." Here is its opening sentence:

> When Eduardo de Majia left Barcelona on an overcast, grey-yellow day in the fall of 1873, he left behind his wife and his two sons, and he took with him trunks and barrels of medicaments,

bitter syrups, dried herbs, astringent tonics, white powders of various kinds, and sixty-three vials of tinctures.

I noticed that I wrote to her…"Page 1 'white powders of various kinds' is very weak after the more specific things which precede. Try one of: nostrums, infusions, lenitives, paregorics, carminatives, balsams—all words fitting to the tradition and period.

"'Bitter syrups' also sounds a bit dodgy. 'Syrup' is defined as 'any *sweet* thick liquid.' Rethink this one.

"And come to think of it, 'astringent tonics' sounds a touch unlikely."

Well, I admit.

It possibly *is* a strange way to spend one's days.

The ideal editor must accept the uniqueness of each text and deal with it on its own terms. I try not to impose anything of my own style but rather seek to understand a book's rhetoric and then work to ensure that the writer performs that rhetoric to the top of his bent. I also feel quite strongly that an editor can only *suggest* changes; the writer must be ultimately responsible for the work.

The level and depth of editorial meddling is dictated not by some abstract theory but by the typescript itself. Sometimes good editing is the ability to see when little or none is needed. There are some writers who are so painstaking and meticulous and who have so burnished their manuscripts that editing is more or less a formality. I'm thinking here of such writers as Keath Fraser, Caroline Adderson, Annabel Lyon, and Mary Borsky.

Some writers operate in what I think of as "closed systems." You can't go inside them except in superficial ways. This is because they've perfected a style and vocabulary that is so idiosyncratic or mannered that an outsider, an editor, cannot really contribute. Terry Griggs would be a good Canadian example. Ronald Firbank springs to mind. How did Robert Bridges edit Gerard Manley Hopkins? All that an editor can usefully do with a closed-system writer is say, These stories are stronger than these, so let's drop the weaker ones. This was exactly the process with Terry Griggs's extraordinary collection *Quickening.*

At the opposite end of the scale are writers whose work cries out for intercession. This is not to be negatively critical. A writer's style is the outcome of, among other things, temperament. Some writers write in a passionate outpouring of words and that approach seems to them necessary and natural. Steven Heighton writes in this way and in my editing of his work I always attempt to prune his lushness, concentrate, suggest the dryness of *fino* rather than the sugar of *oloroso,* the marksman's rifle rather than the shotgun blast. He is always good-natured about my plaintive nagging. In the *New Quarterly* special issue on my editing work Steve reproduced a letter I'd sent him about a story which appeared in his collection *On earth as it is.* The story was "Townsmen of a Stiller Town" which takes place in a morgue, an important detail given my first quoted note.

I wrote in part…"P. 22. If Basil had been drinking rye his breath wouldn't be 'briny.' What about 'a breath as foul and harsh as formaldehyde'?

"P. 20, middle of page. 'Joliffe's pipe on its side, sifting ash over papers.'

"You *cannot* say this. 'To sift' is a precise action of riddling material over a grill—metaphorically, I suppose you could 'sift through archives.' But a *pipe* can't *sift.*

"*Please* please an old man and change this.

"Sorry to fuss so much but getting things *right* will mean that your work will live. Get them wrong and wild dogs will gnaw at your corpse."

Possibly the loving combat I'm always locked in with Steve comes from my own temperament, from my own neurotic writing methods. I write an initial sentence usually many times over until it strikes me as perfect in diction and rhythm. Then I do the same thing with the second sentence. But joining the second sentence to the first changes both and so I rewrite both. This slightly mad process goes on, sentence by sentence, for weeks.

(I noticed in the revised text as it appeared in *On earth as it is* that "sifting" had been changed to "leaking". "Leaking" is too "liquidy" for ash but there comes a point in editing where to push harder is to risk damaging the writer's spirit or trust.)

When *The New Quarterly* published a special issue on my editing work, the editor, Kim Jernigan, wrote, in a letter, "You have, as you must know, a reputation for being FORMIDABLE." I have no idea how this slander got abroad but Steve Heighton amplified it in his *New Quarterly* contribution.

> How do I know what John is like with the others? I know because whenever I happen to meet other writers he's edited, we always end up huddled together and asking, in hushed tones, "So, what kind of thing does he write on *your* stories?"
>
> I usually answer with a few choice samples of Metcalfian marginalia: "Another EXCREMENTAL metaphor." "Oh Christ, Heighton, are you KIDDING?" And my personal favourite, which appeared, in large caps, between the lines of an unmedicably ailing story, later put down: "YOU CAN ONLY SAY THAT ABOUT HORSES, YOU DINK."

Steve's approach to story writing is not merely intuitive. Getting the rough shape down on paper—a process I suspect he might think of as *receiving* the shape—is, for him, "sacred."

From *Writers Talking:*

From editing *Quarry* I've learned that many talented writers who have studied creative writing formally have not assimilated the technical stuff and blended it, as they have to, with their very own brain and body fibres—they haven't forced the stuff down into themselves but have let it float mouldering on their minds' surface where it binds their thought and mutes their voice and makes them awkwardly careful and self-conscious about what they write. Which often looks to have been churned out by a committee, or on an assembly line.

Related to this "intuitive approach" is my attitude towards the first draft. I consider first drafts sacred. Not unchangeable—I write up to ten drafts of a story and I usually rewrite every sentence—but sacred nonetheless. On the day of a First Draft I rise early and drink far too much coffee and then sit down at a quiet carrel in the library and stay there until the first draft is done. Fifteen, twenty, even thirty pages, handwritten, poured onto the page in a kind of trance. And almost every word of it is AWFUL. Sometimes it takes twelve hours and by the last syllables my fatigue is obvious and my handwriting and syntax almost incoherent, but besides being burdened with a neurotic need for a tentative kind of closure—that first draft done and in my hands—I like to think my one-day drafts have a kind of emotional coherence and sustained vitality that I might not be able to get if I wrote the story in a dozen sittings. Others can write stories that way—stories much better than mine—but if I want my finished work to be true to my temperament, I believe my working habits have to be in harmony with my temperament...

I try to elicit the form from the central themes and images, the central metaphors of the story rather than settling for an existing or inappropriate form and imposing it on the work. I try to find the form that's radically appropriate. So that "Five Paintings of the New Japan" is presented in five sections, each of which draws on a famous painting for its imagery, its colours, its tone, its pace...

...So was it a good thing, all this "early success"? It didn't make me lazy. But it probably made me too confident. It led me to believe that if I keep putting in the hours, the writing would keep getting better, the responses more positive, which of course are no sure things. The imagination can tire temporarily as surely as the body can, and as for the public's response to the work, the writer has no control. All a writer can directly control and exert is will—effort, focus, craft—and although will is clearly essential to the enterprise, it is never enough. Magic and surprise often refuse to be conjured, and all the industry, technique and intelligence in the world are useless. Part of the art of becoming a writer, I see now, is learning how to lose—learning to relinquish certain cherished hopes, to accept that a book has refused to gel.

Which brings me to my hooking up with the Porcupine's Quill. You, John, read the manuscript of Asian stories I was working on and told me the Japanese ones were alive and the others not. You also wrote to me that "it is too easy to get published and praised in Canada." I wanted to believe you were wrong on both counts—for one thing, a larger publisher had already expressed interest in the book—and so I continued on my hopeful course. Six months later you wrote again and repeated your offer to work with me on a book of Japanese stories. I was surprised and flattered by your persistence. It made me take a cold, close look at the non-Japanese stories, and finally, reluctantly, I had to agree with you. I'd had a larger structure in mind, involving stories from all the countries where Mary and I travelled, and I was trying to force the material to conform. In the case of the weakest things, magic-realist tales of Bali and Malaysia, I'd been like someone doggedly performing CPR on a bog man. I decided to go with you and the Porcupine's Quill. Two years later the Japanese stories appeared as *Flight Paths of the Emperor*, and three years after that a second collection, *On earth as it is*.

In *Workbook* he wrote:

> As the lives of writers, along with everyone else, accelerate and fragment—as access to sacred as opposed to logistical time decreases—so the timeless slowly vanishes from our world.

Steve fought through to the ability to make writing that overwhelms, enraptures us, that makes us see again our world as we saw it once in childhood, the world that, in Cheever's words, lies *spread out around us like a bewildering and stupendous dream.* He fought through to writing that makes us really *see* the flirting-down of a Red Admiral's wings on a buddleia bush, the oddly comical legs, winter twigs, of the scurry-bursts of a lapwing running, such simple things that are, paradoxically, only captured and enshrined by the most intense and sophisticated deployment of words.

Steve's *Selected Poems 1983–2020* appeared in 2021. David Helwig's memoir *The Names of Things* was published in 2006. David lived in Kingston for years, and he and Steve had in common friendship with poet Tom Marshall. I wondered if the title was in Steve's mind when he wrote the elegy for his mother, "The Waking Comes Late."

THE WAKING COMES LATE

Year by year the lindens he planted with his mother
tap deeper into the hills, root higher into the winds,
the slender limbs at midwinter stripped, the skies
Frisian blue. And on the lee slope a few hundred
spruce, once seedlings, now fill in
a solid sun-annulling acre,
though they turn out to be balsam fir, not spruce,
her mistake and his, or maybe his alone—
in those days he assumed all evergreens
were "pines," or "spruce," whatever,
beyond his ego's stunted reach it was all whatever,
all lazy approximation. Now he believes little matters more
than knowing right names.

But the waking comes late.
In the early evening of a life, with dusk
redoubling in a still hectare of hemlock,
tamarack, redcone cedar, you might stir
out of self-induced coma and stare
years down into the mind—
                                        too late, you might fear, this insight,
like others before it, might wane, the crucial life-change
fail to hold.
                Out of the spruce swale
he climbs a knoll into a third and final stand
they sowed a few weeks before she died,
during a brief and happy remission,
she looking years younger, quietly pleased how the steroids had

puffed her face enough
to fill in wrinkles, pad out the bones.

In ambering October light they dug
nursling birches into the knoll's bare scalp—
so now with every spring, it too seems
softened, freshened, aging in reverse,
while under the earth the roots of each
in fierce secrecy radiate like veins, fusing
further down into riches,
where all the mothers,
unfinished
unfolding,
remain.

This crystalline poem, a work of great simplicity and unobtrusive sophistication, is perhaps the most fitting way, for me, although usurping, to say my own farewells to Steve and at the same time urge upon readers the rich pleasure of these stories, the work of one of Canadian writing's elect.

John Metcalf
Ottawa, 2025

Five Paintings of the New Japan

A NATIONAL GALLERY

I. SUNFLOWERS

I WAS THE FIRST foreigner to wait tables in the Yume No Ato. Summer enrolment was down at the English school where I taught so I needed to earn extra money, and since I'd been eating at the restaurant on and off for months it was the first place I thought of applying. It was a small establishment built just after the war in a bombed-out section of the city, but when I saw it the area was studded with bank towers, slick boutiques, coffee shops and flourishing bars, and the Yume No Ato was one of the oldest and most venerable places around. I was there most of the summer and I wish I could go back. I heard the other day from Nori, the dishwasher, who works part-time now in a camera store, that our ex-boss Mr Onishi has just fought and lost a battle with cancer.

"We have problems here every summer," Mr Onishi said during my interview, "with a foreign tourist people." He peered up at me from behind his desk, two shadowy half-moons drooping under his eyes. "Especially the Americans. If I hire you, you can deal to them."

"With them," I said automatically.

"You have experienced waitering?"

"A little," I lied.

"You understand Japanese?"

"I took a course."

"Say something to me in Japanese."

I froze for a moment, then was ambushed by a phrase from my primer.

"*Niwa ni wa furu-ike ga arimasu.*"

"In the garden," translated Mr Onishi, "there is an old pond."

I stared abjectly at his bald patch.

"You cannot say a sentence more difficult than that?"

I told Mr Onishi it was a beginners' course. He glanced up at me and ran his fingers through a greying Vandyke beard.

"How well do you know the Japanese cuisine?"

"Not so well," I answered in a light bantering tone that I hoped would disarm him, "but I know what I like."

He frowned and checked his watch, then darted a glance at the bank calendar on the wall.

"Morinaga speaks a little English," he said. "He will be your trainer. Tomorrow at 1600 hours you start."

"You won't be sorry, sir."

"I shall exploit you," he said, "until someone more qualitied applies."

NORI MORINAGA LEANED against the steam table and picked his nose with the languid, luxurious gestures of an epicure enjoying an after-dinner cigar. He was the biggest Japanese I'd ever seen and the Coke-bottle glasses perched above his huge nose seemed comically small.

"Ah, *gaijin-san!*" he exclaimed as he saw me, collecting himself and inflating to his full height. "Welcome in! Hail fellow well-hung!"

I wondered if I'd heard him correctly.

"It gives me great pressure!"

I had. I had.

Nori Morinaga offered me his hand at the same moment I tried to bow. Nervously we grinned at each other, then began to laugh. He was a full head taller than I was, burly as a linebacker but prematurely hunched as if stooping in doorways and under low ceilings had already affected his spine. He couldn't have been over twenty-five. His hair was brush-cut like a Marine's and when he spoke English his voice and manner seemed earnest and irreverent at the same time.

"Onishi-san tells me I will help *throw you the ropes*," he chuckled. "Ah, I like that expression. Do you know it? I study English at the University but the *gaijin-sensei* always says Japanese students must be more idiomatic so I picked up this book"—his giant hand brandished a thick paperback—"and I study it like a *rat out of hell*."

He grinned enigmatically, then giggled. I couldn't tell if he was serious or making fun of me.

Nori pronounced his idiomatic gleanings with savage enthusiasm, his magnified eyes widening and big shoulders bunching for emphasis as if to ensure his scholarship did not pass unremarked. I took the book and examined it: a dog-eared, discount edition of UP-TO-DATE ENGLISH PHRASES FOR JAPANESE STUDENTS—in the 1955 edition.

"We open in an hour," he said. "We are *oppressed for time*. Come on, *I'm going to show you what's what*."

Situated in a basement, under a popular *karaoke* bar, the Yume No Ato's two small rooms were dimly lit and the atmosphere under the low ceiling was damp and cool, as in an air-raid shelter or submarine. I wondered if this cramped, covert aura hadn't disturbed some of the earliest patrons, whose memories of the air raids would still have been fresh—but I didn't ask Nori about that. The place had always been popular, he said, especially in summer, when it was one of the coolest spots in Ōsaka.

A stairway descended from street level directly into the dining room so on summer days, after the heat and bright sunshine of the city, guests would sink into a cool aquatic atmosphere of dim light and swaying shadows. The stairway was flanked on one side by a small bar and on the other by the sushi counter where I'd eaten before. An adjoining room contained a larger, more formal dining space which gave onto the kitchen through a swinging door at the back. Despite the rather Western-style seating arrangements (tables and chairs instead of the traditional *zabuton* and *tatami*) the dining area was decorated in authentic Japanese fashion with hanging lanterns, calligraphic scrolls, a *tokonoma* containing an empty *maki-e* vase, *bonsai* and *noren* and several framed, original *sumi-e*. The only unindigenous ornament was a large reproduction of Van Gogh's *Sunflowers* hung conspicuously on the wall behind the sushi bar.

"Onishi-san says it's for the behoof of the American tourists," Nori explained, "but I'd *bet my bottom* he put it there for the bankers who come *in the wee-wee hours*. It's the bankers who are really interested in that stuff." He sniffed and gestured contemptuously toward *Sunflowers* and toward the *sumi-e* prints as well, as if wanting me to see he considered all art frivolous and dispensable, no matter where it came from.

I didn't realize until much later the gesture meant something else.

Nori showed me around the kitchen and introduced me to the cooks, who were just arriving. Kenji Komatsu was head chef. Before returning to Japan and starting a family he'd worked for a few years in Vancouver and Montreal and his memories of that time were good, so he was delighted to hear I was Canadian. He insisted I call him Mat. "And don't listen to anything this big whale tells you," he said affably, poking Nori in the stomach. "So much sugar and McDonald's the young ones are eating these days. This one should be in the *sumō* ring, not my kitchen."

"*Sumō* is for old folk," Nori said, tightening his gut and ironically saluting a small, aproned man who had just emerged from the walk-in fridge.

"*Time is on the march,*" Nori intoned. "*Nothing can stop it now!*"

Second chef Yukio Miyoshi glared at Nori then at me with frank disgust and muttered to himself in Japanese. He marched toward the back of the kitchen and began gutting a large fish. "Doesn't like the foreigners," Nori said with a grin. "So it is. You can't pleasure everybody."

The swinging door burst open and a small white form hurtled into the kitchen and disappeared behind the steam table. Nori grabbed me by the arm.

"It's Oh-san, the sushi chef—come, we must hurry."

Mr Oh was a jittery middle-aged man who scurried through the restaurant, both hands frantically embracing a mug of fresh coffee. Like all the elder folks, Nori explained, Mr Oh worked too hard...We finally cornered him by the walk-in fridge and Nori introduced us. Clearly he had not heard of Mr Onishi's latest hiring decision—he put down his mug and gawked as if I were a health inspector who'd just told him twenty of last night's customers were in the hospital with food poisoning.

The *yukata* which Mr Oh insisted I try on looked all right, and in the change room I finally gave in and let him Brylcreem and comb back my curly hair into the slick, shining facsimile of a typical Japanese cut. As he worked with the comb, his face close to mine, I could see the tic in his left eye and smell his breath, pungent with coffee.

"You look *marvellous,*" Nori laughed on my return, "and you know who you are!" He winked and blew me a kiss.

Mr Onishi entered and snapped some brusque truculent command. When the others had fled to their stations he addressed me in English.

"I hope you are ready for your first shift. We will have many guests tonight. Come—you will have to serve the aliens."

From the corner of my eye I could see Nori clowning behind the grille, two chopsticks pressed to his forehead like antennae.

As I trailed Mr Onishi into the dining room, two men and a woman, all young, tall, clad smartly in *yukata,* issued from behind the bar and lined up for inspection. One of the men wore a pearl earring and his hair was unusually long for a Japanese, while the woman had rich brown, luminous skin and plump attractive features. Mr Onishi introduced the other man as Akiburo. He was a college student and looked the part with his regulation haircut and sly, wisecracking expression.

With patent distaste Mr Onishi billed the long-haired man as "your bartender, who likes to be known as Johnnie Walker." The man fingered his earring and smiled out of the side of his mouth. "And this is Suzuki Michiko, a waitress." She bowed awkwardly and studied her plump brown hands, the pale skin on the underside of her wrists.

My comrades, as Mr Onishi called them, had been expecting me, and now they would show me to my sector of the restaurant—three small tables in the corner of the second room. In this occidental ghetto, it seemed, Mr Onishi thought I would do the least possible damage to the restaurant's ambience and reputation. Michiko explained in simple Japanese that since my tables were right by the kitchen door I could ask Nori for help as soon as I got in trouble.

The *tokonoma,* I now saw, had been decorated with a spray of poppies.

"We open shortly," Mr Onishi said, striding toward us. His manner was vigorous and forceful but his eyes seemed tired, their light extinguished. "We probably will have some American guests tonight. Your job will be to service them."

"I'll do my best, sir."

"And coffee—you will now take over from Michiko and bring Mr Oh his coffee. He will want a fresh supply every half-hour. Do not forget!"

For the first hour the second room remained empty, as did the tables of the front room, but the sushi bar was overrun within minutes by an army of ravenous, demanding guests. "Coffee," cried Mr Oh, and I brought him cup after cup while the customers gaped at me and hurled at Mr Oh questions I could not understand. The coffee yellowed his tongue and reddened his eyes, which took on a weird, narcotic glaze, while steam mixed with sweat and stood out in bold clear beads on his cheeks and upper lip. Orders were called out as more guests arrived. Mr Oh's small red hands scuttled like sand crabs over the counter, making predatory forays into the display case to seize hapless chunks of smelt or salmon or eel and then wielding above them a fish-silver knife, replacing the knife deftly, swooping down on speckled quail eggs and snapping shells between thumb and forefinger and smearing the yolk onto bricks of rice the other hand had just formed. Then with fingers dangling the hands would hover above an almost completed dish, and they would waver slightly like squid or octopuses in currents over the ocean floor, then pounce, abrupt and accurate, on an errant grain of rice or any garnish or strip of ginger imperfectly arranged, and an instant later the finished work, irreproachable and beyond time like a still life or a great sculpture, would appear on the glass above the display case from which it was whisked within seconds by the grateful customers or attentive staff.

The process was dizzying. I was keenly aware of my ignorance and when I was not airlifting coffee to the sushi bar I was busy in my own sector studying the menu and straightening tables.

Around eight o'clock Mr Onishi entered the second room, carrying menus, followed by a man and woman who were both heavyset, tall and fair-haired. The man wore a tailored navy suit and carried a briefcase. The woman's hair was piled high in a steep bun that resembled the nose-cone of a rocket, and her lipstick, like her dress, was a pushy, persistent shade of red.

"Take good care with Mr and Mrs Cruikshank," Onishi-san said in a low voice as he passed me and showed them to their seats. "Mr Cruikshank is a very important man—a diplomat, from America. Bring two dry martinis to begin."

Mr Cruikshank's voice was genteel and collected, his manner smooth as good brandy. "How long have you been working in this place?" he inquired.

"Two hours," I said, serving the martinis.

"Surprised they'd have an American working here." With one hand he yanked a small plastic sabre from his olive, then pinched the olive and held it aloft like a tiny globe.

"I'm not American," I said.

There was a pause while Mr and Mrs Cruikshank processed this unlooked-for information.

"Well surely you're not Japanese?" Mrs Cruikshank asked, slurring her words a little. "Maybe half?"

Mr Cruikshank swallowed his olive then impaled his wife's with the plastic sword. He turned back to me, inadvertently aiming the harmless tip at my throat.

"*Nihongo wakaru?*" he asked in plain, masculine speech. *You understand Japanese?* I recognized his accent as outstanding.

"Only a little," I said.

"I'll bet he's Dutch," Mrs Cruikshank said. "The Dutch speak such beautiful English—hardly any accent at all."

"You'll find it hard here without any Japanese," Mr Cruikshank advised me, ignoring his wife, drawing the sword from his teeth so the gleaming olive stayed clenched between them.

"*Coffee*," Mr Oh called from the sushi bar.

"I'll only be serving the foreign customers, sir."

Mr Cruikshank bit into his olive. "Some of the foreign customers," he said, "prefer being served in Japanese."

"Or maybe German," said Mrs Cruikshank.

"I can speak some German," I said. "Would you like it if—"

"*Coffee*," cried Mr Oh from the sushi bar.

Mrs Cruikshank was beaming. "I was right," she said, lifting her martini glass in a kind of toast. "*Wie geht's?*"

"We'd like some sushi," Mr Cruikshank interrupted his wife, who was now grimacing at her drink as if trying to recall another German phrase.

I fumbled with my pad.

"An order each of *maguro, saba, hamachi,* and—why not?—some sea urchin. Hear it's full of mercury these days, but hell, we've got to eat something."

"Yes, sir."

"And two more martinis." He pointed at his glass with the plastic sword.

"Got it."

"*Danke schön*," roared Mrs Cruikshank as I hurried from the room.

While waiting for Johnnie Walker to finish the martinis I noticed an older guest rise from the sushi bar and stumble toward the washrooms. As he saw me, his red eyes widened and he lost his footing and crashed into the bar, slamming a frail elbow against the cash register. He righted himself with quick slapstick dignity and stood blushing. When I moved to help him he waved me off.

Johnnie Walker smirked and muttered as he shook the martinis and for a moment the words and the rattling ice took on a primitive, mocking rhythm, like a chant. The older man began to swear at him and reached out as if to grab his earring, his long hair. *Shin jin rui*, the old man muttered—Strange inscrutable creature! I'd heard it was a new phrase coined by the old to describe the young.

"Wake up old man," Johnnie snapped in plain Japanese as he poured the martinis. "Watch out where you're going."

The man lurched off.

"Always drunk, or fast asleep in their chairs."

"*Coffee*," cried Mr Oh from the sushi bar.

II. THE DREAM

"TELL ME SOMETHING about the restaurant," I said to Nori, sweeping my hand in a half circle and nodding at the closed bar. "How old is the place?"

Nori finished his Budweiser and balanced the empty tin on a growing tower of empties. "It was built after the war ends," he said, belching—and I couldn't help noticing how casually he used the word *war*. His expression was unchanged, his voice was still firm, his eyes had not recoiled as if shamed by some unspeakable profanity. That was how my older students reacted when The

War came up in a lesson. No doubt Mr Onishi would react the same way. But not Nori. For him the war was history, fiction—as unreal and insubstantial as a dimly remembered dream, a dream of jungles, the faded memory of a picture in a storybook. He wasn't much younger than me.

"What about the name," I said, "Yume No Ato? I mean, I can figure out the individual words, but I can't make sense of the whole thing." *Yume,* I knew, meant "dream," *no* signified possession, like an apostrophe and an "s," and *ato,* I thought, meant "after."

Nori lit a cigarette and trained a mischievous gaze on my hairline. His capacity for drink was larger than average for a Japanese but now after four tins of beer he was flushed, theatrical and giddy. He wrinkled his broad nose, as if at a whiff of something rotten, and spat out, "It's a line from a poem we had to study in the high school. Ah, Steve-san, university is so much better, we have fun in the sun, we make whoopee, we live for the present tense and forget all our yesterdays and tomorrows...I hated high school, so much work. We had to study this famous poem."

He stood and recited the lines with mock gravity:

"Natsu kusa ya!
Tsuwamono domo ga
Yume no ato."

"It's a haiku," I said.

"Aye, aye, captain." He slumped down and the tower of beer cans wobbled. "Do you watch *Star Trek?*"

"I'm not sure," I said, "that I understand it."

"Oh, well, it's just a TV show—about the future and the stars."

"I mean the poem, Nori, the *haiku.*"

"Ah, the poem—naturally you don't understand. It's old Japanese—old Japanese language, old Japanese mind—not so easy for us to understand either. It's Matsuo Bashō, dead like Shakespeare over three hundred years. Tomorrow and tomorrow and tomorrow. We had to study them both in school. Full fathom five and all that."

"But about that last line..."

"*Yume no ato?*"

I nodded.

"That's the name of the restaurant. You see, when Mr Onishi's uncle built the place after the war he gave it that name. It's a very strange name for a restaurant! Mr Onishi was just a boy then."

"What does it mean?"

"I don't think Mr Onishi would have called it that, but when his uncle went over the bucket he didn't want to change the name. Out of respect."

I finished my own beer and contributed to the tower of cans. The other staff had gone upstairs to the *karaoke* place but they'd drunk a lot of Bud and Kirin beforehand and the tower was growing high.

"I wonder," I said, "if the words mean 'when the dream is over'?"

Nori took a long drag on his cigarette. "I don't think they do," he finally said. "And besides, the dream had only just begun... The uncle was smart and he built Yume No Ato to attract foreigners as well as Japanese and it's done really well, as you can see." His eyes brightened. "*We're going great guns.*"

Mr Onishi's telephone began to ring from the back of the restaurant, where he was still working. We heard him answer.

"The first line," I said, "is 'Ah! Summer grasses,' right?"

Nori seemed to be weighing this, then blurted out, "*Yume no ato* means...it means what's left over after a dream."

Mr Onishi's voice could be heard faintly. I surveyed the shaky tower, the ashtrays, the skeletons of fish beached on the sides of our empty plates.

"Leftovers," I said, ironically.

"There's another word."

"What about vestige? No? Remnant?"

Nori stubbed out his cigarette like a game-show panellist pressing a buzzer. "*Remnant!*" he cried, "*your choice is absolutely correct, for five thousand dollars and a dream home!*" Suddenly he grew calm, thoughtful. "So many foreign words sound alike," he said. "There's a famous Dutch painter with that name."

"You mean Rembrandt?"

"That's him. A bank here in Umeda just bought a Remnant for nine hundred million yen."

"*Yume no ato*," I said, "must mean 'the remnant of dreams.'"

Nori furrowed his brow, then nodded.

"Funny name for a restaurant," I said. "You like game shows?"

As if in a fresh wind the paper *noren* in the doorway behind the sushi bar blew open and a haggard phantom came in. Mr Onishi. He seemed to look right through us. Nori suggested we clean up and leave. We began to pile the chopsticks and empty plates onto a tray. I glanced up and saw Mr Onishi beckoning Nori.

"Please go examine the guest toilet," Nori told me.

The guest washroom was immaculate—I'd cleaned it myself two hours before—but I spent a few minutes checking it again so that Nori and Mr Onishi would know I was thorough. For the second time that night I was intrigued by a notice in the stall, pencilled on the back of an old menu and taped to the door—

TO ALL FOREIGNERS:
OUR TUBES ARE IN ILL REPAIR, PLEASE
DO NOT THROW YOUR PEEPERS
IN THE TOILET.

When I came out of the washroom Mr Onishi was gone. "The boss looks awful," I whispered to Nori, my smile forced. "When he was on the phone before—maybe a guest was calling to complain about the new waiter, eh?"

"Possibly," Nori said, "but more likely it was a banker."

"What, at this time of night?"

Nori shrugged. "The elder folks, I told you, they're working late. And early, too—there was a banker here first thing this morning to talk at Mr Onishi."

"Bankers," I said, shaking my head. "Not trouble, I hope."

Nori laughed abruptly. Arm tensed karate-style he approached the tower of cans.

III. THE KERMESS

KAMPAI!

A month has gone past and the whole staff, *gaijin-san* included, are relaxing after a manic Saturday night in the Yume No Ato. August in Ōsaka: with other waiters and students and salarymen we sit in a beer garden under the full moon above twenty-two storeys of department store merchandise, imported clothing and cologne and books and records, Japanese-made electronics, wedding supplies, Persian carpets and French cigarettes and aquariums full of swordfish and coral and casino-pink sand from the Arabian Sea, appliances and appliqué, blue china chopstick-holders computers patio-furniture coffee-shops chefs and friendly clerks and full-colour reproductions of well-known Western portraits, etchings, sketches, sculptures, landscapes that Japanese banks are buying like real estate and bringing back to Ōsaka, anything, anything at all, SPEND AND IT SHALL BE GIVEN, endless armies of customers and ah, summer tourists billowing like grain through the grounds of Ōsaka's most famous department store. SURELY, quoth the televangelist from the multitudinous screens, SURELY THE PEOPLE IS GRASS.

(For a moment the tables shudder as a tremor ripples through toxic earth under the Bargain Basement, and passes.)

KAMPAI! Western rock and roll music blasts from hidden speakers. In a few minutes the *O-bon* fireworks are due to start and we've got the best seats in the house. The plastic table sags and may soon buckle as another round of draft materializes and is swiftly distributed. A toast to this, a toast to that, *kampai,* KAMPAI, every time we lift our steins to take a drink, someone is proposing another toast: in a rare gesture Komatsu toasts the wait staff (Akiburo and Johnnie and Michiko and me) because (this in English) we were really on the balls tonight and made no errors at all. *Kampai!* Akiburo toasts Komatsu and Mr Oh and second chef Miyoshi in return, presumably for turning out so much food on such a busy night and making it all look easy. *Kampai!* Mr Oh raises his glass of ice-coffee in thanks while second chef Miyoshi, drunk and expansive, in a rare good mood, toasts Nori for not smacking his head in the storeroom when he went back for extra soy sauce, *kampai* (this translated by the delighted Nori, who immediately hefts his stein and decrees a toast to Michiko, the waitress, simply because he's mad about her and isn't it lucky she doesn't speak English?).

The blushing Michiko lifts her heavy stein with soft plump hands and meekly suggests, in Japanese, that it might be possible, perhaps, to maybe if it isn't too much trouble drink a toast to our own skilful bartender, Johnnie Walker, without whom we would hardly have survived the night, it seems to me, after all, or maybe we might have? *Kampai! Kampai!* The flesh of Johnnie's ear lobe reddens around his pearl stud. He smirks and belts back another slug of whisky.

"To Onishi-san," he says in English. "To Yume No Ato." And he quickly adds some other remark in harsh, staccato Japanese.

"KAMPAI!" I holler, hoisting my stein triumphantly so that beer froths up and sloshes over the lip of the glass. But no one else has followed suit. They are all gazing without expression at the table or into their drinks. Johnnie Walker's head hangs lowest, his features hidden.

Komatsu glances at his watch and predicts that the fireworks will start in thirty seconds.

I turn to Nori. "Did I do something wrong?"

Miyoshi and Mr Oh both snap something at him. I can't make out a word.

"Well, not at all," says Nori, softly, "I guess people just don't feel like talking about work after a busy night."

I purse my lips. "I have the feeling you're not being completely honest with me."

"Of course I'm not!" he says loudly—and I wonder if we've understood each other.

At that moment the fireworks start. Everyone at our table looks up, relieved. "*O-bon*," Nori says to me, relaxed again. "Tonight the ancestors return." Flippantly he rolls his eyes, or only seems to—I can't be sure because his Coke-bottle lenses reflect the moonlight and the fiery red glare of the first rockets. One after another they arc up out of the dark expanse of Nagai Park, miles to the north, then slow down and pause at their zenith and explode in corollas of violet, emerald, coral, cream, apricot and indigo. *Hanabi,* they call them in Japanese: fire-flowers. The steins are raised again, glasses rammed together, toasts made and spirits drawn skyward by the aerial barrage.

My flat is somewhere down there on the far side of Nagai Park and now I picture a defective missile veering off course and buzzing my neighbourhood, terrifying the old folks, plunging with a shriek like an air-raid siren through the roof of my flat...

Nori grabs my arm with steely fingers. "Steve-san, listen—do you hear what I hear?" I'm still concentrating on the look and sound of the exploding flowers, but suddenly I pick it out: the bouncy unmistakable opening bars of "Like a Virgin."

"It's the Madonna!"

"I hear it, Nori."

He lumbers to his feet. "You want to dance? Hey, get up! Come off it!"

Michiko and Johnnie Walker are already up beside the table, strobelit by the fireworks, shaking themselves to the beat, Michiko with a timid, tentative air and Johnnie with self-conscious abandon. The older staff sit motionless and watch the exploding rockets. Nori glances at them, at Michiko, at me, and I can tell he doesn't want to lose her. As she dances her small hands seem to catch and juggle the light.

"Life is so curt," he pleads. "You only lived once!" He gives me a half smile, a sly wink, and I'm no longer sure he doesn't know exactly what he's saying.

KAMPAI! Nori hauls me to my feet and heaves me from the table in a blind teetering polka, out toward Johnnie and Michiko, his big boorish feet beating a mad tattoo on my toes. Komatsu and Mr Oh, the elders in the crowd, link arms and start keening some old Japanese song. Steins raised they sway together to a stately rhythm much slower than Madonna's, their voices rolling mournfully over the antique minors and archaic words. The rockets keep exploding. Their sound takes on a rhythm which seems to fall between the beats of the opposing songs—then as I watch, one of the rockets fails to burst. Like a falling star it streaks earthward in silence and disappears over the city.

IV. GUERNICA

I woke early the next morning with a headache and a burning stomach. I'd been dreaming. I dreamed Michiko had come home with me to my flat and we stood together hand in hand on the threshold, staring in at a gutted interior. The guilty rocket, however, had not actually exploded—it was resting in perfect condition, very comfortably, on an unburnt, freshly made futon in the centre of the room.

Michiko took me by the hand and led me into the ruin. When the smoke began to drown me she covered my mouth with her own. Her breath was clean and renewing as wind off an early morning sea and when she pulled away the smell of burning was gone. She removed her flowered kimono and stood naked before me. The nipples of her firm small breasts were now the accusing eyes of a seduced and betrayed woman—then I was naked too, and utterly absolved, and we were lying side by side amid the acrid wreckage by the futon. She climbed atop me and took me inside her, slowly, making small articulate sighs and rolling her head back and forth so her dark bangs rippled like a midnight waterfall across my nipples, and the blue-black hair was curved as space-time and full of sparks like the Milky Way, which in the Japanese tongue is called *ama no gawa*, the river of heaven.

I wanted to come, to fill the gathering space inside her, and I wanted to run my tongue down the soft pale line of hair from her breasts to her belly and on up the wooded mound of Venus and lick the nectar from her tender orchid, as the Japanese poets say, but then it came to me that Nori had meant to tell me something important—about Michiko? About a poem? Or was there something I'd asked him that he hadn't answered?

Summer grasses... Something left over after dreams...

What a stupid time to be thinking about poetry.

I woke embarrassed but with a feeling of desperate tenderness for Michiko, to whom I'd hardly ever spoken and who had inspired, I thought, no more than a generic interest on my part. It was like missing a lover who'd slept beside me all night and had just left and gone home before I woke.

Well, I reflected, a dream like that was better than the constant waitering nightmares I'd been having until recently, and still woke from now and then. Usually I'd enter the restaurant and be told I was two hours late and none of the other wait staff had shown up and the restaurant was full and we were booked solid until midnight. Other times I would realize I'd forgotten a couple or threesome who'd been seated two hours ago in the back corner of the second room and would they believe now it was just an honest mistake and I'd really been busy and meaning to get to them all along? Sometimes they were the Cruikshanks, and sometimes Mr Sato, who (Nori had told me) had been a professor at the university in Kyōto but was demoted and now taught primary kids in Nagai, and that was why he drank so much and was so cold and pedantic when he spoke to you. In fact the unrequited dream-diners could be just about anyone, because the summer had been busy and now I was serving both foreigners and Japanese alike.

It had been the busiest summer in years, Komatsu said, and we were attracting more tourists than ever before—so why the visible anxiety whenever talk after hours came round to the restaurant? Mr Onishi did not look like a man with a flourishing business. Perhaps he was ill and everyone was worried? I'd been reading articles lately about the soaring incidence of cancer in Japan, the spread of big business and factories into the countryside, toxins in the soil, polluted water, poisonous seafood...

"I think you'd better level with me," I told Nori the night of my dream.

Miyoshi was standing by the walk-in fridge, reading the *Sangyo Keizai*, and Komatsu was behind the steam table chopping onion. But I had the feeling they were listening to us, and so did Nori.

"Not here," he whispered.

"Ah, such good news," growled Miyoshi, lowering his paper with an unpleasant smile. Since he hardly ever spoke English I knew the remark was aimed at me. "Such good news about the yen!"

Nori shook his head. "For some the war has never ended."

"*Nihon ichiban!*" Miyoshi cried. "Japan is number one!"

"And he wasn't even born till after," Nori said. "I don't understand."

"Maybe we should talk somewhere else," I said.

Nori nodded but Komatsu set down his knife and said quickly, "No. It's all right. Steve-san is part of the restaurant now—we should tell him the truth." Eyes pink and glistening, he walked out from behind the steam table and pulled the newspaper from Miyoshi's hands.

Miyoshi scowled, did an about-face and marched into the fridge.

"Look at this," Komatsu said, handing me the paper.

"You know I can't read Japanese."

"Of course. Don't read, just look—the pictures."

In the lower right-hand corner of the front page several well-known pieces of European art were reproduced in hazy black and white. One was a Rousseau, the second a Gauguin, the third a Brueghel. I couldn't read the caption beneath but I could make out the name of a prominent Ōsaka bank, written in *romaji*.

"And Van Gogh," Komatsu said, sniffling. "I hear they have just bought another costly painting by Van Gogh—so many paintings they are buying and bringing to Japan."

We could hear Miyoshi in the fridge, muttering to himself, furiously shifting things around.

"They're buying everything in their sights," Nori said, his usual gusto tangibly absent.

I told them I knew a bit about these purchases, but didn't see what they had to do with us.

"Well," Komatsu started, "they need some place to put these paintings…" His voice tapered off on the last words; I sensed I was being counted on, in customary Japanese fashion, to finish the sentence mentally so that everyone would be spared embarrassment.

"Chagall, too," Komatsu resumed, "and Rembrandt and Picasso." *Bigasshole,* it sounded like, but I knew who he meant. "Costly things…they need to find a place to put them all…"

"Like an art gallery," I said.

Komatsu rubbed his eyes with a corner of his apron. "I'm afraid so."

It had been just like *Dallas,* Nori groaned, describing how the bank had first made polite offers to the dozen businesses operating in the block where they meant to build, and most were politely accepted. But several proprietors (including Mr Onishi and the owner of the Idaho Caffeine Palace, a large coffee shop dating from the late forties) had refused to consider them. Secretly the bank had made more attractive offers, then a final offer which the firm's representative begged Mr Onishi to accept, because if a negotiated settlement proved necessary then payment would revert to the level of the initial sum—or, conceivably, somewhat less.

Mr Onishi had ignored the bank's covert threats and a negotiated settlement proved necessary. Unfortunately it did not involve negotiation. The bank produced lawyers who showed that actual title to the land had belonged to the bank until the end of the war, and they argued that the transfer of deeds had been improperly handled by the overworked civil authorities of the time.

The young lawyers (I could just hear them) moved further that since the art gallery would be a public facility of great benefit to all citizens of the prefecture and would attract hundreds of thousands of foreigners to Ōsaka, it was in effect a civic institution, albeit privately owned, and the city should urge Mr Onishi to come to terms.

"The court is asking Mr Onishi to accept," Nori said, "but he just says no."

"*Nihon ichiban*," we heard faintly from the fridge.

Komatsu took the newspaper from me and walked back around the steam table. He began to giggle, like a bad comedian setting up a punchline. "They're going to tear us down," he said, laughing openly. "Soon!"

Nori was chuckling, too, as the Japanese often will when speaking of their own misfortunes. Komatsu was laughing harder than I'd ever seen him, so I knew he really must be upset.

I paused respectfully. "Listen, I'm really sorry to hear this."

Komatsu roared with laughter. Nori continued to cackle. I asked them if they knew when these things were going to happen.

"There's no time like presently," Nori said, slapping me on the shoulder a bit harder than he needed to. "Come on, it's a busy night tonight, we'd better get happening."

"Please take coffee now to Mr Oh-san," Komatsu said weakly.

Miyoshi was still marching around in the fridge.

V. THE STARRY NIGHT

SEPTEMBER IN ŌSAKA is just as hot as July or August, and this year it was worse. Though many of the tourists were gone, the Yume No Ato was busier than ever: Mr Onishi's struggle with the bank was now common knowledge, so old customers came often to show their support and the sushi bar was crowded with curious locals. Meanwhile enrolment was picking up at the school and I had to cut back on my hours as a waiter.

Mr Onishi was upset when I told him, but since I knew now of the epic struggle he was waging each day in the courts (Nori got the details from Komatsu and passed them on to me) I found it hard to feel angry in return. The boss, after all, was showing tremendous pluck. Sure, he was of another generation, a hardy breed of industrious survivors, and as a child he would have absorbed with his mother's milk the bracing formula of *bushido,* but this was valour way beyond the call of duty. He was giving Japan's second-biggest bank the fight of its life. Already the original date for demolition was three weeks in arrears...

I heard that after receiving the court's final decision, Mr Onishi sighed and said, "*Yappari, nah.* It is as I expected. They will build a museum and a new country and fill both with foreign things."

The demolition was set for the end of September and the Yume No Ato was to close a week before.

On the last night, a Saturday, the dining room was booked solid from five until closing with regular customers, both Japanese and foreign. We assembled by the bar a few minutes before five to wait for Mr Onishi and at five sharp he emerged from his office. He marched up to us, a menu tucked under one arm like a swagger stick, then briefed us in a formal and highly nuanced Japanese that I could not follow, though the general tenor of his speech was easy enough to guess. Or was it? Sometimes I wondered if I'd ever done more than misimagine what these people felt and believed.

A current of laughter rippled through the staff and Nori nudged me appreciatively, forgetting for a moment that I did not understand.

Mr Onishi dismissed us and we hurried off to complete our preparations as he climbed the stairs and opened the door. A long shaft of dirty sunlight pierced the cool gloom, and a few seconds later our guests began to descend, bringing with them the hot muggy air of the street.

"Meet me in the back," I told Nori.

We stood in the kitchen on either side of the open rice machine, slowly filling it with the contents of two clay cooking pots. Thick billows of steam rose between us and Nori's face was intermittently clouded, his eyes nacreous, indistinct, like a man under a foot of water.

"So what did Onishi-san just say," I asked, scooping the soft, sweet-smelling grains into the machine.

"He was apologizing."

"Apologizing," I said.

"Sure. He was apologizing for letting the bank close the Yume No Ato. He says it's all on his shoulders. He feels responsible for the jobs we will lose. He says he is sorry because he has felled us."

The steam was thinning and I could see Nori clearly. His big face was pink and sweating.

"He says his uncle was a soldier in the old navy and after the war he built this restaurant with his own two hands. So he says that by losing the restaurant he has felled his uncle, too."

"But isn't his uncle dead?"

Nori put down his pot and gave me a faintly disappointed look. "For many years. But so the old people believe—they can fell the dead as well as the breathing. Like being caught *between the devil and the deep blue sea, neh?*"

I nodded and stared into the rice cooker, its churning steam spectral and hypnotic.

"I feel sorry for him," I said.

"So it is, all the while. The big fish eat the little."

There was a harsh grating sound as he scraped rice from the bottom of his pot.

It was the busiest night of the summer but the customers were gentle and undemanding and the atmosphere, as at a funeral reception, was chastened and sadly festive and thick with solidarity. The foreigners left huge tips and Mr Oh grunted graciously whenever I freshened his coffee. It fell to Michiko to serve the disagreeable Mr Sato for the last time and though he usually deplored the grammar and fashions of her generation, tonight he was tolerant and even remarked at one point on her resemblance to his own daughter. The Cruikshanks were among the last to arrive. When they left, just before closing, Mrs Cruikshank said she trusted I wouldn't have to go home to Germany just yet and surely with my good English I could land another job.

The last guests, our oldest customers, intoxicated and teary-eyed, staggered up the stairs around midnight and we dragged together a few tables and sank down for a last meal. Mat and Nori and second chef Miyoshi filed from the kitchen bearing platters of steaming rice and salmon teriyaki; at Mr Onishi's behest Johnnie Walker opened the bar to all staff. And now, though I'd felt more and more a part of things over the last months, I sensed my saddened colleagues closing ranks, retreating into dialect, resorting to nuance, idiom and silence, a semaphore of glances and tics and nods. Nori loomed on the far side of the table with Michiko beside him. They were talking quietly. In the shadows by their chair-legs I could see two hands linked, like sinuous seacreatures, twined and mating in the deep.

Johnnie had finished the last of the Johnnie Walker Red and was now working on a bottle of Old Granddad. Mr Oh was not drinking. He sat mutely, his agile hands wrapped around one beer tin after another, crushing them and laying them to rest among the plates and ashtrays. Komatsu and second chef Miyoshi were smoking side by side, eyes half-closed, meditating on the fumes that rose and spread outward over their heads.

Mr Onishi, I suppose, was in his office. At one-thirty he came out and told everyone it was time to leave. There were some last halfhearted toasts and deep bowing and then we all stumbled upstairs and outside. The night air was cool and fresh. We looked, I thought, like a beaten rabble. As if wounded, Nori tottered over and proffered a scrap of paper the size of a cheque or a phone bill. "Here," he said, his speech slurred, "I almost forgot. That poem they called the restaurant for... Remember?"

He and Michiko swayed before me, their features painted a smooth ageless amber by the gentle light of the doorway. Behind them the brooding profiles of bank and office towers and beyond those in long swirling ranks the constellations of early autumn.

I took the slip of paper and held it to the light:

Ah! summer grass / this group of warriors' / remnant of dream
(this poem by Matsuo Bashō, lived same time as Shakespeare)

So long and take care of yourself. Nori.

He shrugged when I thanked him. "We had to study it back then. A real pin in the ass."

"Drop by the school sometime," I said. "Please, both of you..."

I knew they wouldn't come.

Gradually the rest straggled off alone or in pairs and I headed for the station. Waves of heat rising out of sewers and off smokestacks and the vacant pavement set the stars quivering, like the scales of small fish in dark water. In the late-summer heat of 1945, after the surrender, Japanese armies had trudged back through the remains of Ōsaka and there was little where these buildings now stood but rubble, refuse, dust and blowing ash. A stubble of fireweed and wildflowers bloomed on the ruins, rippled in the hot wind. There was nothing for the children to eat. I heard these things from a neighbour, a toothless old man who had been a soldier at that time, and I heard other things as well: how faceless Japan had been, how for a while it had been a different place—beaten, levelled and overrun, unable to rise—waiting for the first touch of a foreign hand. For a sea change, into something rich, and strange.

On the train to Nagai I had a half-hour to experiment with the words on Nori's farewell card. By the time I got home I had the translation done, though the line "*Yume no ato*" was still troublesome and I found it hard to focus on the page.

Ah, summer grass!
All that survives
Of the warrior's dream…

I keep thinking I should send a copy to Nori.

The Beautiful Tennessee Waltz

JASON, ŌSAKA, 1983

I FELL OUT OF LOVE with my friends at the American Dream. We all knew the honeymoon was over. To them I was no longer exotic and alluring like the refinished Chevys in which patrons of the Dream drank malteds and Manhattans and cans of Budweiser—because with each meeting my Japanese improved toward fluency, and I began to say things they considered out of character. I told them I did not regret, as they sometimes did, having been born after the fifties and outside of America. I explained that in English the word "dream" meant not only reverie, promise, hope and ambition, but illusion. I became more and more of a disappointment to them.

And they to me. From the beginning I'd been subject to their mild, well-meaning condescension, but I reminded myself where I was and let them be masters in their own house. Then I began to mature. I learned their language as quickly as a child, and like any clever child grew smug and distant toward my "elders," began to sense their deceit and doubt their infallibility. More and more I saw how their condescension disguised a paralyzing reverence for everything Western. This wasn't their house, after all, but a crass parody of my father's world, a pastiche, a cut-rate cathedral of imported icons.

"I suppose you must be comfortable here," they would say. "We want very much for you to feel at home."

"Well," I told them, "it's not quite what I expected."

They tried to reason with me. "Japan is changing," they would say, "like everything else. This is the future. These days young Japanese are thinking more internationally."

I told them that in theory that was a fine thing, but their bar looked pretty American to me.

Ah, so the style was authentically American?

After a fashion, I said. But in fact its decor oppressed me, like their endless questions—and my own impatience and ingratitude. At first we had seen each other as spiritual guides to remote Promised Lands, then discovered our maps were obsolete, our purposes at odds. We were falling out of love, but at first we would not give up. I pestered them with queries about Mishima and the Emperor. I patronized them, and they patronized me. They continued to insist I must be American.

Though my friends saw themselves as modern and Western and Americanized (and in many ways they were) the ritual and delicacy of our last meetings proved to me how deeply the old values had been instilled. These rowdy, irreverent students made falling out a kind of sacrament. Their compliments on my Japanese became strident, almost liturgical. They stopped mentioning my "quaint obsession" with the old culture, and when I ordered sake (only old people and foreigners drink sake) they smiled beatifically and said nothing. There were parting gifts, of course, but only one really mattered: the skeleton key of language. I was glad to take it with me.

I began to frequent the little coffee shops in my own neighbourhood—a shabby precinct of squat, crowded apartment blocks, corrugatediron roofs, tangled fire escapes and aerials—where I shared a kitchen and a six-mat room with Fumiko, a college student who waited tables on the weekend. At first my infatuation with her lent a halo of glamour to our dingy surroundings, and I could almost imagine how things had looked before the war, when this had been one of the more elegant sections of the city.

I learned about the old neighbourhood from Mrs Yumeta, the owner of a local coffee shop. She explained that the area was rebuilt immediately after the war when good materials were hard to find. Food was scarce too, she added. After the last bombing hardly a building was left and you could see a long way over the smouldering rubble. Back then most houses were flimsy. Only the Western-style buildings survived. If you bombed us again, Mrs Yumeta laughed, much more would be left standing.

A few coffee shops, I thought, would have to be among the survivors. Like Kamakura with its little shrines, the neighbourhoods of Ōsaka seemed to have a café in every block. Mrs Yumeta explained that they'd appeared with the Americans after the war, and in the names of many I saw a lingering reflection of those times: Yan Kee Café, American Life Coffee Spot, Lik's Café Américain, the Idaho Caffeine Palace, even an American Dreem. But these shops did not have three-thousand-yen cover charges like the bars. Their interiors were dim and tranquil. When I got tired of rice I could order little sandwiches on spongy white bread. The middle-aged or elderly proprietors liked to sit with me and talk, and often they refused to let me pay for my meals or drinks. Finally I was able to get by on my paycheque.

Every Sunday, while Fumiko waited tables in Umeda, I visited two or three cafés. There were so many in the neighbourhood that I rarely had to visit one twice, which was ideal since I wanted to meet and talk with as many Japanese as possible. Most of them belonged to that pivotal generation that had seen the old Japan beaten and radically altered by the West. These aging proprietors were a living bridge between the old and the new, East and West, the virginal, untarnished culture and a rapidly evolving hybrid. I believed they would help me embrace the Japan I had read of and idolized.

My education proceeded. I heard of famines before the war, bitter poverty and the privileges of caste, military festivals, endless lines of soldiers parading across the memory as in a yellowing newsreel, and the Emperor Himself appearing one sunny spring day in a cortege in Nagai Park as blossoms fluttering down from plum trees were crushed to red pulp under the royal tires. The school curriculum was very different then. The Emperor was a deity whose unbroken lineage began with the God of the Sun. Of course no foreigner could lay claim to such august descent. Foreigners were gangly, unwholesome and vicious. They rarely bathed. They smelled like rancid butter.

"Of course we laugh at these things now," Mrs Yumeta told me on my second visit to her shop. The New American Café was conveniently situated three minutes from my door and five minutes from the park, but the reason I had come a second time—and continued to come religiously in the following weeks—was Mrs Yumeta's aggressive hospitality. While many of the other proprietors would not accept my money when it came time to pay ("*Sensei*," they would say, referring to my status as a teacher of English, "you are the first foreigner to visit our shop, you have honoured us, forgive me but it would be impossible to accept your money"), and while others brought unrequested gifts and snacks and hot towels to my table, Mrs Yumeta asked me to accept several expensive gifts after my first visit. A fine silver pen, a lacquer mug. "So you can have your own cup when you return, *Sensei*. And with the pen—you can write to your friends about the old Japan, and my story."

Of course it wasn't just gifts that made me return, or her need to have me listen; I had other reasons to seek her out. During the week my plans and my illusions continued to fall apart, as if the seismic tremor rumbling through the city in recent weeks were undermining everything. For a long time I'd found consolation in Fumiko, because seeing her I was still reminded of the courtesans of the Floating World whose portraits I'd always loved; they were inhabitants, I thought, of an orderly, coherent circle, where myths and meanings were commonly understood. But as I came to understand Fumiko's words I found her less and less consoling. Now she would say things that seemed out of character. Hairline flaws began to taint her beauty, like cracks in a museum mask. Sometimes I snapped at her. For the first time I understood what it meant to be foreign.

Sundays I took refuge in Mrs Yumeta's shop.

Mrs Yumeta was heavy and small and when she walked she stooped as if expecting the low ceiling to collapse at any moment. Like the walls and the two circular tables by the door her face was cluttered and messy, a collage of lines and thickly, erratically applied makeup. (The walls were covered with posters of American show bands of the '40s, old calendars, framed portraits of Bogart, Bacall and Hepburn; she explained that she'd studied and loved traditional Japanese flower arrangement but a coffee shop must have exotic decorations.)

The small round windows on either side of the door reminded me of her eyes. The panes were tinted umber like the colour round her iris, an unwholesome, tainted shade, as if she never left the smoky shop for the somewhat fresher air outside; the shop's light, a muted amber, was matched or mirrored by her complexion so she looked like a figure in a sepia print.

I sat at the table nearest the door and farthest from the stereo. Mrs Yumeta had a slight hearing problem ("the bombing," she explained) and played her music loudly. Old American Favourites, she said, rummaging through a heap of old magazines and unopened mail for the record jacket. "Some people were interested in the big bands before the war, and American movies too, but it was…unsuitable for people to show such a feeling."

"Western things were seen as a bad influence," I suggested.

"That was the official idea," she said. "I think the generals had already decided on war and didn't want us involved with foreigners in any way."

Mrs Yumeta slowly exhaled a chestful of smoke until the little shop seemed filled with it, like a dim lobby during an intermission. This was the time I watched her finish a whole pack of Larks without rising from the table.

"I became interested in the music after the war. Near the end my husband—he'd been an officer in Malaya but he was wounded and sent home—my husband said to me, 'If the Americans win'" (in Japanese there is some ambiguity, she may have meant *when* they win) "'they will be the new masters. The *Sensei*. Everything they do we will have to admire, not despise.' He said it with great contempt, and disappointment. He was much older than me.

"At the end of the war I was ready to change with the times. The people who couldn't adapt died off…those who hadn't been killed in the bombings. Listen—this one's my favourite."

I recognized the song. I remembered my mother singing it, half facetiously, on various occasions. Probably I'd heard it a few times on nostalgic radio shows:

I was dancing with my darling to the Tennessee Waltz
When an old friend I happened to see;
I introduced him to my darling and while they were dancing
My friend stole my sweetheart from me…

Mrs Yumeta would always break off whatever she was telling me to sing along with the droning, scratchy, primitive recording. *I remember the night and the Tennessee Waltz, now I know just how much I have lost...* She had no English but she could sing the words perfectly. She could even mimic the wistful, drawling quality of the unknown singer's voice. ("I must find you the record jacket," she repeated.)

One time, the last time I visited her shop, she rose when the song started and spread her arms wide and sang as if performing for a full nightclub or auditorium—

Well I lost my little darling, the night they were playing
The beautiful Tennessee Waltz

—and I recalled her polite disappointment of a few months before when she first learned I did not know the words by heart. I could not even satisfy her request that I demonstrate the waltz. "You're like the young people here in Japan," she taunted me amiably. "You've forgotten everything."

Mrs Yumeta was a skilful narrator. She revealed her knowledge in tantalizing fragments, gliding forward and backward in time with what seemed a meandering senility. But I knew she had some purpose in mind. Perhaps it was only my imagination, or wishful thinking, but it seemed she was drifting toward something final and momentous.

"My brother was a poet," she told me. "While he was still attending university in Kyōto his first book was published. I didn't really understand the poems, many people called them eccentric, but I was proud of him. Critics praised his book, they said it combined the most interesting aspects of Western poetry with the great Japanese tradition. My brother worked hard to translate it into English because he wanted to have it published overseas.

"Soon after he finished the translation he became convinced that the authorities were having him watched. At the time we thought he was being ridiculous, but the next year when the government decided to remove Western literature from all curriculums he spoke against it at the university and was arrested. Within a month he was shipped to a labour camp in Manchukuo.

"For about a year we received letters and poems, then a message came from the government informing us that he had died suddenly of typhoid. I suspected this was untrue but could do nothing. My husband, who by that time was a colonel stationed in Kyūshū, had been disgusted by my brother's actions and terrified they would discredit the family and ruin his career, so when news arrived of my brother's death he seemed relieved. Still, when I begged him to take a post in Manchukuo to find out exactly what had happened he agreed to try—partly, I suppose, for his own reasons. But he was not a bad man. He felt sorry for me.

"Unfortunately the authorities refused his request and sent him to Malaya as soon as the fighting began there."

I asked her if she still had a copy of her brother's book; she told me her copies had all been destroyed in the bombing. "So much was destroyed," she said. "We were all left with nothing. I felt my past had disappeared entirely. Photographs, gifts, letters...I was lucky enough to inherit money from wealthy relations of my husband who were killed in Kōbe. So I have been able to make a new life..."

She lifted her hands in a kind of priestly gesture to indicate, or consecrate, the new world she had made. I wasn't sure if she was being ironic—the shop was small, musty and sepulchral, as if no one had entered since the day it was built. Mrs Yumeta's fingers began to waver, like a bandmaster's, to the beat of an instrumental piece that was quickly becoming familiar. By the time of my last visit I could hum along with most of her favourites.

When her favourites ended she always returned to the past.

War. Her mother and father died early in the bombings. Her husband returned from Malaya in 1944 with a shattered arm; until the end he was forced to wear a cast and sling. (He had been hit, she insisted, with a large stone hurled by an American prisoner-of-war, who had unfortunately been shot for it. *Wasn't that an unusual kind of wound for a Japanese officer to suffer?* Ah, but the prisoners were being mistreated, everyone was willing to admit that now, and men driven half-mad by hunger will do rash things. *But why Mr Yumeta?* Many guards suffered similar injuries, though few had the good fortune to be sent home. Her niece came every day for a month to sit by his bed and comfort him.)

Children. The couple had one child—a girl—but she'd died in infancy before the war. And in the closing days of the conflict an exhausted Mrs Yumeta had miscarried.

The occupation. The American soldiers she met after the war *were* loud, but not especially smelly or vicious as she had been taught. One, in fact, had become something of a friend. Mrs Yumeta often remarked on our uncanny resemblance.

Childhood. As a girl she had fed the birds in Nagai Park, and as a young bride she had fed them in the garden of her husband's home. (Taking a bag of bread crusts she went to the open door and stood at the threshold to demonstrate.)

Yes, exactly here it must have been. This shop was built over the ruins of the old house. These birds—you would think they were the same ones as ever. *Neh?*

On this occasion I was drunk, a little dizzy, so I did not move from the chair. I had been drinking a lot on recent visits. I watched

Mrs Yumeta stand in the doorway tearing strips of crust and tossing them out into the bright chilly air. It was mid-fall and the last of the summer heat had vanished; for a moment a fresh draft penetrated the shop. From outside an impatient squabbling, birds struggling over the bread.

"When he returned from Malaya my husband was able to tell me things he couldn't say in his letters. The year before, my brother had suddenly appeared in the company of intelligence officers and a group from the Ministry of Propaganda at a POW camp near the place my husband was stationed. They were having him speak to the prisoners, in English, about the decadence of Western customs and ideas and about the hopelessness of their cause. This was meant to persuade them to lend their services to the Ministry, which would then let them warn their compatriots by radio about the futility of further resistance. My husband said my brother seemed cooperative, even zealous, and apparently had not been beaten or drugged. Of course there's no telling what might have happened to him before, but at the time the only thing that seemed important to me was that he was alive. I wanted to rush out and announce to the neighbourhood that he had seen reason and was not a traitor after all—you remember I told you how it was for me, alone here, when my brother was first arrested then interned. But my husband would not let me talk to the neighbours. He seemed very strange, I wondered if the injury had somehow affected his mind. He suffered terribly from nightmares. And he told me things I could hardly believe—that the war was going badly for Japan, that it would soon be over and when the Americans won they would be the masters here. He told me he was deeply worried about my brother's activities; he himself had gotten involved because when my brother realized he was stationed nearby he'd honoured my husband by suggesting he help the Ministry, as he put it, 'persuade the prisoners to cooperate.' My husband would never tell me exactly what he'd had to do in the camp, but he was anxious, he said, because in his capacity as a—an investigating officer—he'd heard prisoners' warnings about what would happen to all such men after the war. He admitted that what he was most afraid of was his relationship to my brother. He seemed sure that my brother would come in for special treatment when the war ended. In fact he felt certain the whole family would be destroyed and its fortunes confiscated. And he was right—my brother died during his trial in 1946 and my husband's family were killed in the final bombing of Kōbe.

"'I myself have done nothing unless told,' he insisted, and at the time I believed there could be no stronger justification for his actions, whatever they were."

She lit another cigarette and looked away. I had a feeling she knew more about her husband's activities than she was letting on, but I said nothing; her words were beginning to strain under the weight of their confession, and I felt I should grant her whatever freedoms she required for a swift, painless passage through her story.

Suddenly she changed the subject and despite several broad hints would not return to her past. We discussed the problems of small businesspeople, which were the same all over the world. She complained a little, as she often did, about the young people who frequented her shop on school days. They were arrogant and impolite. They were allowing the cultural tradition to die out. They seemed to her like—foreigners.

I left with a package of expensive Kyōto sweets, promising to return the next Sunday, but problems at home kept me away for several weeks. My relationship with Fumiko had been crumbling for some time and on the night of the fall's most serious tremor it dissolved completely. Then, a few days after she left, the principal of my school said he had had complaints from students about my behaviour. I was arrogant and condescending, they claimed, about things Western and things Japanese. But I love Japan! I protested, I revere the culture! *Gakk'chosan* said nothing. Nobody is ever fired in Japan. He waited politely for my resignation, and after a few moments I gave it.

The next Sunday, jobless, virtually broke, I returned to Mrs Yumeta. I found myself wondering when I would hear about her husband's death, which had grown more and more implicit, a pale thread woven subtly but visibly into the fabric of the story. I began to sense his death would be the climactic chapter, as it seemed to have been in Mrs Yumeta's life; I couldn't help speculating on the kind of conclusion and revelation it might bring. But that Sunday I learned nothing.

A few days later I had a shock. On my way home after another unsuccessful job hunt I stopped at the Café Pittsburgh for a bite to eat, and the white-haired gentleman behind the grill asked why I'd never patronized his shop before. I explained that I usually went to Mrs Yumeta's. He couldn't hide his surprise.

"You are the only one who ever goes there," he said. "You and the odd stranger to the neighbourhood."

I agreed I was usually alone there, but wasn't Sunday a quiet day in all coffee shops?

Not in his, he said. But then Yumeta-san had never done any business, even during the week. Neighbours avoided her. She didn't need their business.

As he leaned over the sizzling grill a vein of sweat trickled between his eyes. His breath smelled of whiskey.

"She is a strange woman," he said in a low voice. "The war. They say she killed her husband. Some kind of minister in the old government. I hear he had a bad leg and during the bombing—"

He withdrew across the grill, grinning with shame as the Japanese sometimes do. Probably he thought he had embarrassed me by mentioning the bombs.

"Rumours," he said, shrugging. "Who can say for sure?"

IT WAS LATE NOVEMBER. The weather had turned gloomy and cold. That morning, briefly, snowflakes delicate as sifted flour had blown out of the northwest. Japanese winters come down from Siberia, Mrs Yumeta explained. The winter of '45–'46 had been a cold one. She had sheltered two families in the newly built coffee shop until spring…

I was broke. The schools had either heard of me from *Gakk'cho-san* or weren't hiring. I had nothing left but a ticket to Vancouver. I told Mrs Yumeta I had to go home in a few days—there had been a death in the family, something unexpected—and as I spoke I couldn't help relishing the sense of advantage that such news confers. It hardly mattered that it wasn't true. If my stories could not tantalize Mrs Yumeta at least they could surprise her. I assured her I had not been close to the deceased who, according to the Japanese euphemism I politely used, had simply disappeared.

I regretted she might have to end her story prematurely, as I would not be able to return.

Mrs Yumeta lit a cigarette and looked shrewdly over my left shoulder, as if she'd expected me to say something of the kind. I began to feel impatient. I sensed I was being kept in the dark for reasons even she might not fully grasp; suddenly I was tired of being teased with fragments, as I had been since coming to her country. So when she began to speak, in what I took to be a deliberately evasive way, about her husband's career in the military and his stiffly patriotic views, I broke in and with very Western directness asked what exactly had happened to him.

"My husband?" she said. "Yes, you must want to know..."

Her favourite record was playing. The opening bars of "In the Mood" erupted from hidden speakers at an urgent, alarming volume, like a siren in the room's still air. She smiled sadly. "Poor Mr Glenn Miller," she said. "A perfect American. Like my husband, he died too soon."

Mrs Yumeta broke off and looked away toward the door. From outside there was a muted commotion—the birds congregating for their daily meal. She stiffened as if about to rise to go to them, then leaned toward me across the table. She frowned and fumbled for a cigarette and for the first time I was almost sure she was performing.

"The fire-bombs started to fall just after midnight, when most of the neighbourhood was asleep. The sirens didn't start until after the first bombs had exploded. By the time we got out into the street everything was burning.

"My husband began to rush around trying to help people whose clothes had caught fire. There were many like that. He was naked, he had removed his *yukata* to smother the flames. I remember he struggled with his cast and he was badly flushed and sweating. Together we helped a neighbour—an old woman born around the time of Perry—into the middle of the street away from the flames. She was dead by the time we set her down.

"This seemed to finish my husband. He wept and clutched his bad arm, he was ashamed of his pain—then suddenly he was reminded of something. He leapt up and shouted that he had to go back into the house. I begged him not to, I screamed at him to stop but he wouldn't listen. When I tried to grab him he pushed me away. I insisted there was nothing we needed so badly but he turned from me and ran back into the burning house. I tried to follow but a neighbour held me and would not let go. A few moments later the roof collapsed.

"In the morning all we could find of him"—Mrs Yumeta paused and raised her upturned, empty palms above the table, in a gesture that struck me as indecently dramatic—"bones. Really there was nothing left. And of course no trace of whatever he went back to find. About that I have always wondered..."

Her tone was suggestive. The photograph of a lover? His uniform, perhaps, his decorations...Her upturned palms still hovered above the table, conspicuously empty. Whatever he had turned back to save had disappeared with the rest of the old world, with *bushidō,* geisha, colonels and their swaggering dreams, the cryptic smiles of a billion Buddhas. *In a gust of wind the white dew on the autumn grass scatters like a broken necklace*...The coffee shops and American bars that sprouted from the debris must have gleamed with a pledge of reformation, wholeness, survival. In the smell of brewing coffee there would have been a bracing freshness that promised change, like the scent of a shifting wind. But the new story had never got past its introduction. The old one was not yet finished and never would be. *I have been left hanging,* Mrs Yumeta's expression seemed to suggest.

"This shop is built on his ashes," she said finally, letting her hands fall to her sides as a melodramatic riff moaned from the speakers. Everything seemed staged, but her tears welled up suddenly, prodigally, and I felt guilty and cynical for my detachment. But I have reason to doubt her, I thought, remembering the old man in the Café Pittsburgh...

Like Mrs Yumeta I was trapped between worlds. There had been a time, I supposed, when it was easier to believe in things.

Now I was paralyzed, unable to leap forward into faith and compassion or retreat into sarcasm and incredulity. I could picture myself asking the immense question, Did you kill him? and imagine her look of disbelief, then feel her conviction that I have made an error, some quaint and terrifying mistranslation—but no, she has heard correctly. *No,* she is saying: *no, I didn't kill him. It was you.*

The story, I discovered, was not quite over.

The morning after the attack, for the first time ever so far inland, seabirds had appeared in large flocks and swooped low over the ruins. Afraid they were scavengers looking for scraps of flesh, the survivors tried to drive them off, but the birds continually returned, screeching and flapping, alighting on broken rafters and shards of scorched metal…

Mrs Yumeta smiled and looked away. The Japanese consider it rude to dwell on their misfortunes. She glanced at her watch and spoke gamely: "They'll all be gathered by now, the birds, it's time. And listen—it's our old favourite."

And it was. Mrs Yumeta stood and spread her arms wide and began to sing, then took me by the hand and drew me to my feet. "Come," she said, "this is the last time. You're American, show me how to waltz."

Somehow, to my surprise, I did.

I remember the night of the Tennessee Waltz, now I know just how much I have lost…

We turned and glided through the sluggish air of the little café. Dust swirled up from the floor and settled on racks of unused cups and piles of old magazines. As we danced I could feel her cheek trembling at my chest; her mouth was pressed against it so that when she sang out, without understanding, "my friend stole my sweetheart," the words seemed to resonate inside me.

"You're a good dancer," I said softly, the song ending. "There. I really have to go now."

As Mrs Yumeta drew the back of her hand over her eyes I politely looked away. Her face would be a lurid mask of drying tears and smudged makeup; it was better that I didn't see. And now, years later, as I remember leaving, I see myself taking leave of a different Mrs Yumeta, much younger, a bride, a fiancée who does not turn away or hide a face blurred by tears and flattened with time; when she reaches through the room's dim air to turn off her music, so the birds are suddenly audible, the arm is slim and supple and glides with a whisper of silk sleeves over skin.

"There," she says—the voice smooth and youthful—"there, you can hear them. They always come. They are as punctual as you were, *Sensei*."

Taking her bag of crusts she walks me to the door, then presents me with a small jar of homemade pickles she has somehow concealed on herself till then. "Ginger," she says, "and mountain herbs. The art is almost forgotten."

She pulls open the door: a mob of gulls, cranes and herons fills the narrow walk, cawing and flapping, edging forward. A light snow is falling and the feathers of the gulls, grey with soot, seem to whiten before our eyes. I smell brine, a hint of the Inland Sea. The road is a scribble of fading footprints. As Mrs Yumeta tears and throws out crusts to the strange birds I kiss her smeared cheek and tell her I hope to come back when everything is cleared up at home; but the one Japan I would have returned to is dead, or murdered, and I am no longer certain it ever lived.

"Goodbye," she echoes me in Japanese—*sayōnara, sayōnara*—though the old word does not really mean "goodbye," but *Well, if it must be so, so be it.*

"A Man with No Master..."

AMANOGAWA AMERICAN ENGLISH SCHOOL, ŌSAKA, DECEMBER 1987:

A FEW DAYS before Christmas, when my teaching job was due to expire, I was kidnapped by the Japanese mafia.

I heard the front door of the school swing open a few minutes before my one o'clock lesson. I turned from the coffee machine with a counterfeit grin, ready to greet an early student. Two *yakuza* stood in the doorway. The stocky one wore mirrored Ray-Bans and the tall one's tiny eyes stole from side to side, taking things in. Roach-brown leather jackets, pressed black slacks and pointy, patent-leather shoes. Permed hair, of course, though the tall one had only a few curls left on his shiny head.

"*Konichi wa!*" I said loudly. "Interested in improving your English?"

The sunglassed one glared up at his partner who glared at me.

"Ah, forgive me," I said in clumsy Japanese. "I see you don't speak English. Perhaps a beginners' course, then?"

The tall bald one unzipped his jacket halfway and took a few strides into the room. He rubbed his fingers over a small pockmark on his cheek. A bullet scar. Tattooed on his hand and wrist under a Seiko quartz was a long thin samurai sword, crimson.

"I'm afraid," I spread my damp palms, smiling, "I'm afraid you gentlemen may have made a small mistake. Perhaps you're looking for the pool hall? Or the *pachinko* house up the way... Next block, both of them."

"No mistake," said the bald one in guttural Japanese. With one slick motion, as if drawing a knife, he whisked a cigarette from inside his jacket and jabbed it into his mouth. "We have come for Principal Kobayashi. Is that her in the back?"

"You're just hearing the television. *Miami Vice*."

Ray-Ban's sullen mouth showed interest; the bald one nodded down at him, then cleared his throat.

"You—usually wear that hat when you teach?"

I removed a scarlet toque and dangled it in front of me by its flossy white pom-pom. The two men stared.

"The theme of the next lesson," I said, grinning feebly, "is Christmas in Canada."

Ray-Ban shoved past me, heading for the TV.

"This is Japan," the bald one said, "and the mistake is yours."

There was a fierce cry, a crash, and the TV went dead.

LIKE A SAMURAI steed careering through the shifting tides of a Kurosawa battle scene, the sleek black Toyota Crown surged forward, accelerating whenever a break appeared in the herd of tiny honking cars, shuddering to a stop at red lights and whenever the deadly press closed in along Motomachi Dori. Ray-Ban-san was driving. The bald one, still smoking, turned from the front passenger seat and held out his pack.

"What are you going to offer me next," I heard myself babbling, "a blindfold?"

"*Eh? Nani...!*"

"Sorry," I said, switching to Japanese. "I'm sorry. But if you wouldn't mind telling me—I mean, if it's not too much trouble—where are we going?"

Ray-Ban geared down dramatically and the bald one's answer was swallowed by the engine's braying. His full lips had not opened but I knew he'd said something because his cigarette had wagged up and down like a stern, censuring finger. I glanced at his scar.

"... *school*," I caught now, "*has made ... foolish mistake.*"

"Pardon me?"

"*... costly, too. Very ... and unethical.*"

We screeched to a stop.

"But I told you I don't know anything about it!"

"Of course not," the cigarette bowed. "You are merely the foreign *sensei*. Your principal is responsible and she will have to pay for this mistake."

Ray-Ban revved the motor and my pulse raced.

"Please, where are we going?"

"The other school warned her one time already. They did not want to call us but you left them no choice."

We roared off and Ray-Ban cackled as the Crown thundered through the intersection.

"I THINK I'D LIKE TO GO HOME NOW," I found myself saying. "IF YOU'D JUST DROP ME OFF? THE LIGHT UP AHEAD WILL BE FINE."

"*... unfortunate for you that your principal was not ... school when we arrived ...*"

"THAT LIGHT WAS YELLOW!"

The bald one asked me if I would like to calm down. "*You have nothing to fear*," his cigarette bobbed, the barrel of a carelessly held handgun. "*But ... have to keep you with us until ... contact your principal. We could not…warning her about meeting us. She… might call…police."*

I admitted she might. We braked and he tried to smile, his bullet scar squeezed to a dimple. "You have nothing to fear. As soon as we reach her, you will be returned to the school."

"'Set free,' you mean."

"Your Japanese is very good," he said, "for a *gaijin*."

I took a cigarette shakily. The Toyota charged under the green light and swerved round a traffic island on which a single officer stood. "*Omawari, neh?*" the bald one said; it was the slang term for "policeman," and meant "thing idly standing around."

We braked for a light near the north gate of Umeda Station. As the bald one passed me his gold lighter I glimpsed the red sword tattooed on his wrist. *Katana,* I thought—and fumbled the lighter.

"I hope you will not be fired," Katana-san growled sympathetically, "for abandoning your English class."

"I'll just tell them I was kidnapped."

"Yes," he nodded quickly, "they will understand if you say that. In Japan everyone knows all about us."

He was watching me.

"You—usually take this long to light a smoke?"

Ray-Ban gripped the gearshift with adolescent gusto and the engine howled. We covered the intersection then veered off the street down a sudden ramp into a large, empty basement garage, jarring to a stop seconds later. The two men leapt out and Ray-Ban pulled open my door. He barked out some harsh staccato command.

"We will telephone the school now," Katana-san said as I followed them through a swinging steel door and up dim flights of stairs, "and I will speak to your principal. You did say she would be back after lunch…?"

I nodded, trying to catch my breath.

"*Sensei*," he said, firmly taking my arm, "you look terrible. Perhaps in future you should get more rest!"

Under his watch, the tattoo-sword was lined with scarlet characters that dripped like blood from the blade.

I WAITED WITH Ray-Ban on a blue suede couch in a dingy, airless sitting room. The end tables were crammed with dirty cups and glasses and dog-eared piles of pornographic *manga*.

"It's Snoopy," Ray-Ban announced in English. From behind his glasses he nodded at the TV, tore open a can of Budweiser.

A Charlie Brown Christmas in Japanese: Charlie's voice plaintive and befuddled, like some of my students, struggling and overworked; Lucy roaring like a samurai field marshal. I looked away. Above the droning set hung a woodcut of *ninja* in training and an autographed still of James Cagney.

"Bad news," Katana-san said, swaggering into the room. RayBan finally grinned—I hoped at something on the screen.

"I am sorry to tell you that your principal is still out of the school, so we will have to keep you with us for some time."

"But she told me she'd be back after lunch—she's always on time!"

Katana-san glanced at the television. "I spoke to one of your students," he said. "Your principal did come back after lunch. And when she found you had abandoned the class, she left at once to find another teacher."

"But I didn't abandon the class, you kidnapped me!"

I caught myself. Ray-Ban cackled and slapped his knee three times; Linus was on stage delivering the Christmas passage from the Gospel according to Luke.

"You have nothing to fear," Katana-san repeated, smoothing the unruly wisps on his buffed skull. "And kidnap is a very *strong* word, do you not agree? I feel it would be better for all of us if you did not use such a strong word…"

Ray-Ban aimed a large black pistol at the TV set and changed the station. A car chase, it looked like—the last few seconds of *Miami Vice.*

"Especially when you talk about us hereafter. We would like to let you go, of course, but we have to be certain you will not say…unfair things about us to the police. Unkind things…"

"Who? About you?"

Ray-Ban fired another round at the TV and a *sumō* match appeared.

"So say nothing," Katana-san said. "That would be best. We rarely have problems with the police here and everyone is happier that way."

A wrestler rolled like a giant beachball from the *sumō* ring. Ray-Ban fired another round. MTV—Madonna. BLAM. *Miami Vice.* BLAM. *Peanuts* again.

"You have nothing to fear. I explained to the student that you were called away by an emergency, so, if you go back, you will not have lost face."

"*If* I go back? Emergency?"

"I said you had a heart attack."

"I'm twenty-eight years old!"

Hurt, Katana-san stared at the floor, smoothing his wisps, then glanced at the TV. Linus was summing up.

"A *mild* heart attack. You have nothing to fear, Japanese people will believe anything about foreigners. And you did look pretty bad coming up those stairs."

"I *feel* pretty bad. I feel *terrible!* I've been kidnapped by gangsters!"

Ray-Ban offed the TV with a single shot and turned to me.

"*Sensei*," Katana-san said gruffly, "I think we already agreed about not using words like that. Am I wrong?"

I eyed the dark stain my palm had left on the arm of the couch.

"We have been very patient with you so far. We are trying to be...*obliging*." He jabbed his mouth with another cigarette. "Hospitality is an important part of our, our cultural heritage here—our code."

I peered up at him. His bullet scar dimpled into a smile.

"Let's go for lunch," he said.

RAY-BAN, slurping beer, gawked through his glasses at the TV set mounted over the long counter. From the corner of my eye I made out the opening scenes of *Seven Samurai*.

"How long does it take to make one phone call?" I said in English. Ray-Ban ignored me. The aged proprietor, a skeleton in grease-stained apron and paper cap, mumbled to himself in Chinese as he flipped over our sizzling *okonomiyaki*. His wrinkled forehead shone with sweat and periodically he grabbed a grey rag and swabbed it dry.

"*Mō ip'pon!*" yelled Ray-Ban, slapping his empty beer can on the counter. The old man quickly replaced it.

Katana-san emerged from the gloom at the back of the restaurant, his face a black flag.

"She is still out." He shook his head. "And the students are gone now, too. I got an answering machine. I called her home number as well. Another answering machine."

"I don't suppose you might have left some kind of message?"

"Quiet!" Ray-Ban spun from the TV and glared.

Suddenly I was annoyed. "You know, something like, 'Hi, this is the Mob. We're holding one of your teachers hostage and we intend to extort several hundred thousand yen from you at our earliest convenience. We can be reached at the following number'..."

"I sense your irony," Katana-san said, seating himself close on my other side. "Perhaps with foreigners this is a sign of nervousness?"

Ray-Ban guffawed and rattled his beer can on the counter. With one blow, I saw, a samurai had just cut his hairy opponent in half.

"You look pale again, too. Tired. Perhaps with a little food...?" Katana-san gestured expansively at the grill where our *okonomiyaki* were browning. The old proprietor swabbed his brow and glanced up at us with a nervous smile.

"And beer—perhaps that would help. Suppose you take a beer."

I nodded numbly. "Could you make it something stronger?"

"A Kirin for me," he barked, "double Suntory for the prisoner."

I looked at him. His scar dimpled again.

"A joke!" he said, draping his arm round my shoulder. "Granddad here doesn't know more than a few words of Japanese, just brand names and numbers, that's why we always come. I was making a joke!"

I felt myself smile.

"Besides, the *okonomiyaki* are very good. True, the old man is Chinese, but he has run the shop for a long time. Did you know this place is over forty years old? I know you *gaijin* are interested in our history, so think of our, our little outing today as a kind of, well—a kind of historical tour."

"I hadn't thought of seeing it that way."

"You must try."

The old man piled the steaming greasy pancakes onto plates and set them before us, along with my whisky and two more beers. Ray-Ban ignored his meal and stared up at the TV.

"A wonderful film," Katana-san said, nodding at the screen, cheeks bulging with beer and food. "I have seen it many times. You—uh—would like another whisky?"

"If possible. Please."

"You're not touching your lunch."

"*Kill him*," snarled Ray-Ban, beating a thin metallic knell on the counter.

"He knows every scene," Katana-san explained, swallowing. "The film is an important one for us... Probably you think of us as uncultured people...?"

With his eyes the old proprietor signalled at my glass. I nodded gratefully.

"And it is true that I, for example, have never been to the university. But I enjoy a good meal, a bath, the *sumō*"—he stuffed a chunk of *okonomiyaki* into his mouth—"and I do try to read as much as possible."

"*Arigato*," I told the old man.

"Mishima, for example, and many of the Japanese classics. And I have read *The Godfather*—you know it?—three times, in translation."

"Ah," I said between slugs of whisky, "that's good. Wonderful."

"But better in English, I suppose?"

Something on the screen made Ray-Ban laugh. I smiled again. The knot in my gut was dissolving in whisky, chest growing warm.

"...I really must try to read that original..."

"Maybe," I said, covering my mouth, "maybe we'll bring in a special course for mobsters. Criminal English 101."

Katana-san blinked and pursed his lips, then released a hearty laugh and brandished his empty beer can at the proprietor. "Now you feel better," he said, "I can see it! Not so pale. And such fine Japanese!"

"*In the belly!*" cried Ray-Ban. "*Like a dog!*"

Katana-san guzzled beer and jammed his mouth with the moist, delicious-looking pancake. For a moment he could not speak and sat back chewing, cheeks puffed out, stabbing the air with his chopsticks.

"*Mmmmmbb*," he finally brought out, "in some ways, you know, we are the only warriors left. The only real Japanese. The older people... the older people are like robots with their factory jobs, working on and on, so obedient—like peasants—and as for the young students you teach, well, you know how... how *frivolous* they can be. Like small children. You know, in a way our people keep alive the warrior's tradition. Like the forty-seven *ronin*—you know them?—or your Robin Hood. We are outside the law, certainly, but we are always fair. Why, just look, that other school called us instead of the *omawari* when your principal broke the rules of fairness!"

"You still haven't told me what she did."

Katana-san dispatched my remark with a slash of the chopsticks. He signalled for another round. His eyes were glassy, vague, as if focused on some faraway object.

"Nothing," he said staunchly, shaking his flushed head, "*nothing* is better than to live with intensity and honour. For some people, my friend, an ordinary life would be far too... too ordinary! Unbearable! We are the warriors of our time and our code will always be more important to us than the laws of the land, which change with every government. We are like... like the *ronin*—warriors without a master."

I nodded and looked down, unsure how to respond; I tried to read the time on his watch.

"Of course this is difficult for you to understand."

"Of course."

"There are not many of us left."

Shouts, screaming from the TV. We had to pause. The rattle of musketry rose, then fell. After a few moments I said, "That inscription on your tattoo...I've figured out a few of the characters—'man,' 'without'—but some of the others...your watch is kind of in the way."

"*Hold them!*" shouted Ray-Ban, shoving aside his untouched food. A sudden rumble of drumming hoofs; Katana-san had not heard me. He spun around and raised his beer can to toast the warriors in the television.

"No," he said at last, turning back to me, "there is nothing like living with that kind of honour." And his earnest eyes seemed to issue a challenge. The drug deals and knifings my students always spoke of—I was not about to bring them up.

He blushed. "Come now, *Sensei*—you must eat!"

"You're not going to hurt Kobayashi-san, are you?"

Ray-Ban turned to us at once. Katana-san gazed up at the TV, nodding, reaching into his jacket and exhuming a cigarette. "I suspect," he said, "that is very unlikely. *Very* unlikely. We prefer to leave civilians alone. The injured party has simply asked us to, ah, secure a token of your school's regret for its...its unethical mistake. It should be a very simple transaction."

I drained my glass.

"It is really too bad we cannot reach her yet. Things will move very quickly once we get through. We carry out this sort of business all the time."

"Of course."

He lit his cigarette and exhaled. "You have little to fear."

Ray-Ban laughed again and turned to me, nudged me in the ribs. The old man bowed over the grill and set a plate of fortune cookies before us. I had never seen this done before in an *okonomiyaki* house.

"True, it is unusual," Katana-san said, "but times are changing—even here." He crumbled his cookie, shook his head and frowned. "*Yappari, nah!* The fortunes are in English, too!"

I unfurled my own:

SOON YOU WILL BE CROSSING THE GREAT WATERS

Wonderful.

"Translate," Ray-Ban said, thrusting his slip at my chest.

"*Soon,*" I improvised, "*soon you will meet with a . . . a slow, very painful, and untimely end.*"

He snatched the slip from me and held it to his glasses. Katana-san passed me his own.

"*He who lives by the sword,*" I said, "*dies by the sword.*"

He grinned shrewdly. "I know more English than you think," he said, signalling for the bill.

Unsteadily we rose. Katana-san muttered something at Ray-Ban who was still slouched on his stool, motionless, gaping up at the screen. A scruffy barbarian had just fired his matchlock at an unarmed samurai, and missed.

KATANA-SAN, face flushed and slack, explained that he and his men went to the *sentō* each day at five sharp, and since he'd still not reached my principal there was no need to break with tradition.

"Besides," he said, holding the door for me with a grin, "a foreigner can always use a bath."

Dating to well before the war, the *sentō* was situated in the heart of thriving Motomachi Mall; Katana-san explained how the huge shopping centre had spread around and absorbed the bathhouse a dozen years before. "It is our favourite *sentō*. When they built the mall they wanted to tear it down, but we—we let them know we considered their plans a little, well... unwise. For historical reasons."

We passed through a temple-gate wooden door and the *sentō* assistant—a wire-thin student with granny glasses—dropped his comic book and shot from his chair and bowed deeply, repeatedly. Without straightening up or raising his head to look, he motioned with both hands toward a further door. Katana-san did not offer any money.

We stumbled into an empty change room. Under the harsh fluorescent light the white tiles on the walls and floor looked new, as if recently replaced. In one corner a miniature Universal Gym and in the other a Coke machine, couch, two chairs and a TV.

Outnumbered, armed only with swords, the Seven Samurai continued to resist the barbarous onslaughts of their scruffy, fire-armed opponents. But I'd seen the film before; I knew their time was at hand.

"We strip here!" Katana-san said, slurring the words a bit. "I bet you have never been before to the *sentō*?"

"Today's been a first in a lot of ways."

"For me too. I have never yet seen a foreigner naked. Not in person, that is. Naturally I have seen a lot of films..."

Ray-Ban was standing stark naked in front of the TV screen like a patient receiving some New Age therapy. His back, turned toward us, was a rainbow palimpsest of tattoos. There were wings on his shoulder blades, an eye on each buttock, and along his spine a milk-white Snoopy on horseback slaying with a purple lance an Oriental dragon.

Katana-san had a black handgun tattooed on his muscular belly and around either nipple two slightly faded Rising Suns. And, on his penis, a faint inscription, pale blue.

"What are you staring at?"

"I can't make out the third and fifth characters," I said. "It's not Bashō, is it?"

"Bashō?"

"I've always admired *haiku* poems," I said. "Their brevity."

Hurt, Katana-san seized my clothing and stuffed it with his own into a locker. There was a sharp metallic clanking as he shoved the jumbled clothes to the back of the box, tossed in his Seiko and slammed the door.

"Follow me."

As soon as we entered the steaming bath-room the five or six elderly men soaking themselves in the far tub thrashed youthfully from the water and scurried past us to the change room, eyes downcast, hands daintily dangling white washcloths over their loins.

"The owner must love you guys. Does this happen every time you come in?"

Ray-Ban laughed with surprising warmth.

"We take care," Katana-san said, smoothing his curls, "to go to a different *sentō* each night of the week. We would not want to hurt anyone's business. The school, the *okonomiyaki* house, the *sentō*—these businesses are as important to us as our own."

The tiles in the bath-room were greying badly, much older than outside but had been kept meticulously clean. The light was softer, bulbs instead of tubes; we seemed to be moving back in time. Squatting on low wooden stools, we washed at the antique faucets.

Katana-san's tattooed sword was faded on the wrist where his watch had covered it, but I made out two more characters: *sensei*—master—and *shimpo*—progress. *A man with no master moves forward*...

"*Oide*," Katana-san nodded, leading me to the first tub. We clambered in and I gasped at the water's heat.

"Always heard it was dangerous—hot baths after drinking."

"Oh, this is not hot at all," Katana-san said with a smile, his head lolling back on the porcelain rim of the tub. "There are two more tubs to go, each hotter than the last."

"Maybe I'll just cool off a bit first. In the change room."

"We would prefer you to stay with us, please. I will telephone your principal again when we are through. Come now, *Sensei*—relax and enjoy yourself!"

The second tub was piercingly hot. My skin prickled painfully and I was instantly dizzy, breathless; Katana-san's scar was a gory red, his damp skull bright as a buffed helmet.

"I've heard this kind of—kind of water is—terrible for the sperm count."

Ray-Ban scowled at me and moved to the next tub.

"Blood pressure too."

"You know," Katana-san said thoughtfully, "nowadays people lack the will to endure pain. I believe that our people are...are *survivors* because they have that will. The will of the warrior!"—his finger burst like a sword from the steaming water and wagged in admonition—"with the strength to live with intensity."

He rose abruptly and goose-stepped into the next tub.

"And, of course, some discomfort..."

The third tub, smoking, churning with bubbles from the air jets, was a cauldron at roiling boil. After I'd lowered myself in I could no longer speak. Suddenly everything was clear: with liquor the *yakuza* had lulled me into a false sense of security and now after I'd passed out in the boiling water I would be left to drown. Pink, lifeless as a steamed lobster, I would be hauled from the tub in a few hours and my death put down to foreign inexperience and stupidity.

SOON YOU WILL BE CROSSING THE GREAT WATERS.

"*Mā, jūbun da neh!*" said Katana-san. *Enough is enough!*

I got up with difficulty, reprieved.

"Time for a sauna."

Five minutes later, basting on the damp scorching bench between my captors, I was sure my drunken fears were well-founded. I was trapped. The sauna was tiny, dim, a muffled box, the pine walls stained and warped and soon to decay, I was sure, with moisture. The brazier in the corner, topped with rude, steaming slabs of granite and glowing from beneath, was a primitive firepit. I was trapped in a cave, a burial site. No one would hear me when I cried out. The men were silent. Waiting. Katana-san, it was true, seemed to be dozing—leaning back, hands folded on his chest like a marble knight on a tomb—but I sensed Ray-Ban was wide awake.

I pointed out how dark it was in the sauna and asked him if he would like to take off his sunglasses. He didn't respond.

Just as I touched the floor and reached for the handle the door swung open with a fresh cool draft. Hashimoto, my best student, stood naked before me.

"*Sensei!*" he shrieked. "Such a surprise!"

I heard startled grunting behind me, violent movement. Hashimoto's eyes and mouth formed O's of wonder as the dead warriors awoke, sprang from the shadows and gripped me by the arms.

"Tomorrow's lesson," I got out in English—"explain to you then."

"*Nan'tte?* What was that? What did you tell him?" Ray-Ban shook me by the arm and I saw red. I turned and shoved him, hard. Katana-san grabbed me from behind.

"Stop! Stop it!"

"I'll get help," Hashimoto cried, scuttling over the wet tiles toward the change room. I broke free and tried to follow but Katana-san caught me at the door. I watched Ray-Ban dash into the change room and charge at Hashimoto, who had managed to grab a hand towel. "Call the police!" Hashimoto yelled as he flew past the assistant's booth—but the assistant was gone.

Towel in hand, Hashimoto reached the front door and streaked out into the mall. The door swung closed on the screaming of shoppers. Ray-Ban stopped himself at the threshold and spun around, fists clenched.

"He will call the police!"

Wearily, Katana-san blinked his bloodshot eyes. "I don't think he will have to."

"The *gaijin*"—Ray-Ban edged close, forefinger pointed, face sweating—"the *gaijin* is a problem!"

"It does not pay to bother the foreigners. Get dressed."

"It will be no bother."

Katana-san turned to me, frowning. My knees were teetery and I was glad for his grip on my arm. "You have nothing to fear. We have our code. We have never yet hurt a foreigner"—he tilted his head, squinting, and by the harsh fluorescent light I saw that his bullet wound was really an old smallpox scar—"Well, there *was* that one time...My assistant here was involved, in fact. But since then I have been watching him. He is very useful to us, you see, but not...not altogether..."

Ray-Ban had already forgotten us and was closing in on the TV. He seemed to be mumbling. He flexed his back and Snoopy's lance skewered the dragon, which bled sweat and water. The final stages of *Seven Samurai* flickered over the screen: struck by a musket ball, the slender, weary knight collapsed, hurling his sword away from him as he died.

MOTOMACHI MALL swarmed with Christmas shoppers pushing carts full of crammed bags and sparkling parcels and worn-out, cranky children. Everywhere young girls, dressed up as elves, timidly passed out flyers. Some of them looked shaken. From far off, under the great clock set over the mall's far entrance, the jangling drumbeat and faint glitterings of an approaching parade.

"This way," Katana-san growled, all but devouring a cigarette. "The *sentō* boy saw him running this way. And we can call your principal from the pay phones up ahead. If we get her to pay damages at once, the *omawari* will not want to do a thing—not after the fact."

He checked his watch. I glimpsed the sword again and recognized another kanji. I tried to focus on the inscription, translate it, stay calm.

A man with no master moves forward like... like...

Ray-Ban held me by the arm. The two men's heels slapped double time on the tiles and bystanders, furtively watching, made way. "If you say anything," Ray-Ban hissed in my ear—and I could smell the stale Budweiser on his breath.

"There," Katana-san pointed, glancing back at me over his shoulder. On a billboard between a Nintendo shop and a Benetton's I saw one of Principal Kobayashi's posters:

ENGLISH LANGUAGE
MADE NOT EXACTLY EASY BUT
HELPFUL FOR YOUR BETTER LIFE.

AMANOGAWA AMERICAN ENGLISH SCHOOL
ŌSAKA, 521-3651

Unmistakably it was tacked up over another poster.

"In several key locations"—Katana-san raised his voice over the growing jangle of the parade—"your principal has covered up the advertising of a rival school with her own. That is strictly illegal, and so we have been called in to gain reimbursement."

We were approaching the pay phones at high speed. A salaryman glimpsed us, hung up, turned and dashed away.

"Let us hope I can reach her now."

... moves forward, fearless and very fast, like ...

We came to a halt. Katana-san ground his cigarette underfoot and jabbed his calling card into the machine.

Like time, I said to myself, that must be it. *Fearless and very fast, like time. A man with no master moves forward, fearless and very ...*

Ray-Ban squeezed my arm. I turned to him, glaring, then froze: reflected in his dark lenses were countless tiny screens, all of them in turbulent flux. I spun round and stared past the phone booths at the TV shop that now commanded his attention. Absently he freed my arm and shuffled off like a blind man, bound for the store's towering window; he stopped before it and stood frozen, his body haloed with light. The televisions inside were stacked five storeys high and a dozen across and as far as I could see in that two-second span each screen held a different image, from cartoon mice to calm anchormen, from preening rock stars and manic talk show hosts to Clint Eastwood cleaning a gun and the Prime Minister pointing a finger and *sumō* and soccer and ads for ginseng-tonics and well-aged whiskies and the spiralling Wheel of Fortune…

Katana-san had covered his ear with one hand and leaned deeper into the glass booth to escape the clamour of the nearing parade, the beat of drums and clang of cymbals, the frantic farting of the tubas. He seemed to be arguing, shouting. Ray-Ban was frozen under the window. I turned away and walked a few steps, still faint, then began to run. A few seconds later I heard shouting from behind. I sped up. I could see the parade ahead—I'd almost reached it now—the first float led by a team of cardboard reindeer towing a fat waving Santa on a Styrofoam sleigh. I passed the float at full speed, weaving through crowds, making for the huge clock face that stared from over the far entrance. Ranks of people applauding the parade now watched me. Parcels flopped from fumbled bags and a Christmas elf, already shaken, set eyes on me and dropped her flyers and fled.

"*Come back!*" I heard Katana-san yelling. "*Please!*"

Applause and shouts of approval at the passing floats echoed from the high ceiling of the mall. Bands marched between the floats, playing Christmas carols, and a rabble of schoolchildren appeared, singing along, dressed up as samurai and geisha. More cheering and applause—but up ahead and behind me those sounds were mixed with shouts and cries of alarm. "*Sensei…Sensei, please!…come back!*"

I knocked over a full shopping cart and a second later almost tripped on a hand towel. I kept running. I swept past the long applauding ranks and through a multinational gauntlet of stores and ads in a dozen tongues and flashing signs and shoppers staring in that vast mall boundless as the world, past papier-mâché dragons and *sumō* wrestlers sparring on a cardboard ice floe and men dressed as penguins and polar bears and three pious bearded wise men and a squad of *ninja*.

Someone screamed directly ahead. Three policemen charged straight at me, holsters slapping at their thighs. I stopped and froze. Some of the floats had halted too and the marching bands and bears and *ninja* were piling up behind them. Musicians had lost their place. The jumbling bands made a deafening cacophony.

I knelt down and the cops raced past on either side as if I were a ghost. I glanced back. The two warriors had stopped, spun around and were now in full retreat from the law. Inexplicably I hoped Katana-san would escape.

Raucous laughter now, shouts of surprise, as a last float hove into view: a shining turreted Japanese castle tinselled and decked out with flickering lights, the name of a local college emblazoned on the walls and around the moat a circle of students in business suits. And here at last was Hashimoto, my prize pupil, naked as a babe, his heels pinched and pulled at by yelling cops while those playful students, divinely laughing, raised him onto the float and cloaked his shame in somebody's pinstripe jacket.

Townsmen of a Stiller Town

Smart lad, to slip betimes away
From fields where glory does not stay
And early though the laurel grows
It withers quicker than the rose.

—HOUSMAN,
"To an Athlete Dying Young"

A WASHED-OUT slushy weeknight near the end of winter, the Maple Leafs losing badly to the Canadiens, business dead slow, when a man's voice called in an order from an address none of them had heard before. A pre*posterous* voice, Aunt Helen said, a real live one. She figured the place must be somewhere down near the hospital, maybe just back of it, she couldn't rightly tell—but one thing she did know, a new address meant new customers so would Tris kindly oblige her and put aside his vanity just this one time, for her, and get into his official uniform? Now?

A FEW MONTHS AFTER fleeing high school with a skin-of-the-teeth diploma and going full-time as driver at his Aunt Helen's Pickin' Chickin' franchise (TASTIEST SOUTHERN FRIED CHICKEN IN THE GREAT WHITE NORTH, ran the lot-lettered sign beside a giant neon figure of a grinning chicken lifting a boater off his comb with one wing and with the other wing picking a banjo), Tris Leduc had caged a secret mutiny and begun removing his uniform anywhere he could between the shop and the places he was bound with his deliveries of deep-fried Pickin' Chickin', deep-fried Possum Chips, pan-fried Alabama-Style Biscuits, Toothsome Tennessee Apple Tarts, and Carolina Corny Pone, fresh and steaming from the microwave.

Wearing the uniform had become hateful to Tris. Wearing it on late-night deliveries up to the base had always been a drag because it was so dangerous, though not nearly so bad as it was for the cadets themselves to wear their own uniforms in certain of the city's bars. And as certain locals would tell you, and without being asked, the city of Champlain Locks (pop. 22,501) had more bars per person than any city of comparable size in North America.

One problem Tris had faced since starting part-time when the shop opened a year back was that the massive feathered headpiece reduced his peripheral vision to practically zero, forcing him, even in the dead of winter, to leave the driver's-side window down so he could poke out his beaked, wattled head when turning or pulling out to pass. Not that the cold was any real problem. Even with his comb and his left wing icing over, Tris found the suit unbearably hot, not to mention too tight, though the Pickin' Chickin' International head office in Athens, Ohio, had issued along with the suit a colourfully illustrated, jokey brochure that boasted about how "marvelous improved new elastic advances" in the waist and chest material ensured "our one standard suit fits every possible sized Cock, or Hen." Tris was skeletally thin but tall and had what his Aunt Helen liked to call "a heroic frame"—wide shoulders on a tapered waist, big bones, big hands—and every time he'd locked himself in the staff washroom to squeeze into the suit it was a battle. He felt like a crazy man or a scapegoat cramped into a straitjacket, then tarred and feathered. But hardly a man. Glaring into the mirror before pulling on the last part of the outfit—the headpiece with its goggling eyes the size of softballs—he saw an overgrown kid dressing up for a Hallowe'en party, pale lashless eyes, a face so neutral and unlined it might have been sketched in thin pencil with a few listless, grade-school strokes.

Standing six-foot-three in his red-striped leggings, with the bulky headpiece in place, Tris bore a degrading resemblance to Big Bird.

The first stage in Tris Leduc's separation from the ludicrous suit came during a heat wave in late July. Between deliveries he'd gunned the aging little Samurai down to Juno Beach on the Ottawa and leapt from the car, stripped out of suit and cut-off jeans and T-shirt and dived into the river in his briefs. While he plunged and butterflied outward into colder and colder currents, groaning with pleasure, the laid-off mill workers drinking beer up the way, on Omaha Beach, had sauntered down and resurrected the crumpled yellow outfit lying by the car; and as Tris waded back up into air so humid it felt half again as dense and slow as the water, he saw a troop of hooting guys marching away up the beaches, a huge chicken hoisted on their shoulders like a team mascot or troop hero. The bird was facing backwards toward Tris, gaping beak tilted back as it held a beer bottle overhead with one fingered wing and poured a stream of liquid down its throat, the other wing thumbing the beak in farewell.

Tris did not give chase. He was completely delighted. He lit a cigarette and drove back laughing, cool and happily windblown—the Crash Test Dummies on the radio moaning about Superman—and while picking up his next delivery reported to Marsh McDermott, back of the pickup counter frying drumsticks, that the suit had been stolen.

Marsh was the only high school friend Tris still saw and that was only because Marsh was Aunt Helen's other full-time employee. From four till midnight six days a week he worked back of the counter with fryer and microwave, essentially warming over the prepackaged items the head office shipped them in bulk every month. Marsh's red hair had once been long but now it was brush-cut like a cadet's, which beat the shit out of wearing a hairnet on the job, he said. Besides, with the mills shutting up for good he thought he might as well join the army. HATE U., read the college-style crest on his backwards baseball cap. His lean, red-bristled face was always slick with grease and sweat, a toothpick champed between long yellow teeth, bad gums. He'd taught himself to roll the toothpicks from one side of his mouth to the other with no visible movement of lips, but his big jaw muscles were always working, always pulsing with a tense, directionless energy.

When Tris told him about the suit Marsh looked up from the fryer and smirked around his toothpick, then came over to the pickup counter and turned down the old portable black-and-white TV.

"She's not going to like this, boy." Marsh said everything through gritted, grinning teeth. "That getup cost her. Shit, did you see that?"

Tris turned toward the Plexiglas door and windows and peered outside. An eighteen-wheeler had just shuddered past and now as it cleared the city limits, where Main Street broadened into Highway 17, you could hear it gearing up, gaining momentum as it headed west for Mattawa and Sudbury and Lake Superior, the prairies, the Rocky Mountains and the coast.

"No, shithead, here, the *screen*, on the *screen*." Marsh grinned violently and bore down on his toothpick. "Our champ Mr Henke just walked another one. Man, shit on *me*."

"Yeah," Tris said distantly, "but she doesn't need to know right now, I'll talk to her later. Anyway there's nothing I could of done."

"Hey, you could of fought." Marsh struck a staunch, fistic posture, jutting out his stiff lower lip, cocking up his toothpick at a plucky angle. "For the honour of the franchise, son. It's like they've ripped off our flag or something. Team colours. Hey, don't you buy that stuff Athens sends us all the time about team spirit and loyalty and pulling together and all that shit?"

Tris grinned. "What do you think?"

Marsh's toothpick drooped, he shook his head wryly and leered at the TV, as if primed to tell it a dirty joke.

"Hear that, sports fans? He's not a believer anymore."

"Marsh," Tris said, chuckling.

"He's in a slump. That's all. Eh, Patrice? Slumps pass."

Marsh kept staring at the TV but now with fierce concentration, then toothpick-crushing distress, his taut jaw working as the Jays pitcher hit a batter and scored another run for the enemy. Tris stared at the screen too, but blankly. Through high school he'd been as big a Leafs and Jays fan as Marsh—in fact they'd been fans together—but over the past half-year his interest had waned, flickered, and at last flattened out like the electrocardiogram of a lost patient.

"Marshall? Marshall, something is burning!" Aunt Helen was trundling into the narrow kitchen behind Marsh. *Mawshall,* she called him again, her accent suggesting that what was burning might very well be Atlanta. She'd only ever been South one time, on her honeymoon with Uncle Hector, but as she liked to put it the experience had been, for both of them, formative. (And for Hector, fatal. He'd joined the Champlain Locks Civil War Club and over the years had risen to General and then, at their annual Gettysburg re-enactment, leading Pickett's Charge in full regalia despite the heat, a heart attack had felled him in his tracks.)

Aunt Helen's blue-rinsed hair was as always piled up over her heavy red face. She was wedged into a peach dress suit with padded shoulders, her bulky form supported by ballerina calves and ankles that tapered to dainty points in creamcoloured ice-pick pumps.

She'd overheard them talking about the chicken suit. Now, as Tris lit a Player's and repeated his story, she eyed him shrewdly and he could tell she didn't buy a word, that she believed he'd ditched the thing as she knew he'd wanted to for a good long while. Finally though she did report the theft to the police, insisting Tris come to the phone and give Desk Sergeant Treacy a conscientious description of the missing bird, and a few days later it was exhumed from a dumpster behind the Wholly Donut a half-mile up the strip.

He'd felt different at first. The first time he'd donned the suit a kind of schoolkid giddiness had overcome him and like a local boy on the first day of the Spring Circus he'd been irrepressible, giggling wildly inside the headpiece, Marsh and Aunt Helen laughing along with him until sweat sprang prickling into his scalp and above his lip, and his own ceaseless laughter, muffled inside the headpiece as if in a rubber room, began to alarm him. Still, for a few days it had been a party, a summer holiday, an *escape,* to see familiar faces along the main drag nudge each other and buckle over with laughter as he peeled out of a stop light in the heat of a June noon, window down, music humping, cigarette burning like a fuse in his beak and one wing cocked coolly over the door. Then, summer fading into fall, the laughter had weakened and died out and people seemed instead to look away—to look away with a kind of embarrassment—like folks who'd really prefer not to hear, yet again, a good joke that has done the rounds.

Hear a joke too many times and you come to see its edges—some of them too sharp to touch. Tris was coming to see how, at the heart of every gag, there's a dark, hollow space, a kind of death, a loss.

October and the Blue Jays bathed in radiance under the banked lights of the SkyDome, brought home another World Series; the Maple Leafs were shooting from the blocks. None of it seemed to matter. When Tris's high school girlfriend Amelia quit finding his uniform amusing there was little left for them to laugh about. He could hardly blame her for blaming him—his moods, his restlessness. Hell, he had a job! Not perfect maybe but still he was a lucky fucker and besides, she said, he wore that suit pretty well...Then one night toward the end of fall, driving up a dark side street as he now liked to do to avoid the downtown, Tris hit a detour and had to bear back toward Main. As he waited for a light at the corner Amelia appeared in the windshield's frame and crossed a few feet in front of the car with a big moustached Air Cad. They were walking with a kind of stiff, hypnotized urgency, hand in hand, as if they'd been ordered in a trance to go somewhere fast and were now obeying. When the light went green Tris popped the clutch and screeched around directly behind them onto Main, sensing their startled faces turning as he peeled and fishtailed away.

By the time of the first snow Tris had found a good place to change out of his humiliating suit. A couple of minutes up the strip there was an old derelict drive-in, the Bill Barilko Burger Barn, and after dark he would skid in behind it and pump to a stop at the back of the parking lot by a gutted phone booth. For a moment before he cut the headlights he would stare at the huge graffiti spattered in crimson spray paint across the diner's back wall. Like the wall of the St Valentine's Day Massacre. The words always made him shudder, glance behind him. Finally he would kill the lights and get out and after a few minutes the loathsome skin would lie gutted and buckled in slush by the shattered phone booth.

"It won't be so long, Patrice," Aunt Helen would say in a wronged, resigned tone whenever she caught him out of uniform, "until this enterprise will be your own. Think of your own future if you're not inclined to think of mine." And she would swab perspiration and blue mascara from her tired eyes, like the tears he'd never seen her weep. And now—a slushy weeknight near the end of winter, the Leafs losing badly to the Canadiens, business dead slow—she eyed him as the phone rang for the first time in hours. Crowed, actually: it was a buff plastic rooster, head craned back, the receiver resting in its opened beak. She swiped it up before the second ring.

BETHUNE STREET turned out to be a dark narrow fire-alley that ran off Lock. Tris had passed this way often but never seen it. A new address, 99 Bethune St (rear), and that meant new customers and since it was a dead night and his aunt seemed so tired Tris decided to give in to her wishes. Put on the suit. The headpiece at least. It wasn't so much to ask, surely? Helen Evans was not his mother—that had been his uncle's French cousin Lucie, killed when the pulp mill burned down in '78—but she was as close as he would come.

Tris crunched to a stop in the slushy gravel before a wall of black-washed brick indented by a grey-painted steel door, knobless and riveted like the door of a plane. The door was lit from above by a single bare bulb, the number 99 stencilled in black paint on the steel. Killing the lights Tris got out of the car, threw open the trunk and took out the headpiece. For a moment he smoked and stared at the grey door and its cone of light where a few flakes of wet snow glittered as they fell.

The buzzer by the door seemed to make no sound. The bag of chicken cradled under his arm steamed in the cold air, a few snowflakes lighting on the paper, melting. Through the gauze surface of his eyeholes Tris's gaze was tunnelled to a small circle showing the stencilled 99, then his finger, still on the buzzer.

A quick spatting of footfalls behind the door and it swung inward with a groan. A short bald man in a lab coat stood there with an open-mouthed smile, marvelling as if sizing up a long-lost friend. When he pursed his full lips his look turned knowing, almost scornful. His small dark eyes were shrewdly appraising, skin swarthy, beard fussily trimmed, a fine dash of black along the jawline linking sideburns and goatee.

"Ah. Very good. You do deliver the food in disguise. What a piece of work, that mask! Well, no need to stand on ceremony, or out in the freezing—by all means come in."

The man had a vague unplaceable accent and spoke with theatrical precision, like someone on stage playing a dandy or a connoisseur. He seemed to list slightly to one side; that side of his body was smaller, sunken, as if there were only bones under the lab coat.

"You see there has been a heated debate downstairs as to whether you really do dress up. *My* faith never wavered. One has to believe, though, doesn't one? Even when all the instruments agree it is a dark cold day. Although I had hoped you would go the whole hen. Ah well. Through here, just tag along into the dumbwaiter. You're?"

"Pardon me?"

"But allow me first. Basil Mantha." He held out a shrivelled hand and when Tris took it Mantha squeezed with surprising force, something sharp like a ring jabbing into the boy's palm. The man pulled him on toward another steel door which hatched open to swallow them: the elevator was deep and filled with an anemic green institutional light and against the chrome of the back wall stood a sheeted gurney. There was an odd medicinal smell.

"I'm Tris," Tris said, wondering if his weak voice had escaped the long plastic beak. "Is this a hospital?"

"Well an abattoir it is not, let me put you at your . . . Oh *Christ.*" Basil Mantha's polished head bobbed with fierce flamboyant impatience as he stabbed a finger into the control panel. It was whisky Tris smelled—rye. Cologne too. They were dropping fast. The elevator braked with knee-buckling abruptness and the doors clanked open. "Excellent. End of the line. The lowest circle."

Tris heard his own breathing inside the headpiece.

"*Come* on!"

Like a retired colonel with his dignifying wound, Basil Mantha limped briskly ahead up a broad dim-lit corridor and burst on through a set of swinging doors. Polio, Tris thought. He had to run to get through the doors before they swung shut. Then, headpiece wobbling and chafing, he had to jog to keep up. Mantha was glancing back at him with his beady, satirical eyes: "No, young Tristan. No. You must not. You just leave that chicken head on. By order of the City. If you can call it that. I called *you,* you see, for the novelty—we could use a bit of a. What. A *lift*. We've had such a night. And on Byrna's fiftieth too. Here, through here and we shall fix you a drink, young Dristan, something to unclog those fouled-up sinuses!"

"It's Patrice," Tris said, but Mantha had already bustled through another set of doors.

Tris entered a small grubby room lit by a bare bulb hung on a string above a table strewn with paper, books, playing cards, mugs, a coffee pot, an old black manual typewriter and a half-empty quart of Golden Wedding. The damp cold air stank of coffee and tobacco. The bulb's light was dull and sallow, the air smoky, but Tris, scanning the room with his funnelled eyesight, saw everything with heightened precision: the schoolroom clock facing him from the far wall, the brace of framed certificates beneath it, rows of filing cabinets and dented chrome sinks, and, beside them, afloat in a specimen jar, some kind of brain. The right wall seemed to consist of a door and a long window that gave onto another, darkened room, as in a recording studio.

"Tristan?"

Basil Mantha was reclining in a rollered office chair, the orthopaedic heels of his polished shoes on the table by a pile of books. The titles on some of the spines were French, German. HOUSMAN, read the paperback on top, A SHROPSHIRE LAD. There was a second man and a woman, their lab-coated backs to Tris; the man's big white-haired head was turning slowly from side to side, brown smoke seeming to fume up from him. "Jesus, Baz, you shouldn't have brought the delivery boy down here."

"If you can call him a boy," Mantha said.

With a drawn-out sigh the man worked himself free of his chair and turned around. By the time he reached Tris his glum jowly face had rounded into a grin that seemed to mix sheepish apology with tickled disbelief. He stuck his pipe back in his mouth, held out a shaky hand, blue lashless eyes leaky and twinkling over the bifocals low on his nose. "Well, Baz—I'll be damned, you were right after all." His slack throat shook as he chuckled. "How do you do, son? Norm Joliffe. I'm afraid you'll have to, uh…I'm afraid we're not being too professional tonight, been a bit of a bad one. Here, sit down a minute, take a load."

Tris fell into the only free chair, across from Dr Joliffe and with Mantha on his left. Behind Joliffe was the wide dark window where Tris could not help seeing the obscure, goofy reflection of his goggle-eyed headpiece—though against the dark background it seemed the denizen of a drug-induced nightmare, not a cartoon. He looked away. On his right a woman sat stiffly upright as if in a church pew. She was drunk. Under her drooping lab coat her chest and shoulders seemed fallen, her averted face shrivelled and puckered as a deflated balloon.

"And this is Byrna Starnes, our unit manager." Dr Joliffe spoke gently, sitting back and drawing on his pipe, the bowl trembling where his fingers held it. "The birthday girl."

"Tris Leduc. Congratulations, ma'am."

"It would seem I am due an apology," Basil Mantha said. "And you can hardly deny me now; not with the cock crowing here before you."

"Like I said, Baz—you were right. Hot in there, son?"

Leaning forward to set the bag of food on the table Tris could feel Byrna Starnes's hooded eyes raking him as if she'd bet her life savings on his not wearing the suit.

"Just half," she said.

"Oh Byrna," Mantha said, "you become so solemn when you tipple."

Setting down his pipe Joliffe picked up the bottle and gave Tris a confiding wink. "We'll pour him a drink then, see what he's more of—eh son? Man or bird."

"I could just take it off," Tris said.

“What am I owed then?” Mantha asked. “Armagnac or single-malt next time—was that not the bet? No more of this rye. Malt *does* do more than Milton can to justify God’s ways to man. Now had you bet *cash*—”

“He’s not wearing the whole of it,” Byrna Starnes said with stilted precision. “My sister’s children once saw him wearing the rest.”

“Yeah, well, jeez.” The doctor’s eyes were suddenly wistful, watery above his glasses as he sat up, raised his mug in a toast and nodded toward the window behind him: “May they never get the rest of you son.”

“Hear! Hear!” cheered Basil Mantha—and Joliffe now shook his head and snorted out a hearty, sensible laugh as if he’d just been caught mumbling to himself and wanted to be the first to make light of it. “Well, what do you say, all—should we tuck in? But first—right go ahead, Baz.”

Mantha was posing a Styrofoam up in front of Tris. “Out of mugs,” Mantha said daintily, “do forgive us.” The doctor, muttering something about highway safety, dispensed a small shot and Byrna Starnes tugged open a can of Jolt Cola and topped it up.

“Can you really feed yourself a drink through that thing, son?”

“What if I take it off,” Tris said.

“Please do,” Byrna Starnes said, and a smile grazed the pinched corners of her mouth. “Please. You look ridiculous.”

A paper plate appeared in front of Tris. Dr Joliffe, hand trembling less but still trembling, dug clumsily in the food bag and brought out cans of Mountain Dew, three CollardGreen Cole Slaws, a grease-sodden Banjo Box of Possum Chips, an Alabama Jumbo Bucket of chicken.

“Go on, son, help yourself.”

"Thanks," Tris said, "but I really can't stand the stuff anymore."

He gestured with his beak.

"What's through that window there?"

"May I help you with the neck, dear?"

"Right—*off* with his head." Over the rim of his mug Mantha's small black eyes glittered with irony, and something harder. "No, young Tristan. No, you must not let us make a cannibal of you." He seized a chicken breast and bit into it.

Tris removed the headpiece and set it on the floor. As Byrna Starnes saw his face there was a rueful softening in her hard hooded eyes; Tris had to look away. But Joliffe was watching him too. Mantha too. And his own face in the window. Tris reddened, sipped stiffly at his drink. He liked rye and Coke, he and Marsh had drunk a lot of it for a while, but now the lukewarm sweetness sickened him as if the bubbles were welling from something rotten at the bottom of the cup. Somehow the eyes that watched him seemed both plaintive and predatory.

Finally Joliffe, voice shaky, spoke. "How old are you, son? You in school?"

"Eighteen," Tris said.

"So you're done. For now."

"Yes."

"You like the job?"

"A mind reader," Mantha said, dabbing lips with handkerchief, "is hardly called for in such—"

"Jobs do have their ups and downs, son, no question there. No question at all. Sometimes though...Sometimes a man really does get the feeling he's had enough."

Byrna Starnes smiled grimly. "One does." Then, diluting Tris's Coke and rye further with stale-smelling coffee, spilling some on the table: "Bad driving tonight is it, dear?"

"Not so bad." A dark stain was spreading and blotting into a pad of blank forms: *Name, Age, Race, Place and Approximate Time of Death.*

"He wasn't driving," Byrna said.

"Who?"—but Tris instinctively looked up past Joliffe's face and tried to peer into the dark room behind him. His own squinting face stared back.

"Jeez now, Byrna, you know better than to—"

"Ah, what does it matter," Mantha said, "*sub specie aeternitatis?* Whatever *that* is, eh Tris? Someone else was at the wheel."

"There's always somebody else at the wheel," Byrna said.

"There was an accident?"

"Hit and run, dear. Of a kind."

"To the Great Lay Public, yes, Byrna, hit and run, as you so demotically put it. But to the initiated—since tonight you are one of us, Tristan—the term is, well. Roadkill."

Byrna Starnes shot Mantha a glance that might have bored through steel. Joliffe frowned down at the carnage on the plates before him.

"You're kidding," Tris said.

There was a silence during which Tris listened to the clock ticking and the cola's effervescence expiring in his cup.

DR JOLIFFE RELIT his pipe, drank off his rye and cleared his throat, as if preparing to deliver a complex prognosis. "Know what I'd do if I were your age, son? The whole of life at your feet?"

"I know what *I* would do," Basil Mantha said, "but I suspect young Trismégiste here wants only to know what all the—all the scabby particulars—"

"Here, Baz, have another."

"*I* would go to a city that cherished conversation. Bookstores. Fine wine. No wine here in Winesburg!"

"Maybe seal you up for a bit."

"No wine but winos aplenty. How do they manage? Resourceful of them don't you think?"

"Basil..."

"*I* would look for a place where the alley behind Welfare is not littered with empty Aqua Velva bottles. Where no child cyclist is ever found throttled with her own kryptonite lock. Where people do not glare when they see one pull out a book in a restaurant as if one were holding a rotten smelt. Hah! Did I say *restaurant?* There are no restaurants anymore. Only this—*Pickin' Chickin'*. Only chains." He shoved his unfinished food away, let his head sag forward. His ringed, withered hand moved slowly over the damp scalp, as if feeling for an old scar.

Joliffe sighed wearily as he set the bottle—close to empty now—back on the table. The shake in his hands was gone. He looked up over his bifocals into Tris's eyes with a kind of avuncular sobriety; Tris kept trying to see behind him, through the window, where a pale oblong shape glowed dimly in the darkness through the marbling pipe smoke. At first it had seemed an elongated reflection of the doctor's white hair, yet it did not move when he did.

"It was a fight at Henderson's Goal, Tris. The kid's an Air Cad, fresh off the base. French, from just over the river in fact. I uhh, I know his people in fact, they're relations of my wife. I knew the kid when he was, what. Just a kid. Haven't seen him in years, mind you, but still.

"Anyway, the game was on in the bar, Leafs and Montreal I guess and he and a couple other French Cads got into a mix-up with some of the local boys. You know how they are about the Leafs. And I guess they were losing."

"It was pretty bad," Tris said.

"So they took it outside into the parking lot and went at it, I guess a few of the others wound up a *bit* hurt, Cads and local boys too, but not this one. A couple boys knocked him down, thought they'd really hurt him so they tried to scram but he dusted himself off and went after their truck like a damned fool and they didn't see him, that's what they told old Treacy anyway, said he got pulled in under the tires. Drove right over him and crushed his pelvis. Half his gut in the snow. Got him to hospital but it was too late."

Tris felt the cup start to buckle in his hand. "I never even heard the siren," he said.

"The boys in the pickup—they came back. Brought him in to emerg themselves."

"What are friends for," Mantha said bitterly.

"Baz, shut the hell up, OK?"

Byrna Starnes seemed suddenly much drunker than before. She was mumbling something, eyes closed, thin arm crossed over her sunken chest as she rocked herself back and forth. Tris couldn't be sure of her words. *I do,* he thought he heard, *I really do.*

"We don't often see it this bad," said Joliffe, brusquely setting down his pipe and stabbing his plastic fork into a drumstick. "Hardly ever in fact. And he was so damned young. And *family.*"

"And dead ere his prime, Tris," said Mantha. "But men may come to worse than dust. Even golden lads like you Tris. Tall and pretty and six-foot plus. Ah who would not sing for—"

"Jesus, Baz, quit *quoting* that stuff. Leave the kid alone!"

"Hate it here," Byrna Starnes was saying, eyes closed, body rocking. "With all my heart." Tris turned to her gratefully, afraid now of facing Mantha, afraid of the clock above that bald, perspiring head. He knew he was late. Yet he could not turn to check.

He could not tear his eyes from the pale supine form in the darkness behind Joliffe—who was now huddled with Mantha, the doctor flushed, frowning as he scolded and shook his pipe in the small man's haughty face.

Tris felt something come to rest on the back of his hand. It was so light and dry it could not possibly be another hand, it must be a fallen leaf—something that shrunken, weightless. It was Byrna's hand. Her hooded eyes were aimed straight at him though they seemed to overshoot his face and fix on something on the other side.

"It was better the year I was sixteen," she said in a grave, conspiratorial whisper. "You do make me think of him, that one on the French shore. A fisherman. I never knew what he told me, it wasn't English. We were having a bonfire on Juno Beach and Wilf Flowers dared us, who'd swim across the river and back? It was a joke, he didn't mean for anyone to. I was so cocky that night though. Strong. I was sixteen. A good swimmer."

"You swam across the river and back?"

"It's a long way."

"It's a hell of a long way!"

"When I came up on the French shore a man was there on the bank, fishing—fishing, you see, and it was midnight! He was very tall, like you. Handsome. He put his fishing rod down, came over and he had a jacket and I was cold. I let him wrap it around me and then he, he held me and told me something and I got afraid and broke away and dove in. It was farther coming back. When I came in, my friends were lined on the beach shouting with lamps and flashlights, and a few in canoes, they thought I'd drowned you see, they had to help me up the beach. I was too weak to walk. They were saying I was a hero but all I cared was to ask my friend Claire—she was French, you see—she's dead now, cancer, we had her in last March, what was left—I asked her about the words, but I must have addled them all, swimming, she couldn't make sense of it. What he'd said. At all. I so wanted to know."

She closed her eyes and sank back in her chair.

"No one would be waiting for me now, you see. On the beach, with lights."

"Well!"—Basil Mantha clapped his hands—"on that sprightly note! Byrna swimming the Hellespont again. What has become of our bona-fide Ottawa Valley wake? I believe we meant to show our poor grounded chutist back there the time of his, uh…And you too, Tristan. I fear we have made you even *trister.*" Mantha's voice bristled with vindictive scorn. "But then I suppose it never is too early in the morn for a head-on collision with the realities of life. Here on earth, Tristan. The real one. *Bienvenue.*"

"You're drunk," Tris said.

"And you, my boy, are a hollow man, stuffed man, headpiece filled with straw!" A large black beetle scuttled out from under the stained papers and raced over the cable. Lip curling with cruelty, or in pain, Mancha swung his dwindled arm and cracked the flat of his hand down.

"What was the cadet's name," Tris said quickly, turning to Joliffe.

"Not just Juno Beach either. On both shores. I've thought of it too, don't think I haven't. Swim out again like that. Stars would be the lights to guide you home."

"Now Byrna," Joliffe said gently, "don't talk nonsense."

"The cadet's name, Tris? *Mouton Cadet!*" Mantha's voice was raucous, his accent thick. He toasted Tris with the bottle: "One more lamb to the slaughter!"

"I tried once too. Walked out on the ice to where it flows."

"Everyman, Tris, that was his sobriquet. Now Tris you may believe that is something that belongs in the barbecue—sobriquet—right under the spitted, roasting—"

"SHUT THE HELL UP BASIL," Joliffe said and spat something into his napkin.

There was a prolonged silence. For the first time in months Tris found himself wishing he had the headpiece on; he didn't know where to look. He stared down at a table strewn with bones, the scorched rinds of Possum Chips, Joliffe's pipe on its side, leaking ash over papers. *Length. Height. Nature and Extent of Internal Injuries.*

"I should go now," he said.

"You want to know where I'd go, son? With all of life at my feet?" The pathologist's leaky eyes were glazed and wishful; then they went hard and dead as stones. "Where I'd go is somewhere folks didn't butcher each other over a goddamned, stupid, piddlyass..."

As his voice trailed off he shook his drooping head.

"I could have swum the Channel then... I *ran* that group of friends."

"I have to get going," Tris said. "I should get back."

Tris picked up the chicken head and set it on his lap, then stood. A bone crunched under his shoe. He turned the head uncertainly in his hands, like an enormous hat.

"I'll see you to the door, son," Dr Joliffe said, starting to rise from his chair, but then he sagged back and did not try to stop himself. He, Basil Mantha, and Byrna Starnes all slumped gravely around the table staring at the boxes, bucket, bones and cups, the little Rorschach smear Mantha had made of the beetle, the green evil splat of a collard slaw slathered over some forms. Above the clock's ticking, the slow drip of a tap and a steady electric humming that seemed to come from somewhere past the darkened room's door and window. And Byrna Starnes, weeping.

"Don't go," Basil Mantha said.

AFTER WHAT SEEMED a long time Tris heard himself mumbling, "I'm sorry, it's late" and at once Mantha wobbled upright, grabbing the bottle, but instead of heading for Tris he cut a teetering half-pirouette and stumped toward the second room. "Smart boy," he said pulling open the door, the empty bottle slipping and smashing. "Smart boy to slip betimes away, from fields where honour does not, ever..." He hobbled into the dark. Tris squinted through the wide window but could not see him. The lights blazed on, a blinding radiance, and when Tris could look again Mantha stood dramatically spotlit in a bare room under a ceiling striped with fluorescent tubes, the tiled walls and guttered floor glaring white, a blackboard on the far wall scribbled with figures, a microphone dangling mid-air.

Beside him on a table of shocking chrome, under a sheet, the body. Two yellow feet splayed out at one end. Through the window Mantha was skewering Tris with a glare of triumphant allegation, an attorney facing the accused with clear evidence of his crime. He seemed set to speak into the microphone—then with one theatrical sweep of the hand he uncovered the body, the face blanched, unblemished, a grisly pink zipper of puckered flesh running from armpit to groin and the groin itself a squashed, sunken mess.

Tris jerked away, groaning, dropping the headpiece and bolting up the corridor through sets of swinging doors as the sounds of violent contention faded behind him. He stood jamming his finger on the elevator button. He kicked and shoved at the doors. There was a flustered shuffling and he wheeled around: Basil Mantha, wall-eyed yet stately like a demented lord, was almost upon him. Mantha stopped and stood tottering. The steel doors at Tris's back lurched open and the small man rose onto his toes, put his dead hand on Tris's shoulder and pulled himself close while his good hand slipped bills into the boy's shirt. Lips puckering in his beard he huffed out a breath as foul and harsh as formaldehyde. "Beauchemin, Marc," he said, and pushed Tris firmly through the doors.

SPINNING OUT OF the slippery lot Tris heard behind him the buckshot rattling of gravel against the door of the morgue. He swerved onto Lock Street and then veered again onto Main and raced through the near-deserted, dying business section, past closed or boarded shopfronts and huge, useless signs saying FOR SALE or TO LET, past punctured hoardings scrawled with obscene clichés and then the gaunt teenage hookers being hassled by cops outside Henderson's Goal, then the small wedge-shaped park where the green copper bayonet of the Great War soldier was always sheathed in a hot dog wrapper or a chip bag or condom, his upturned eyes gouged out...Nirvana came on the radio and Tris jerked the volume to full. Over the opening chords of "Come as You Are" the DJ was yelling that Kurt Cobain had heroically recovered from his accidental OD and would be leading us all in song for a long time to come.

The strip melting behind him he was back in the town's strung-out neon peripheries where the signs seemed more than ever to feature vain promises, THE WHOLLY DONUT, THE AVALON BINGO PALACE, SIN-D'S ADULT GIFTS *Where Every Day is Valentines*, Champlain Locks Pentecostal (*He Spent Easter*

On The Cross!), THE NIGHT FRYER, PACO'S TACOS, THE HOLLYWOOD DRIVE-IN (long since closed)—the gaps between them growing longer and lonelier the way spaces between towns would look to the Air Cads on their first night-sorties north over the river into Quebec and on for another hour to the Arctic Circle and the dark, unpeopled treeline and the sea.

The neon banjo-strumming chicken loomed into view, lofty as Goliath, jauntily presiding over the scene. Tris slowed as he passed the shop. His aunt was in the front booth seated upright, with iron propriety, sipping her neat bourbon and glaring at her watch; Marsh, behind the counter, elbows splayed on an open paper and bristly red head in his hands, would be rolling a toothpick in his teeth while he checked out the NHL player stats for the tenth time that day. Neither looked up or out to see Tris edging past.

He pulled in behind the Bill Barilko Burger Barn. He parked by the phone booth and let his forehead sag to rest on his knuckles, white and cold where they clenched the wheel. Then he killed the engine, although he left the lights on against the dark and sat listening as sounds rose to fill the silence: the sly, steady tick of freezing rain on the windshield clicks and weak metallic whimperings from the motor as it cooled, the dying whistle of a CF-18 on the base a mile east, and in the woods behind him a rifling crack: a branch, sap frozen, snapping off.

His headlights blazed against the diner's rear wall. Again he felt his nape and face redden, as if from a vicious slap, as he peered up and out at the words spattered there. Fifty times now he'd faced them. Maybe a hundred. Maybe the last time. There would have to be a last time.

YOUR MAMA HAVE ANY KIDS WHO LIVED ASSHOLE

He dug inside his shirt pocket and pulled out the money Mantha had stuffed in: there were two tens and three other bills he couldn't place at first. He hit the light. Fifties. They were fifties. He turned one over and the snowy owl on the back seemed to regard him with an air of composed, commanding dignity; fanning out behind the bird under a broad, dawning sky was an estuary, or an arm of the sea, and beyond the water a line of low mountains wreathed in snow.

Tris took out his wallet and slipped in the cash. Flicked the overhead light back off. From out in the darkness, like a call, came the gear-grunting of a tractor-trailer on the long highway west.

Shared Room on Union

THEY WERE PARKED on Union, in front of her place, their knees locked in conference around the stick shift, Janna and Justin talking, necking a little, the windows just beginning to steam. We'd better stop, she said. I should go now. It was one a.m., a Thursday night turned Friday morning. Squads of drunken students were on the town. So far nobody had passed the car. *Hey, take it to a Travelodge, man!* Nights like this, that sort of thing could happen—one time a rigid hand had rammed the hood, another time someone had smacked the passenger window a foot from her ear, Justin's fingers in her hair stopping dead.

I won't miss this part, he told her.

I really should go, Jus.

Friday was her "nightmare day," a double shift at the upstyle café/bistro where she was now manager. Thursday nights she insisted on sleeping at her own place, alone. Sleep wasn't really the issue, he sensed. This seemed to be a ritual of independence, and he knew she would maintain it strictly, having declared she would, until they moved in together in the new year. Other nights of the week they slept at his place or hers. They would be moving into a storm-worn but solid Victorian red-brick bungalow, three bedrooms, hardwood floors, in a druggy neighbourhood now being colonized by bohemians and young professionals. Justin and Janna were somewhere on the chart between those categories. In

March they planned to fly, tongues somewhat in cheeks, to Las Vegas to get married.

These separate Thursday nights, this symbolic vestige (as he saw it), tore him up in a small way. He could never take in too much of her. He had never been in this position before—the one who loves harder and lives the risk of it. It hadn't been this way at first. Then it was this way, then it wasn't, and now it was again, but more so. This must be a good thing, he felt—this swaying of the balance of desire—and he would try to work out in his mind why it was a good thing, and the words "reciprocal" and "mutuality" would pop up from somewhere, and the idea of a "marital dance," which he thought he had probably read somewhere, yes, definitely...and his mind would start to drift, unable to concentrate on the matter for so long, and he would simply want her body next to his again. For now, no excess seemed possible.

Okay, he said. I know.

I'll see you tomorrow, Jus.

Great.

From somewhere the remote, tuneless roar of frat boy singing. Possibly the sound was approaching. One of the ironies of existence in this city of life-term welfare and psychiatric cases was that the student "ghetto," on a weekend night, could be as dangerous as any slum north of The Hub or in the wartime projects further up. She tightened her eyes and peered through the misty windshield. She had a vertical crease between her brows and it would deepen when she was tired. That one hard crease; otherwise her face was unlined.

What's that?

The boys seemed to be receding, maybe turning south toward the lake. Then another sound—the flat tootling ring of a cellphone, as if right behind the car. Still in a loose embrace they looked back over their shoulders. Someone was there, a shadow, as if seen through frosted glass, standing by the right fender.

What? Yeah, but I can't talk right now. Right, I'm just about to. What's that? Yeah, I believe so.

I'd better go, she said.

I'll walk you in.

It's OK, she said. She didn't move.

Call you in five minutes, the voice said in a clumsy, loud whisper. *Me you, not you me, OK?* The shadow wasn't there by the fender. There was a rapping on the driver's-side window, a shape bulking. Justin let in the clutch and pinched the ignition key but didn't twist. With his free hand he buffed a sort of porthole in the steam of the window. That middle-class aversion to being discourteous, even to a lurking silhouette at one in the morning.

Open it, the voice said roughly. No face visible in the porthole. Justin twisted the key.

Don't!

Jus, he's got something, stop!

It's not a fake—open the fucking door. The man clapped the muzzle to the glass. Behind the pistol a face appeared: pocked and moon-coloured under the sodium street lights, eyes wide and vacated. A too-small baseball cap, hair long behind the ears, dark handlebar moustache.

Justin got out slowly, numbly, and stood beside the car, his eyes at the level of that moustache. The man put the pistol to Justin's chest. An elongated, concave man. Some detached quarter of Justin's mind thought of an extra in a spaghetti western—one of the dirty, stubbly, expendable ones. A hoarfrost of dried spittle on the chin

Janna was getting out on her side, he could hear her.

Just give him the keys, Justin.

There.

And your wallet, the man said. Nice key chain. And your bag, ma'am. Come on.

Ma'am, he'd said. Justin dug for his wallet. His fingers and body trembled as though hypothermic. The night wasn't cold—mild air was lofting up from Lake Ontario and Justin smelled the vast lake in the air, a stored summer's worth of heat. The pupils in the man's pale eyes were dilated with crystal meth, or coke, Justin guessed, aware again of that aloof internal observer— that scientist—though actually in his life he was impulsive to a fault and in his work he progressed by instinctive leaps instead of careful, calibrated steps. He lacked focus but he had energy, good hunches. Two years past his PhD he was in medical research at the university, assisting in a five-year study of fetal alcohol syndrome. No shortage of study subjects in this city.

The pistol looked small to him, maybe a fake, but his knowledge of weapons was vague. He gave his wallet and then, with a sudden instinct to politeness, reached across the roof of the car and received from Janna her olive suede handbag—to pass it to the man. Janna's crease was sharply incised, her green eyes tight and stony. No plea for heroics there. She looked dazed and indignant, he didn't know at whom.

The man got into the car. Justin, as if waiting to be dismissed, stood by the door as it was pulled shut. Your door too, the man told Janna—the voice gone thinner, higher. She shoved it to, the door bouncing back open— the seat belt buckle. Don't slam it that way! he yelled, a man now sustaining an affront to his property. She got the door closed. Frozen, Justin and Janna meshed glances over the roof. The man was trying to start the car. Something wrong there. On stiff, stilt-like legs, Justin edged around the back of the car toward Janna—Janna retreating, as if from him, though more likely toward the door of her building.

The man swung open the car door and shouted, What kind of vehicle *is* this, man?

It's a Volvo. Volvo 240.

I mean what's its *problem?* The man sprang out of the* car and stood teetering by the door, across from them now, eyeing them with ice-clear but unfocused eyes. Possibly drunk as well. He flapped the pistol in the air as he talked in his breathy, squashed tenor. Justin glanced around. The streets were empty.

I don't know, Justin said. It's a standard. You don't drive standard?

His assumption that a townbilly would know how. Pickup trucks and so on. The man's brow clenched, as if at some inward struggle. Drunk too, yes.

Why didn't you *tell* me?

Well, Justin started. The word soaked up whatever breath he had.

I can't drive fucking stick!

Oh, Justin said, eyes on the wagging pistol. I'm sorry.

I hardly ever drive, the man said, quieter.

It's all right, Justin said.

Just leave the car, Janna said, monotone, a digital voice on a recording. You've got our stuff.

The man's cellphone went off like a siren. Stay there, both of yous.

The pistol aimed vaguely at the space between Justin and Janna. Justin wanted to bridge that space and at the same time move as little as possible. The man had the cellphone to his ear. Janna was rigid. She was a quick, fidgety type—frozen that way she was not herself, a wax replica.

Right, but I said I'd call back. How's that? I don't know why the fuck the thing hasn't come, you call them back yourself! I know, I know, that's why I said don't use them anymore, didn't I? Yeah. That's right. And pineapple on just half this time, right? And don't call back. I might be longer, there's no car now. No, I don't want to now. I'll deal with it.

He jabbed the cellphone into his jacket. He looked to either side.

Into the trunk, both of yous.

What? Justin said.

The man flicked the key over the roof of the car. It slid off the near side and plinked down among the leaves and rotting oak mast along the curb.

Hurry up!

Just take our stuff, you don't need to—

Panicking, the man trained the gun on them over the roof of the car, straight-armed, both hands on the grip, a cop at a police car barricade. They might be dead in a second and the afterimage Justin would take with him into oblivion would be from prime-time television.

Open the trunk!

Okay.

I've got to fucking *walk* now.

Still thinking and seeing with a weird clarity, Justin bent down for the key and as he stood up he studied the key chain in his hand. A tiny plastic bust of Elvis. A gift from her, last Valentine's Day. He walked to the trunk and opened it. This was all right, though. There would be people passing, and the trunk was spacious, as trunks go. The guy wasn't taking them into an alley and shooting them. And though Justin had forgotten his cellphone tonight, he knew that she had hers, she always did, and maybe it wasn't in her handbag now, sometimes she kept it in her jacket.

I'm not getting in there, Janna said.

Get in, the man whispered.

No, I can't, please.

Janna, please.

Stop! she hissed in a private way, straight at Justin, her eyes round with rage.

The man's skinny arm pushed her toward the trunk and she gasped. Justin, flat-palmed, shoved at the caved chest under the denim jacket—did it without thinking. The man swung the gun and the butt cracked Justin in the side of the head. He saw a screen of blue light, heard a fizzing sound like static or a can of beer being opened, as he sat back into the trunk. A sick, cold feeling, nausea in the bones, plummeted down his spinal column to his toes. Beaten, he tucked up his dead legs and curled obediently into the trunk. She was making a faint blubbering sound as she climbed in after him. No, I won't, she said as she climbed in. I can't. Please.

Get in, Justin and the man said at the same time. Now just move your foot, the man told her, his voice still quiet but in a different way, maybe appeased, maybe appealing for a sort of understanding. The trunk was deep. It snapped closed and after a second there was a sound of steps running off. The sound-space between the strides was long and Justin had an image, projected on the sealed darkness around him, of the man loping away up Union, long arms dangling, almost simian, mouth slack and panting under the droopy moustache. In their politically civilized circle, people didn't use words like "trash" or "skag" about the distressed elements—addicts, parolees, the generationally poor—who made the city's north side seem more like a slum in Jackson, Mississippi, than part of the old limestone capital of Canada. But now in his anger the words occurred to him. And what he should have done. What he would be doing mentally for weeks to come, rewinding the scene, recutting it.

Fucking yokel. Cops will have him by tomorrow. Are you all right?

No. She expelled the word on a faint puff of breath. He was groping in the dark for her shoulder. He found her breast instead and she seemed to recoil, though there was no room for that. In the deeps of the trunk, furled on their sides in mirror image, they lay with knees pressed together, faces close. Her breaths, coming fast, were hot, coppery, sour.

Janna? He found her shoulder and she didn't move.

She said, Could air be running out already? I feel like it is.

No, no way. And the car's ten years old. We'll get some air in here.

I don't feel it.

Breathe slower, he said. Do you have your cell?

In my bag. It's gone. I didn't want to get in. Why did you just get in?

I didn't. You saw, he smacked me. I was out for a second. He would have shot us. My head is—

I can't be *in* here, Justin. I can't! You knew that, too. That I'm claustrophobic.

He'd never seen her this way. Even in private she was always capable, composed, professional, as though feeling herself under constant scrutiny by some ethical mentor. Too much so, he sometimes felt. How she would never miss a day's workout in the spring and summer while training for her annual triathlon, whatever the weather or her, their, schedule. How she would talk of getting "more serious" about the sport next year, maybe doing more events. Even her recreation—nights out, parties, vacations—she undertook in this same carefully gauged manner, pacing herself. Only so much fun. Only this much frivolity and no more. As if she was afraid of some tipping point.

Till now he had not let on to himself how her discipline—what he had so long lacked and craved—was coming to irk him.

I've told you I'm claustrophobic. Why didn't you tell him?

He probably wouldn't have known the word. Christ, my head.

Of course he would know it.

And I didn't *know*. I mean, I thought you were just saying that before. Everyone says they're claustrophobic.

I don't even like when you pull the quilt over us!

To make love, he thought, in an exclusive cocoon, cut off from the world.

I'm sorry, Jan, he said. The throb in his head was worsening and something was gouging into his hip. Maybe a tool? Something useful here? Of course there were no tools in his trunk. He felt the thing, an old ballpoint pen. His mouth was parched.

And I really have to pee, she said.

That's just nerves, he said. His own guts were wheeling. But it calmed him somewhat, being the one in control like this, consoler and protector.

What's that?

A car revved past, humping out a heavy rap number, the octave dropping as it receded, as if in sadness or fatigue. Justin realized that he'd shouted—both of them had shouted for help, though at the last moment somehow he had tightened the syllable to *Hey*.

You forgot your cell, didn't you? she whispered.

There'll be more cars.

They can't *hear* us, Justin. You always forget your cell! I knew it.

People'll be going by.

Not till the morning. I feel like there isn't, there won't be enough air.

Don't worry, there will.

And I *really* have to go.

She'd never sounded so much like a small girl. Or girly woman. And sometimes he'd longed for that, for a small, unshielded part of her to give itself over to his chivalry and guardianship. But this went too far. Her stomach (invisible now, though as he jabbed the LED on his watch, 1:22 a.m., he got a subaquatic glimpse of her nestled form)—her stomach had a washboard look, tanned, much harder and stronger than his own. She was crying, whimpers mixed with convulsive little intakes of breath, like a child post-tantrum. Finding her hands he held them close between their chests. The trunk seemed to be rocking slightly as if from the adrenalin thump of his pulse, their hearts together. Spending the night together after all. He'd studied murky ultrasound images of curled fetuses, and one time twins—soon to be FAS siblings—the victims of ignorant, careless or despairing parents. Entombed in their toxic primordial sea, the two had seemed to be holding each other in a consoling embrace.

Help, help, she was calling weakly.

Another car passed, slower. Again he yelled involuntarily, aware of a swelling node of panic he was compressing under his heart.

Might have let us go if you said I was claustrophobic.

Okay, Janna. He tried to speak normally. A laryngeal whisper came out. Let me think.

I mean, he won't want us to die in here! He doesn't want to go to jail for that!

You're going to be fine, Jan.

How the fuck do *you* know if I'm going to be fine! You didn't even remember I'm claustrophobic!

Janna.

You're supposed to be a doctor!

I'm not a doctor, you know that. Jesus.

You're crushing my *hands,* Justin!

Her whine seemed to split his head. This felt like the most savage hangover—worse than the worst he had undergone in university and grad school, before he met Janna and set his life on a stabler footing. A student of booze, he had been. My years of research, he would quip.

Jesus, Janna, calm down.

Why is no one walking past? Most nights I lie there and it's, it's. It's like an endless parade of people walking past. Yahoos shouting.

Someone will. Don't worry. We'll call. I—

I just *knew* you wouldn't have your cell. How can we call if—

Shut up! I mean *call.*

This just fuelled her. She wrung her hands free, panting in the tight space. No, no, you're *not* a doctor and it's lucky. You've got no—no—you can never just be *together,* can you, Justin? Why can't you just *arrange* yourself for once? It makes me crazy! You're always—

I'm telling you, enough.

Oh, your bedside manner.

Her breaths were shallow, the sour smell filling the trunk.

You're going to hyperventilate, Janna. That's the only way you won't get enough air, if you hyperventilate.

I can't help it! Get me out of here, Justin!

What are you doing?

Okay. Okay—I'm on my back, I'm pushing up with my feet. You do it too.

Janna—

Like a leg press. I'm strong. It's an old car.

Ten years isn't old for a Volvo. This came to him from somewhere—a line from some ad? His father, years ago? She was grunting, doing her press. At the fitness centre she used a personal trainer and was toying with the idea of becoming one herself.

After a few seconds he rolled onto his back and tried it. It was tight, the angle too acute.

Come on, she breathed out, please please please please. Come on, come on.

The only motion, a slight flexing of the metal. Then more of that suspensioned rocking, below. A passerby might think lovers were in the back seat of the car.

I hear something, he said. He wanted to cover her panting mouth with his hand. Listen.

Oh God, it's someone. Help! she said, but with no breath in it.

Hello! he yelled, amazed at how the enclosure, and somehow the darkness too, seemed to stifle the shout. He squirmed out of his leg-press crouch as steps approached. This move involved shoving contortions, Janna crying out weakly, cursing him as his knee met her shoulder, he guessed. He didn't care now. This was the point in the old film where the hero slaps the hysterical woman and she gets a hold of herself, grateful, admiring, won over.

He got his mouth up against the crack of the trunk, near where it latched. Hello! Help!

The footsteps stopped.

In here, please! We're in the car!

The trunk, Janna whispered.

We're in the trunk!

Footsteps approached. They sounded heavy, solid. A good thing.

Someone in there?

Yes.

Yes! Janna called with a sob. Her breathing was slower, though still shallow.

What, there's two of you?

Yes.

What are you doing in there? A faint slur yoked the words

together. The voice was low and throaty—older. Actually, the voice sounded a bit tickled.

We got locked in. A guy robbed us.

No way! What a fucking drag! I never seen anything like this.

Please, Janna said.

Can you just open the trunk? Justin said. The key might be in the lock there. Or maybe on the ground somewhere.

Hmm. Not in the lock.

Or just call the police. My fiancée is claustrophobic.

Yeah? The wife, she's got that too, as a matter of—

Have you got a phone?

What's that? Oh yeah, at home. Let me see if I can see a key around here.

The key chain is of, uh…it's Elvis, his head.

Not having much luck here. The man started to whistle softly, in tune. *It's now or never.*

I think I'm going to pee, Janna whispered.

Hold on, Justin said. Would you please hurry up, mister?

Hey, I'm doing my best for you, chief!

Maybe you should just go call the cops.

No! Janna said. The key has to be around here!

He might've just stole it, the man said. It's not on the road here.

I don't see why he would have, Justin said stubbornly, hoping the words into truth.

Why didn't he take the car? Nice car. I like these European cars.

He tried, Justin said, reaching to hold Janna's quivering shoulder. He couldn't drive standard.

A momentary silence, then the man burst out in snorty guffaws. Oh now that's too good! he said finally. Guy couldn't drive standard!

I can't hold it, Janna said. Oh God.

It's all right, Justin whispered.

Oh *God,* get me *out* of here, *please!*

Go call the cops now, please! Justin yelled.

All right, yeah, I will so. I will now. But I was just wondering something first...

What?

Got nothing but shit for luck these days. Never the luck, the wife says. If you know what I'm saying. Could you give me a little retainer?

A what?

You know, a retainer. It's legal talk, like on TV. A fee. He paused and then said, firmly: Slip me out some money, whatever you got. I need it. Then I'll call the cops for you. There's a pay phone up the street.

I told you, we were just robbed!

Justin, wait.

We don't have a cent. How the fuck can you ask—

Justin!

Now hang on a minute, chief—I told you, I'm broke, and I'm going to be doing you a favour. I mean, I prefer not to have anything to *do* with cops if it's up to myself. This is going out on a limb for me. It's not like you can't afford it. Look at this car. This fucking *Volvo.*

But we—

It's OK, Janna said, I have something. Some money.

What? Justin said.

Just slip whatever you got through the crack, here by the latch. I can pry, maybe. I got some keys here.

My keys, Justin said. Janna, what are you—

I always keep a twenty separate, she said, in case.

Of course, Justin whispered.

What?

Of course you do, he told her, and now in his mind he saw, not with doting amusement but a stressed rage, Janna opening doors with her hooked pinky, or with the same fey digit keying in her pin at the automatic teller. This although, he'd explained, on any given day a person encountered a dozen infectious agents which, if you were weakened enough, could make you ill or worse. But she was strong—probably all the more so for her years of working with the public at the bistro, where she also did the pinky thing. Where it must be seen as a stylish or campy affectation, not another symptom of her leery, meticulous nature.

A twenty is good, the man said. Try to slip it through here.

No! Justin said. Put the money away, Janna. He was groping in the dark, flashing the LED, trying to find her hand.

Justin, for God's sake, I'm going to get us out of here. Someone has to.

Let her give me the money, asshole. The voice was closer now, the man kneeling, it seemed. I think you can slip it out here.

How do we know you'll even help us, Justin said, if we give you the money?

It's like you got a choice here? The voice was sneering. Justin inhaled sharply. Then the man added, *Duh!*—and this, for Justin, was the end. This soft little *duh*.

Fuck you! You can take our keys and your phone call and your—shove them up your ass, if you know how to find it. And I'm going to find you tomorrow! The cops are going to—

A horrific slamming beat down on them from above, then it seemed to emanate from all directions, a pummelling they felt inside, slower and steadier than their bolting hearts, as the man hammered the trunk with a fist or the flat of his hand. It could have been a street gang smashing the car with tire irons, bats.

Justin rushed his hands to his ears and then to Janna's ears, to protect what was left of her nerves. Stop! he cried. The slamming went on, Janna making a steady high whine of pain or terror. He tried pushing up on the trunk with his fist to absorb the vibrations. He rammed his palm upward once, a feeble counter-blow the man nevertheless must have felt, because now he whacked the metal harder and faster. Justin curled on the floor of the trunk, clamping his palms over Janna's ears, then over his own, back and forth. Though their bodies were jammed together at many points, in this extremity he was fully alone. She must feel the same. He guessed she must feel the same. The beating ended. Heavy footsteps stalked away. The night was quiet again. She was breathing slower—small, sobby catches of breath coming at longer intervals. There was a smell like ammonia and he thought he felt dampness through the right knee of his jeans. He rested a hand on her hip. She seemed to be drifting into a kind of sleep, or a gradual faint, her nervous system, he guessed, no longer able to take the stress.

Now that he didn't have a conscious Janna to coax along, the full weight of his own fear and anger returned. He sobbed for a moment, no tears, eyelids clamped on dryness. Not for the first time he wondered if they actually could suffocate in here. Maybe that was why she'd lost consciousness. His breathing felt tight, but that could just be fear. The trauma of his head blow. A car passed, then another, and he made no effort to cry out.

After a time, soft footsteps approached.

Hello! Please help us! He tried to shout gently, afraid of ripping Janna from her stupor.

Is someone in there? A soft tone, a sort of eunuch voice—the vocal equivalent of the footsteps. Justin explained things, trying to sound calm, murmuring through the crack through which he felt, just once, a cool breath of air. The man listened with a few faint sounds of encouragement. He seemed to be kneeling close to Justin's mouth. The man was an orderly, he said, on the way to the hospital to start his shift on the maternity ward. It was almost five a.m. He would flag down the first car he saw, he said, and get somebody to phone the police, or he would find a pay phone, or call from the hospital if all else failed. That would be ten minutes from now. He would run. The odd, adenoidal voice trailed off, and soft steps—rubber-soled, Justin guessed—jogged away into the night.

Justin left his head against the cool of the metal, his mouth as near as possible to the crack from which that one clean breath of air had seemed to seep. As another draft reached him, tears surged into his eyes with a wide-angle shot of great vapourless skies and fenceless emerald meadows...like a tourist still of the prairies, although he could *smell* the fields. There would be air enough, at least. The police would come soon.

Surely, whatever happened, they would live differently now.

A car was nearing slowly. It cruised past. Perhaps the police, searching for the Volvo they had been told to look for. But the car didn't double back. Another passed, then another. The sparse traffic of early dawn. It was 5:12. In the eerie light of his watch, her sleeping face was peaceful except for the abiding crease between her eyes. Now she was nestled hard against him in the cold, his arm tight around her, his hand splayed wide on her back to cover as much of her as he could. Were old married couples ever buried in the same coffin? he wondered. He had never heard of it, but surely it happened. Or was there some law against it? Another half-hour passed and the little pre-dawn rush hour seemed to end. Why was he not mystified, or at least puzzled, by this latest lack of help, or by its slowness? He felt just numb. There was never any telling. Now and then other cars came from the west or from the east, but none slowed or stopped. Real help would come eventually, of course—the sidewalks would soon be thronged. Another hour or two. Three at most. What was another hour or two in a lifetime together?

A CURIOUS THING he noticed in the years after: In company, he and Janna would often discuss that night, either collaborating to broach the story on some apt conversational cue (which they would both recognize without having to exchange a glance), or readily indulging a request from guests, or hosts, to hear it for the first time, or yet again. And even when passing through a troubled spell in their marriage, they would speak of each other's actions that night only in proud, approving ways. Janna with her granite will, he would say, had faced a claustrophobic's worst nightmare and remained the more rational of them throughout. *She'd probably have got us out of there hours earlier if I'd just listened.* Justin, she would insist, had been competent and forceful the way she had always wanted him to be and had kept her from totally "losing it." Justin would then profess chagrin at how he himself had lost it, screaming at their potential saviour, though in fact he was partial to the memory of that recklessly manly tantrum—and on Janna's face, as she watched him replay the scene, a suspended half smile would appear, a look of fond exasperation. But when the story was done and they left to drive home, or their guests did, a silence would settle between them—not a cold or embarrassed silence, but a pensive, accepting one—and they would say nothing more of that night or its latest rendition. When they were alone together, in fact, they never spoke a word of it.

Those Who Would Be More

Now and then, the man and his boss discuss the weather

Principal Eguchi ordered Scotch instead of beer. Scotch for both of us. We were meeting in Brain Noodle, as we did every week after the Saturday-afternoon cram class I'd been teaching for her since my arrival in Japan ten months before. In public like this, she was always formal with me, but today she was practically rigid and her English had developed a limp.

"You've promoted us from beer to Scotch," I said.

"I have—pardon? Promoted you?"

I knew that Brain Noodle's manager and chefs and wait staff all considered Principal Eguchi a troubling phenomenon—a tall, polished woman who owned her own business and drank quantities of beer in public. And now *Scotch*. She was not sipping.

"A manner of speaking," I said, waiting for her to slip out her pocket dictionary and demand details. I'd never had a student in Eguchi's school as meticulous about learning English as Eguchi herself, as if she had founded her American English school simply as a pretext to improve her own grasp of the language. Officially we met each Saturday to discuss the students and any problems that might have come up during the week, but largely these meetings—like our other encounters—were tutorials for her. I didn't mind. My salary was good, Eguchi was intriguing on a number of counts, and the food at Brain Noodle was superb.

Today the dictionary remained in her pearl handbag, though she did snap the bag open to take out her matte silver compact. She wore as much makeup as any woman I'd ever met. It was applied kabuki-style and, in times of stress, fine-tuned in public. She was a good-looking woman and I never saw the point of this hyperbolic rigour, but of course I said nothing.

"Is everything all right, Ms Eguchi?"

"Would you care for another Suntory!"

"Should we order first?"

She seemed confused. Her eyes were always evasive—she tended to focus on my mouth when I spoke, which usually made me light a cigarette or reach for the toothpicks sheaved in shot glasses along the sushi bar—but today her eyes could find nowhere to land.

"Uh, Ms Eguchi..."

"Some of the parents are compliant," she said in a rush, finally meeting my gaze.

"Compliant? You mean—in sending us their children?"

"They say the children are so happy in the *juku*."

"Oh, oh, you mean 'compliment.' As in—"

"Too happy, the children. Too much play, not enough work. These parents are..."

I sat back. "Oh. These are complaints."

"Several complaints. More than several. How many is several, *Sensei?* In English?"

"Well...I guess around three or four."

"Ah. How many is many?"

"There've been *many* complaints?"

"They say that recess is half the class, *Sensei!* That means, two hours or more."

I could only nod.

"And, you refuse to assign the housework."

"Four hours seems like a pretty long time to keep three- and four-year-olds at a desk. On a Saturday."

"You have said this before, *Sensei*. And I have said: Short recess, no problem. But not like this."

"Some of the children aren't even three yet!" Several. Many.

"Their parents are electing to send them here. You are paid to teach them."

I thought of how some of the smaller pupils couldn't even understand the simple Japanese I had to use to give instructions. I'd tried before, diplomatically, to convey my feelings about the *juku* to Eguchi; she'd simply told me that Westerners—especially of my generation—could never hope to understand Japan.

"Perhaps I feel I have not given you enough time off," she said, inscrutably.

"Have you told these parents that we learn English *during* the recess?"

"But how, *Sensei?*"

"Like I said before. I play games with them. They learn to count. They learn verbs."

"English for playing the game is not what the parents want to learn for them."

I had to look away. I signalled the waiter for two more Scotches.

"All right. I can try shortening the recesses."

"Thank you, *Sensei*. But…"

"But only by so much."

"But I have *promised* these parents, Sensei!"

She was looking at me in a kind of agony. I had seen this before. She was imploring me to take her meaning so that she would not be obliged to finish her sentence, to strip matters to the root. I decided not to help out. I finally sensed what was going on.

"I have promised to give shrift to their compliance, *Sensei*. I am very sorry. So sorry." The Scotches arrived. The waiter glanced at us sidelong. I picked up my Scotch and drank it off, then stood, eyes stinging.

"I gather you mean that I'm fired."

"No!" she said, aghast. "Only that I must replace you at once!"

Each day, the child brings to the teacher an apple

A month into my stay in Japan I began to notice oddities in the primer I had been using to teach myself the language. I'd bought it in a used bookshop on a cul-de-sac in downtown Tokyo. It was close enough to the Ara River that you could smell the water—sour, swampy—as you emerged from the cramped interior. The shop was about fifty feet deep and maybe six feet across—four feet if you deducted the width of the high shelves on either wall. I suppose at one time the space had been no more than an alley between buildings that would have sprouted from the ruins left by the American air raids of '44 and '45. I was in a hurry (on my way to meet Principal Eguchi for the first time: job interview) and didn't spend long comparing the different primers that crammed a good three feet of shelf space. I chose one of the less foxed and fretworn paperbacks: *Japanese for the Beginners and Those Who Would Be More*. The authors shown in the discoloured photo on the back—bespectacled, beaming under a cotton-candy froth of flowering cherry trees—were professors in Kyōto, a pair of elderly and venerable linguists. The book had been published in 1969. I supposed they would be dead by now. It cost just a hundred yen.

The vocabulary for lesson 1 was unsurprising: *thank you, pencil, dog, floor, home, why, when, this, that, him, her, good night* and so on. It was when I started memorizing the words for the next lesson that I noticed an oddness of tone and trajectory. This was a few weeks later, when my honeymoon with the new was waning, giving place to spells of fatigue, commuter claustrophobia, sensory saturation—all the usual markers of culture shock. Among the cats, the cars, the uncles and aunts, houses, doors, windows and other basic vocabulary, the word *shitai* appeared: "corpse." The authors, Drs Sato and Okubo, then perkily urged me to translate a number of Japanese sentences into English, including *My mother's pencil is on the table, When Father comes home, he sees the good dog,* and *When I looked through the window, there was a corpse on the floor.*

I flipped to the appendix to check my translations. All correct. Then, after a dozen or so other standard phrases, this: *My uncle says that there are some corpses in that house.* Bolder now, I tinkered with the sentence and, seizing some lyric licence, settled on: *In my uncle's house are many corpses.* It went on like that. The oddness was diverting enough, but more than once, trying to study while packed among standing, dozing salarymen on trains that were like human trash compactors, I glanced up and looked around, spooked, like a man reading a tepid letter that swerves mysteriously into threatening tones.

In my second month I moved a backpackful of worldly goods into a midget flat not far from the bookshop and the river. I spent little time there. I ate in noodle shops or sat in the park with a book when I wasn't working, commuting. The flat never began to look lived in. Its vacant echoing never ceased—that audible sign that a tenancy has taken root. I was grappling now with lesson 3, which focused on the use of the past tense and introduced new vocabulary. The Second World War, or some discreetly unnamed facsimile, made its first appearance. I wasn't completely surprised. Among the new words that I committed to memory were *rifle, battle, ruin, bomb.*

My aunt stayed with us here for dinner last night.

The sun was bright that day and the wind was warm.

My uncle has a rifle that he found after the battle.

A rifle is no match for a bomb.

I will, I shall, I am going to return

In my last lesson that Saturday, before Eguchi fired me, I'd introduced my students to the future tense in English. It seemed important that the toddlers in the class become acquainted with its nuances. As for the four-, five-, and six-year-olds, the concept would be novel for them as well, since there is no actual future tense in Japanese. *Tomorrow I go to the store. Next week I finish my studies. Before long I go home to Canada.* That was futurity, Japanese-style—simple, logical. By the end of the lesson, and not for the first time, I felt frustrated, mildly ashamed of my mother tongue with all its traps and catches, countless irregularities, fine print, provisos, codicils...If Japanese had a clear, military order and concision, English resembled a sprawling civilian bureaucracy. Hard to get a definite answer. Harder to find your way around. Week by week, just as Eguchi alleged, I was extending the children's recess.

Japanese may have been the more logical tongue, but months into my study of it I was still not fluent; when I gave the children instructions in Japanese they would titter and shout out delighted corrections. My best student, Yukon, would approach me at recess or after the class to footnote these corrections with the mild and beguiling pedantry of a six-year-old happily instructing an elder. Yukon was the "class name" her mother had asked Eguchi to have me use when addressing the girl. I could see the word's attraction from the mother's point of view—it was Canadian, yet in sound it was close to several Japanese given names, and easy to say. All sixteen children had been assigned class names, either by their parents (Clint, Rocky, ABBA, Milk Shake, Waylon, The Phantom, Marvin, Miami, Mickey Rourke) or by Eguchi, who favoured the sort of name she found in the chunky Victorian classics she was grinding through to improve her English: Dorothea, Clelia, Silas, Clement, Edmund, and—for two-and-a-half-year-old Toshiko Watanabe, who, you could tell from her lumpy form and cowpoke wobble, was still in diapers—George.

Once the controlled chaos of recess was at its peak, Yukon would often withdraw from the action and skip over to join me by the chain-link fence that separated the schoolyard from a cool, high, sound-swallowing oasis of bamboo, an exhaling green jungle in the heart of Tokyo. I would be smoking while watching the kids (this was the late eighties, and Japan), seeing how their games would permutate, blind man's bluff into tag, tag into hide-and-seek, intrigued by the brisk negotiations that momentarily broke the flow of play—though the flow, in fact, never really broke, not until I stopped it and herded the class back inside. There was something atomic, or quantum, in this constant, shifting action and repatterning, as if the players were linked so closely to a primal source of energy and motion that they would naturally re-enact it whenever conditions allowed.

Yukon would take my free hand and look up at me in her stern manner, her brow crimped hard under the pageboy bangs, lips clumped together as if ready to scold. Her skin was coppery dark.

She spoke with a slow, dignified formality—possibly a personal style, but more likely her way of making sure I got the Japanese.

Sensei, chotto ii kangae ga aru yo… "*Sensei,* I have a little idea. It might help you."

"Is my Japanese improving, do you think?" I would always ask, flicking down my cigarette and swivelling my shoe on the butt.

"It certainly is, *Sensei!* However, you still talk like a woman."

"I know. My verb endings. I know I have to be less polite."

"And what did you have for your snack today, *Sensei?*"

A quarter pack of Camels, I thought, but I told her, "A muffin and milk." Often at this point I'd have to break off to holler at one or more of the boys. It might be Clement or The Phantom hunkered down on the head of a smaller child like Rocky—a portly, bespectacled five-year-old who wore a tie and looked like a miniature banker—or maybe it was Mickey Rourke, whose name none of the kids could begin to pronounce, trying to wedge Dorothea into the tiny window of the plastic playhouse. "*Damé yo!*" I would call and stride over, gathering George up in my arms to get her clear of the scrimmage, then bringing her back to the fence and holding her, hoping she would again make it through the afternoon without needing a change.

"Tell me, *Sensei,* do you have all these games at home in America?"

"Canada. Yes, we have versions of them."

"Please demonstrate." This she would say with commanding gravity, and often I would, though one time instead I told her the story of how, in Mexico some years before, I and the woman I was with and some other travellers, one of whom had children, started a game of blind man's bluff in the plaza of Oaxaca City. Local children began to gather. We thought it was because of the novelty of seeing adults at play, and gringo adults at that, but no, it was curiosity about the game itself. When one of our number, fluent in Spanish, asked if they wanted to join in, they said that they would like to but didn't know the rules, had never seen the game before. Play, we urged, and they did join in, and before long they had taken over, as we adults and two children backed out one by one, winded and laughing. We left them there, playing in the lamplight in the darkening plaza under ancient Montezuma cypresses while their parents looked on, visibly tickled. And now (I told Yukon) what I wonder is this: Has their game spread outward from that plaza, all through the state of Oaxaca, maybe across the mountains and into the next state— maybe throughout the country? All Latin America? Wouldn't that be something?

Yukon, still holding my hand, gravely watched her surging schoolmates. She seemed to be giving my story consideration.

"Can you stay and keep teaching us, *Sensei?*"

George had dozed off, her head in the crook of my neck, a line of yellow drool snailing down my collar and onto the tie Eguchi insisted I wear.

Yukon added, "*Gaijin-sensei* are forever leaving."

"I think I will go home for Christmas," I said. "I've been away from home for a few years. Eight years now. Imagine not seeing, say, your parents for that long."

"I hardly ever see my father," Yukon said. "I do see his bathrobe. It's white!" Long pause. "If I might ask, will you see your father at Christmas?"

"Well, actually, no." I released her small, cool hand and felt my shirt pocket for my cigarettes, then remembered George on my shoulder. I took Yukon's hand again and explained that my parents had passed away some time ago.

"I used to have two grandfathers," she said after a moment, then smiled.

"I should be back after Christmas, though."

"Perhaps blind man's bluff came to Japan from Mexico," she said with force.

I nodded and made a thoughtful face; I saw no reason to quash the fantasy. It wasn't impossible, after all. And it was good to be reminded that if reprehensible things could spread, spilling outward from their origin to stain the world, better things might spread as well.

Upon meeting, the two conceived an inward affinity

Principal Eguchi had hired me in January. She had asked me to meet her at a place called Brain Noodle. I'd wondered if, over the phone, she'd been mispronouncing "Brine Noodle" or something else, but no. When I entered, five minutes early, she rose from a stool at the sushi bar, her hands brushing her skirt as if bits of food might be clinging there, though at her place there was nothing but a glass of beer and an ashtray with a few butts of exactly even length and a fuming cigarette.

"Welcome," she said, splaying her hands, though not widely or ostentatiously, as if quietly indicating ownership of the restaurant as well as her school. "Please join me."

I was feeling buoyant. I had just arrived from tropical Singapore—where for a year I'd been teaching at an academy expressly tooled to generate dutiful, dream-free logicians—and I was finding the relative cold of Tokyo reviving right to the marrow. And the rush-hour uproar, the near-slapstick tumult of the streets and subway: welcome changes after the embalmed order of Singapore. Energy is optimism and I was ready to start over, one more time. A fresh start might sedate the fear that my years of travel were bringing me no closer to that place where the heart of life beat strongest, and were instead stealing from me the chance of belonging anywhere. I was about to turn thirty and it struck me as old. Old, at least, to have no connections or home, no woman, no child or even niece or nephew—and young to have no parents. Mine had died in a traffic accident several years before, while I was teaching at an American school in the tea-fragrant foothills of Uttar Pradesh, near Dehradun. Paradise, I'd believed. The news had not found me for several weeks. My older brother and our relatives had not forgiven me, as far as I knew, for being so irresponsibly unreachable.

She was tall for a Japanese woman, fit, smartly dressed. A charcoal skirt suit over a blindingly laundered white blouse. Hair back in a tight chignon. Black-frame glasses of a style that would seem hip, youthful, a decade later, but at this point did not. In fact, they seemed chosen to make her look older. More formidably set apart. Her makeup was laid on thickly enough that it was hard to guess her age. Asian adults look about ten years younger than Caucasians of the same age; she looked a little over thirty. Her expression during our meeting and through the months that followed was a repeating slide show of purposeful impatience, contained anxiety, and an openness, kindness, that came in what seemed accidental leaks and which she was always quick to deal with, like something that shamed her—a tampon, a bottle of pills or other sign of carnal frailty—flipping from a purse onto a floor.

Eguchi ordered beer for both of us without asking what I wanted. Hot sake was what I wanted but beer was fine. I was hungry and hoped we might order before discussing terms. She barged straight into them. Talking, she looked me over surreptitiously but steadily, as if interviewing not a potential English teacher but a sketch model or stunt double.

"I have made the schedule for you. Here are your hours."

It should have worried me that she pronounced it "oars." She handed me a neatly typed stack of sheets. Her fingernails were painted cerise, but clipped short.

I scanned the top sheet.

"So it's true, what I've heard—we work Saturdays here."

"So it must be," she said, "for everyone."

"Hmm."

"You will find it the same at each school. And the Saturday is a half day, with the smaller children. An easy day."

"Oh…are small children easy?" I was trying to be droll, to disguise my disappointment, but it sounded almost aggressive.

"Here, yes. Especially if you are not the mother. You…don't like children?"

"It depends on the child," I said frankly—an obvious mistake. Since I never settled in any place for long, I'd developed the habit of saying exactly what I thought. I'd come to expect not to know people for long. With her gaze on me narrowing, I made a recovery, as I had to—I had just a few hundred dollars to my name. "But mostly, yes, I like them. I'd even say I admire them, if that makes any sense. And like I said on the phone, I have lots of experience."

She made a close study of my mouth. "You have none?" she asked.

"Pardon…? No, as I said, I have lots."

"Ah! And how many is lots, *Sensei?*"

"Well…it depends what we're talking about. Flights, money, continents…" I reached for a cigarette.

"I mean *children,* of course."

"Six or seven would be lots."

"Six or seven! Very good, *Sensei!*"

I studied her, trying to get a read. She turned to the waiter, frowned, and signalled for more beer. The brisk demeanour seemed certain to rule out any advances by Japanese men, though her air of professional competence and energy was, to a foreigner of my background, attractive.

"I myself have none of them," she said.

"Oh," I said, "no, I meant that I—"

"But, so it goes, I do have hundreds, at the school. I think they are happy there. But we must work hard."

"*Hai, dozo!*" screamed the waiter, setting down two beers like live grenades and fleeing.

"Is it six, then," she asked me, "or seven?"

I lit my cigarette and offered to light hers. "Well…"

"Ah!" she said. "By the way, as tomorrow is the weekend, you'll be starting."

Passive aggressive

Around three months into my stay, lesson 4 introduced scads of more advanced vocabulary, including nouns such as belief, disappointment, delight, stamina, entrails, and lethality. In the next lesson, "Expressing the Tense-Future in Japanese," I was asked to translate a number of sentences climaxing with *Tomorrow at sunrise, they intend to shoot me*. Lesson 5, around four months into my stay, helped me learn to manage the oft-used passive voice in phrases that built on the work of preceding lessons:

Tomorrow it is quite possible that I shall be shot.

Next week, perhaps, it is more likely that I shall be shot. By the end of next month, at the very latest, I am almost certain that I shall be shot.

The lesson also contained some completely fresh material, like the sentence *Kodomo-tachi made mo korosare-mashita:* "Even the little children were slaughtered."

I was now sure that the authors, consciously or not, were trying to discourage their students from pursuing further study. Perhaps they hoped we would leave the country altogether. At one of my Saturday meetings with Eguchi, I did mention the book and its oddness, but in a subtle way, having learned enough about Japan that I figured specificities would embarrass her. Anyway, I couldn't remember the authors' names, and Eguchi was distracted by business matters, so we let it go.

In the next lesson, toward the end of the rice-planting festival in June, casualties continued to mount and this flashcard narrative appeared: *When the bombs began to fall, there was nowhere for my children to hide. Many children were left without mothers or fathers. All through the night, we searched.*

Ghost in the looking glass

July in the schoolyard, sunlight searing through the breezy peaks of the bamboo to cast moving, ink-sketch shadows onto the asphalt. Yukon canters over and stops, dons a solemn face, takes my hand. A question is coming. In my years abroad I've developed into a decent linguist and my Japanese is now good enough for sustained dialogue.

"*Sensei,* can *gaijin* have babies?"

"Yes, they can!" I respond with enthusiasm. "That's why there are so many of us."

"I don't see many. Once I saw a black man. I was scared of him, but now I'm not."

"My parents had me, for instance."

"I never did see a *gaijin* with a baby. A real *gaijin* baby."

George is in my arms again, drooling against my neck; generally she requires a nap at some point during our now two- to three-hour recess.

"Then you'll have to go to Canada someday, to see. Maybe I'll go back and you can visit me."

For a moment she's pensive.

"What are bears for, *Sensei*?"

"For chasing and eating Canadian children. That's why there are so few of us."

"I thought you said that there were so many?"

"Well—I survived."

This Lewis Carroll logic seems acceptable to her.

"I wouldn't be discouraged by a bear," she says.

"Would anything scare you?"

"I suppose an extremely bad dream might. Do you have bad dreams, *Sensei?*"

"Yes. But I don't remember them."

Silence for a moment.

"Then how do you know you have them?"

"I see their tracks in the morning."

"I dream more when Father is away," she says, "but they're not always bad. But he's *always* away."

"That's why I don't have a baby. Because if I did, I'd be away, in Japan."

Through the looking glass again. She knots her brow. The frown releases in a wide, spirited grin that triggers an answering release somewhere in me. My students' minds offer these brief, sweet truancies from my own.

"Now we're playing hide-and-seek, *Sensei.*"

I look over toward the play equipment. Silas is hunched down on Milk Shake's chest, apparently trying to force a handful of gravel into his mouth. In the distance we hear the mochi-cake peddler in his megaphone truck, inching through the streets, playing a mournful, minor-key jingle, like the theme of a funeral home. Tasty, tasty, mochi-cakes! The sounds and customs of another time.

"I'll join you," I tell her, "as soon as George comes to."

"We would be so honoured," Yukon says, bowing.

People of the Clock

Along with the sometimes macabre lexicon and phrases in my primer, there were dialogues at the end of each lesson that the student was meant to convert into English. Mostly these were untainted by the professors' growing fondness for corpse-filled houses, moaning amputees, children cringing in bomb craters, executions at dawn.

Rather than translate them, I would flip straight to the appendix to read the English versions. Sometimes I would scribble dialogues of my own in the style of the book. It helped me kill hours on the congested, weirdly silent trains I rode back and forth to Eguchi's school and to another school where I sometimes subbed. I read and studied, if with waning discipline, because there was little else to do but be ogled impersonally or doze off on those cars full of sleepers all nodding, twitching in eerie unison as we juddered along through the gloom of tunnels or the sodium glare of stations. Mornings I was the ghost alone among hurried, solid, purposeful burghers; on the night train back, I seemed the only living thing aboard a funeral train of wraiths.

I was aware of a tidal turn gathering somewhere within. For years I'd been in love with being an outsider. Japan, I thought, should have been my Eden, my eventual bride, and would have been, I think, had I been younger. A place I could feel I belonged forever by virtue of not belonging. Never belonging. Islands always rebuff belonging.

But I was falling out of love with distance, absence.

My favourite moment on the ride "home" to my *tatami* closet: as the train crossed under the river and climbed out of the tunnel and shot into the night, a line of huge neon billboards reared across the river like false-front structures in a midway, luminous, festooned, a corporate phantasmagoria of imagery and Japanese characters and twisted English, all mirrored in the sluggish Ara. On a towering billboard, a wry *gaijin*—seemingly James Coburn—sipped whiskey above a slogan set in Gothic script, as if it were a plug for a prog rock band: OF YOU DREAM, BE HANDSOME CAD, FOR YOU PARTY LIFE AND NIGHTIES OF BACHELOR FUN.

DIALOGUE 7: SLEEPING, WAKING

"Who knocks at the door?"

"Open, it is I."

"Please accept my greetings."

"Are you still in bed?"

"Why, what time is it?"

"It has just struck eight. What time is it by your watch?"

"It has stopped. I forget to wind it up."

"Come, my good man, get up!"

"Morning sleep is so sweet. Please go away."

"I don't know how you can lie so long abed!"

"I have nothing better to do; I shall slumber a few minutes

longer."

"But a man's life is so brusque! Come now, up, up, up!"

"Never."

"Then I shall strike you, hence, with my cane."

"No!"

"Have at you, you fop!"

"You are worse than the repeating alarm clock."

On the march, he felt fortunate to have come to no harm

Eguchi was training for the Tokyo women's marathon, coming in mid-November. Sunday mornings I would run with her in the bamboo grove next to the school. The grove was a twenty-acre square with a black asphalt path bisecting it diagonally, and a circular track, a kilometre long, fitting just inside the perimeter. To either side of the narrow paths the bamboo rose in high, hedge-like palisades, so at dusk it was already dark. By day the light was a dim and anaesthetic green, the air almost cool. Where the track came closest to the grove's outer edges, traffic sounds from the bordering streets were loud, yet the streets remained invisible. Eguchi—who confessed that for years she hadn't left the vicinity of her school for more than twenty-four hours at a stretch—would finish these runs by sprinting the diagonal path to Mori Dori and into the schoolyard to check on the Sunday morning class, taught by a gaunt, grim young Texan woman whose students were developing comic drawls, especially on words like *dog* and *house*.

"You are not looking your best this morning, *Sensei*."

We were on our fourth slow lap. Slow, but detectably accelerating. The leaf light didn't do much for her complexion either, but at least her face showed no signs of strain. Mine must have.

I was hungover. The day before, our weekly "meeting" at Brain Noodle had continued through late afternoon, evening, and on into the night.

In a snug salmon track suit with lightning-rod seams, Eguchi ran high on her toes with a silent, gliding gait, smooth but for the steam-house pumping of her arms. The lenses of her wraparound shades turned slowly toward me, seeming to monitor me as coldly as security cameras. Then they slipped down her nose, exposing liquid eyes glinting with irony. "In fact," she said, "you resemble yellow." She slid a finger up the bridge of her nose to push the glasses back into place. On our runs, her English gave up all its gains—the only sign of fatigue she ever showed.

"Look," I panted.

"What?"

"I *look* yellow. You need to let me get more sleep."

"And most of the aliens," she said, "lose weight on the Japanese food."

"It's not the weight. It's the smoking. Slowing me down."

Eguchi smoked nearly as much as I did but it didn't seem to affect her wind.

"Smoking only kills the germs," she said. "In the lungs and chest. It's good for us. Smoking expends the capacity of the lungs."

"I've read that men gain weight. When they're ready to settle."

She laughed huskily, an astonishing sound effect, one that I heard only a handful of times over the ten months I knew her. I turned my head sharply. By the time I brought her face into focus, only the shade of a grin remained.

"What's so funny?"

"Foreign teachers never stay. *Gaijin* never settle here."

"I've seen some," I said, my voice squeezed thin and small. Lap six. Silence but for the sounds of our mutual panting, close and loud in that narrow space. "I've seen some *married.* With a house. Kids."

"Yet in their hearts, home is elsewhere."

"I didn't say *I* was ready to settle."

"No, no. Of course not. Let us now do the wind sprint."

Eguchi seemed to decree these sprints whenever we disagreed—on politics, say, or the way I was teaching for her, especially in the *juku*—or maybe she did it by mischievous instinct whenever I was tired. She surged ahead now, darting with the sleek, silent efficiency of a woodland huntress, me clomping along behind like a puffy old satyr. Her track suit was a flattering fit. At last she slowed to a trot. I caught up. While I was still gasping, she informed me that she'd decided I was a romantic in my view of the teaching. "Like that curious German," she said. "*Do iu hito deshō?* Steinman, *deshō ka?*"

"Steiner. Austrian, I think."

"They are one race, *Sensei.*"

"We read him a bit. Teachers' college. Thought kids shouldn't be wakened too soon."

"Awakened, *Sensei*—in the morning?"

"Metaphorically. Torn from a dream. Pulled into rationality too soon."

"Childhood is not a sleep, *Sensei*—not now. There's no time for that. Ah, time!" She brought the back of her wrist to her face and frowned as she read her Swatch. "Now we do a lap at eighty percent of utter speed. Begin!"

Lately I'd been smoking Peace cigarettes, a cheap local brand.

"Not that I'm *happy* about it," she said, raising her voice over the bellows of my breathing. "When I was a child, we spend plenty of time hunting insects with the nets. The fireflies and the *semi.* What is it, *semi?* Not the cricket..."

"Cicada."

Cheap and unfiltered.

"Your grasp is improving, *Sensei*...We used to bring them back from the fields and the forest and maintain them in the cage with net for walls. We used to name them and play with them like the pets. Summer nights I woke up and came outside after everyone was asleep. To sit and watch the fireflies fly in their cage."

She would not be willing to speak this way, I thought, if we were face to face.

"It's years before, *Sensei*. Now, it's necessary to work harder. Everyone here. It's just too bad, but so it must be."

She smiled uncomfortably. The need to work hard was neurotically national; Eguchi's need to maintain her school in the face of throttling competition and despite being a professional freak—a lone woman boss among a million male ones—was all her own. She would not slack or stint where her business, her baby, was concerned. "There's no help for it—so it must be." Her fallback phrase. *Shikata ga nai*. And though I could now see the wisdom of occasional unromantic acceptance, surrender, I could not impose such a rueful wisdom on my students. A child is a romantic or no longer a child.

"Faster, *Sensei!* Don't stop."

"I need to stop."

"Walk a lap," she instructed. "After, we can walk back to the flat. You can have a bath and a rest again."

"A rest," I said, grinning as I gasped. "Right."

DIALOGUE 9: LOVE & THE ROMANCE

"I am in love with a young gal. I fell in love with her."

"You didn't. You got a fancy. You imagine that you are in love."

"My affection is deep-seated. She has the countenance of an angel."

"You are infatuated with her. Your mind is clouded."

"What? How dare you!"

"You fell into the snare of love. Cupid has snared you."

"Not at all! She has a fine figure, a lovely face, an alluring smile. She has so many personal charms. She walks like a duchess."

"Is that all? Has she good sense, intelligence? Has she good education, good breeding? What of her social position? Has she any big brothers? What kind of man is her father?"

"I know only that I love her dearly. Do not trifle with my love. My life without her would be a life of misery. And what is life without love?"

"You are a shapeless romantic. She may reject you."

"Yet for her, would I chance all."

"Shame on you! Friend you speak non sense."

He had come to behave toward the boss with a befitting respect

"Do you have another book of matches?"

"Here, *Sensei,* you can light it with mine."

"You can call me Curtis, Ms Eguchi. I mean, here we are."

"I prefer to say *Sensei,* even so."

"And you still prefer I call you Ms Eguchi."

"*Sō desu.* There, you see. So easy to light you up."

Even after nine months of this, it was hard to say when she was joking. Her manner was deadpan. Her voice was even, low, and hoarse. Yet during the day, if the phone by the bed should ring and she grabbed it (and she always would, signalling me to be silent), her greeting voice was the standard public female voice of Japan: a breathless treble full of obliging little hiccups and bubbles, all service and subordination. Then she would hang up and, with no apparent self-consciousness, reassume the femme fatale baritone.

"I think maybe I should go back to my place," I said. "I have to teach at the other school, a sub class, first thing."

"Ah, cheating on the side. Is that the phrase?"

"Close."

"You are welcome to stay, *Sensei.* Stay another hour. It's early. Here."

I laughed as if being tickled. "You again."

"How is that?"

"Deeply unethical. Hang on a sec."

"There's none more in the pocket, I think. Don't you worry."

"Packet. You're not worried?"

"Stay, just so. There."

"But *gaijin* all have aids—that's the rumour. And that we're *fertile.*"

"But I am not, *Sensei.*"

"You mean, at this time of the...?"

"In my life. I did want them when I was young. Quite a bit. They never came."

"I'm sorry, Ms Eguchi."

"Now, I could not have them even if I could. I'm a business. And a divorced one. Nobody marries such a woman. Nobody even takes her for the date."

Except, I thought, *gaijin*. I wondered whom I had replaced and who would eventually replace me at the school.

"I'm sorry, Ms Eguchi. I think they're fools."

"*O-seiji desu yo!*"

"No—I'm really not flattering you."

"You're improving, Curtis. *Sensei*."

"This time I want you to look at me the whole time."

I kissed her eyes and tasted kohl.

To describe one's inner feeling

Genki (GENG-KEE): n. or adj.: phonetically eloquent word for vigour, health, high-spirited energy. "How are you today, Curtis *Sensei?*" "*Genki da yo!*" I'm well. Excellent. Fit as a butcher's dog. No English word quite substitutes and I know that for the rest of my life, whenever I feel the way I feel today, *genki* is how I'll want to describe it. It's that kind of day: autumn sky swabbed free of cloud, smog, or the faintest vapour, hardwood leaves in full ignition, the sun bestowing heat in a mood of mellow generosity, unlike summer's violent excess. As I walk, heels snapping, from station to school through the bamboo grove in this elating air, I recall similar days, years ago in my own abandoned country. Sounds carry in clear air and at dusk on fall Saturdays you would hear the caroming hollers of boys playing road hockey on distant streets in all directions compassing outward, while we—the kids of our street, at the navel of the known world—conducted our own passionate match. It seemed the whole universe was at play.

Working briskly, I conclude the lesson (Word Order in the English Sentence) after some fifteen minutes and announce that it's recess, which it will continue to be till the end of class time. Few, if any, of the students can tell time, but even they seem surprised that the lesson is over. Nor will I be giving homework. I will not withhold this day from them. The cold rains of early winter, I've heard, will soon arrive.

I agree to be the spinner in a game of *tanuki*. Standing in the middle of the yard, eyes shut, I pirouette on my heels while the children run off. On the backs of my eyelids they register as a sonar map of scattering laughs and squeals. My right arm sticks straight out as I spin. When I come to a stop I open my eyes, yell "Freeze!" Whichever child I'm pointing at is out and stays frozen. Eventually only one child—today Rocky—remains.

I retreat to the fence beside the bamboo grove and lean back and light a cigarette, which I don't finish. The air is that sweet to inhale. On the east side of the schoolyard, under a rank of mature beeches, Yukon crouches, gathering the gold and yellow leaves layered in a windrow against the fence, layers deepening even now as the wind culls further flurries from the boughs. When I emerge some time later from thoughts of lobbing a football with my father in such weather—striving for and never quite achieving that ideal, high-floating, hosanna spiral—I see she's deputized her little acolytes George and Dorothea to help. I break up a minor fight (Edmund Oyama vs. The Phantom), reconvene the kids and organize a game of animal tag (all animal names to be yelled in English), and still Yukon persists with her project. From time to time she glances over, pretending not to look. Clumsy, comic espionage. I smoke another cigarette, this time finishing the job.

People will tell you, "I don't want a child because it just seems wrong to bring a child into a world like this." High-minded horseshit, in my view. A cut-rate cliché. When has it not been a troubled world? People have children or don't have them for their own selfish reasons, and that's fine and natural. No need to dress up the option as a philanthropic gesture.

For a long time I used that same excuse myself. At teachers' college and in the years after, in the States and Mexico and two

Asian countries. With several women who were interested in complicating our connections, maybe for worse, maybe better, who could say? It meant the end of those affairs, and now, instead of being generationally webbed into the world—which no longer sounded like a trap—I found myself peripheral, placeless, the owner of an accent nobody could pin down, a citizen of departure lounges and unfurnished rental units.

As I pivot my toe on another dead butt, Yukon slowly approaches. George and Dorothea trail. Something is up. Normally Yukon will run up to me, abruptly stop, take my hand, speak gravely. Now in her cupped and sunlit hands something is hidden. She holds it near her chest with great care and ceremony, as if it's a robin's egg, or a living chick. She extends her hands. They open slowly. I see a yellow rose. She peers up at me with a squint, the sun in her eyes, a shy grin. "Here, *Sensei.*" I bend closer, reach out: it's a rose of yellow leaves. She has foliated the leaves in tight, concentric circles, perhaps around a pine cone or a stone or a plum pit. The full shape and the involutions are convincingly floral. A living flower out of dead leaves. I take it from her gently. A red hair-tie near the bottom seems to hold it together. I grip it there, pinched tightly, to hold it together.

Phrases for emergency

"I am looking for my son and daughter. Have you seen them anywhere?"

"I have not. I have been hiding."

"Hiding! Friend, this is no time to hide!"

"Who would not be afraid at such a time?"

"Only think of the needs of your neighbours! Many call out for your help!"

"I will aid you in looking for your children, then. I resolve to help."

"I am grateful."

"When did you last set eyes upon them?"

"This morning, when they left for the school."

"Where would they have gone at the sound of the sirens?"

"To the shelter, it goes without saying! But the shelter lies in ruin."

"Is there anywhere else they could be?"

"Perhaps in the forest. Perhaps they have hidden there."

"Shall I come to assist in your search?"

"I should be much obliged. I should not like to search for them alone."

"In next to no time we shall find them!"

"Come, let us proceed now."

"We shall. Be of good cheer."

The floating world

I may have been jilted professionally, but not sexually, not yet. On Monday, when I went into the school to empty my small desk—and to inform Eguchi that I would be flying to Canada within the week and would need my final paycheque before then—she suggested, awkwardly but frankly, that I should stay with her at least a couple of times before I left. In spite of the firing, I was too amused, and maybe flattered, to turn her down. Men are easily flattered; I should have seen that she was merely feeling in advance the loneliness of a vacant bed. She would not have admitted that she hated sleeping alone, but I knew it. Always, after the night's last sex and cigarette, we would turn away from each other and lie back to back, space between us, to fall asleep, but when I woke up in the small hours she would be furled into me, face on my shoulder or pressed into my nape, sleeping hard.

Actually—be honest—I felt the same way about sleeping alone. Actually, in my sleep, I did the same thing as she did. Pressing myself into her, my heart full. On a cold night of rain, the prospect of a good dinner and drinks and then sex and twined sleep—belly pleasures shared with a keen partner—stirs an expectancy under the heart that's a facsimile of real love. For drifters and outsiders, that may have to do. The night before my flight out, we had an excellent dinner at Brain Noodle, hot sake, appetizers, sashimi and *chanko nabe,* all on her yen, then I walked her home through the rainy streets, sharing her umbrella, which I held. She slipped me a windowed pay envelope as we walked, hips jostling. "I thought it would be better to give it to you now, rather than afterward...after tonight. In the morning." Behind her fogged glasses her look was as deadpan as ever, but her tone was distinctly droll. I laughed, a little drunk. I took the envelope and said, "I can't stay until morning, though. I wish I could. I still have some packing to do and I have to be at Narita at ten."

That night the sex sustained itself not just on the knowledge that this wouldn't be happening again, but also, I felt, on a covert fuel of aggression. She slammed her body against me, worked me mercilessly with her mouth, refused to let either of us rest, all the while locking me into a sexual staring match that was unnerving after almost a year in Japan, where I was no longer used to maintaining eye contact for more than a second, even with her, a lover. Now her gaze was more like an assailant's. *You forced me to fire you,* her eyes seemed to say. *I didn't want to. I wanted this to go on. But my school is too important to risk.* I found that I was angry too, my bites and sucks and thrusts and clutchings all forceful, rough. A firing is like a jilting; even if you fully understand the reason, in your gut you feel panic and anger. For a long while we couldn't exhaust that anger and desire, but at last, after an orgasm that for me was almost painful, as if pulled into being by the roots, I collapsed and we lay side by side, staring into space, for now too tired even to smoke.

"I'll need to go now," I told her. "Soon, anyway."

Her voice was amused: "Go means 'to come,' you know. In Japanese we say 'to go.' *Iku*."

"I think you told me that once. They don't mention that in my primer."

"I suppose you will forget your Japanese."

"I don't think so—not any time soon," I said honestly. "You'll remember to say goodbye to my students for me? Especially the Saturday kids?"

"Of course. I'll say that you are called off by a family emergency."

"Which is hilarious. I have no family."

"You will have."

I propped myself on an elbow and looked at her—she did not look back—and it struck me that she was right. Somehow she knew it and, just then, so did I. The facsimile of love, however convincing, would no longer do.

I lay back down, emptied, my whole body in a flaccid state.

"I won't forget all my Japanese," I said, staring down at my pale paunch, still growing despite all the running and sex. "I'll always remember how to say 'corpse.'"

"Ah, yes, your lesson book. You asked. I intended to tell you. I know the one."

I turned to look at her again. In the near dark I could see how the makeup had smudged around her eyes.

"There was a scandal about that book. I was at a university then and people spoke of it. One of the professors was an officer at the war, and afterward he was imprisoned by the Americans, I can't recall the reason. But the other professor, Okubo I think he was named—"

"That's it—Dr J. Okubo."

"He was *against* the war. He was a pacifier, in the university. So, he was imprisoned as well, but throughout the wartime, by the imperial government. And then in the big firebombing, his wife and children were killed. I can't recall how many children now. Maybe not his wife. But the children, yes—maybe three. It changed him. And the later bombings too …"

"Hiroshima," I said, "and …"

"*Sō desu.* He began to write books, history books, novels and the poetry, even this language book you use. He said Japan was not the aggressive one, but a victim. At the American occupation, they called him the white-washer and forced him to depart the universe."

"University."

"Of course. But he kept on writing."

"I suppose Japan *was* a victim," I said. "You can be a bully and a victim."

"Aliens would weaken the purity of the Japanese race and culture, he believed. He believed the aliens should not remain here." She paused for a moment. "I think that both of those professors have now passed along. I have not heard of that book for a long time. Difficult to find, I think."

"I've gotten to like it. Most of the time, it seems completely normal."

"That's Japan," she said.

"That's any place," I said.

We fell asleep and I only woke at dawn, with Ikuko (her first name, which, out of respect for her wishes, I never used aloud) wrapped around me. She was warm and smelled wonderful. It took some time to disentangle myself so I could get up and clumsily dress and rush out to hail a cab to the station. She didn't see me to the door. Nor did she say goodbye. As the gloom of a wet December dawn crept through the apartment, she pretended to sleep, her face turned into the pillow and hidden by her hair and her hand.

Lesson 12

As the sun rose on that summer morn, the city lay in ruin, with the dead all about. The survivors felt a loneliness so great, words may not describe it.

Omoikiru

On the long flight east over the Pacific, passing under the sun and abridging the day, then the night, I skimmed through the final lessons of *Japanese for the Beginners and Those Who Would Be More.* I was exhausted, but sleep was nowhere. At one point I took Yukon's rose of yellow leaves from my carry-on bag. I was trying to keep it fresh in a baggie; it was already starting to wilt. On airline postcards showing a tiny 747 leading a vee of Canada geese across a clear autumn sky, I wrote a note to Eguchi and, care of the school, to Yukon.

The professors' final lesson was equipped with the usual vocabulary lists, lexically obsolete dialogues, and ordinary sentences alternating now and then with odd ones. *The living mourners remained, yet the house seemed empty with the corpse gone off.* Now and then I was distracted by the in-flight film—*Working Girl*—but as I reached the book's last pages, my attention quickened at the sidebar definition of a verb I'd encountered on several occasions, never grasping the meaning. I'd meant to ask Eguchi about it. *Omoikiru,* the sidebar explained, is a compound verb formed out of the infinitives *omou,* "to think," and *kiru,* "to cut." *Therefore, "Omoikiru" has the meaning: "to cut off all thought of something"; "to surrender the hope"; "to resign oneself to the inevitable."* I put my head back, closed my eyes and wondered—what else?—how I and billions of other non-Japanese speakers had ever gotten by without the word. *For example: To see again those I have cared for is impossible; there is no help for it but to "cut off all thoughts."*

The Dead Are More Visible

A GRAVEYARD SHIFT meant time-and-a-half but she would have worked these January nights, flooding the park rinks, for regular pay. She worked alone and liked the peace of it. In the small office attached to the skaters' warming hut, she kept a thermos of heavily sweetened coffee, her new radio/CD player, a few magazines and a horror or romance novel, neatly packing and taking them home in a duffle bag when her shift ended in the morning dark. Friends would ask if it didn't get lonely. Sure, at times, but if you have to be alone at night anyway, you might as well be working, earning time-and-a-half, instead of alone in the bed.

And working alone saved fuss—dealing with bosses, or with co-workers who always had a grievance to share and wanted you to take their view. Ellen got along fine with them, but they often vexed each other, and who needed to be around that? She'd always found it natural to get along with people. She didn't understand the general crankiness of the world. Often now it seemed easier, if not exactly preferable, to be alone. In earlier jobs she'd had bosses peering over her shoulder all the time—often touching her shoulder, in fact. That groping had died out some years ago and she didn't miss those confidential hands, though she did sometimes miss the looks, all the candid, famished stares that had helped define her teen years and early twenties. Still, she'd never found it as hard to be alone as some of her friends claimed it was. If you got along well with people, you got along with yourself. She believed that as a general rule. In a sense, she was well made for this stage of her life. Look at it that way.

After her first hour or so, flooding the shinny rink and the children's oval, she would come back into the office to warm up while the ice set. She would unzip the front of her black snowmobile suit and slip her feet out of the big Sorels and prop back in the conference chair by the space heater, sipping coffee and reading. Tonight it was *The Shell Seekers* and she would read a good half of its 582 pages before dawn. Harlequins had bored her for some years. No substance, no surprise. They kept you company for an hour or so and then evaporated, leaving no trace. As for horror novels— these freezing nights, nobody around, were just made for them. She liked Thomas Harris and H.P. Lovecraft and lately she'd been rereading early Stephen King.

Depending on the night's coldness, after an hour or two of reading under the lone fluorescent tube she would turn the water back on and pull on her wool gloves and, over them, a pair of industrial rubber gloves, then go out for another round of flooding. Her third or fourth round, near dawn, would finish the night. It took at least three really cold nights to get the rinks up and running in each park, and then there was plenty of maintenance, night and day, after that. This park, unofficially Skeleton Park (it had been the city's main cemetery through the 1800s), was her favourite. She liked its office, preferring the fire-like, toasting heat of the space heater to the electric baseboards in the other, larger offices. And this was pretty much the part of town where she'd grown up. It was changing, of course. Students and young professional types were moving in, renovating the old rental properties enclosing the park on four sides—the handsome Victorian redbricks that gave the park a sort of phony, respectable frame, since just beyond were hundreds of smaller places on narrow yardless streets, much aluminum siding, low apartment blocks of bile-yellow brick. She was raised in one of those smaller houses and had skated here as a child forty years ago.

Technically she still had a boss, but out here she never had to deal with him. Not that he gave her a hard time. They got along. He was a short, fit, swaggery man of about thirty who once had a tryout with an NHL team, she could never remember which one. He treated her like one of the guys to the point of using "man"— while not exactly calling her "man"—when speaking to her. Sure thing, man. Man, I wish I could tell you. You want Skeleton Park this winter, man, it's all yours. Maybe he preferred to think that anyone so much bigger than himself, and possibly stronger, must be a sort of man. Ellen was not only sturdy—her ex-husband's backhanded compliment—but tall. She came from a side of town where most women thickened dramatically in their thirties and before long outweighed their men. The men thinned to sinew, their faces got a wrinkled, redly scoured look as if the skin had been worked with sandpaper, their eyes grew raw and haunted. Ellen had been spared the puffy moon face of her older sisters, only to see her features grow meaty and masculine while her body consolidated, almost doubling itself, like a hard-working farm wife of another era.

Her husband had left, seven years ago. No children. Gavin had never wanted any and now she supposed, accepted, that it was too late. She was forty-six and she no longer registered on men. The many she worked with—almost all of the city's outdoor and maintenance staff were men—were genial and respectful and she never felt so invisible as when they were around: robust, vital men, and they addressed her like a buddy. Or talked about women in her hearing. Maintaining the rink during the day, seeing the boys play shinny or smaller children chug around the oval in their wobbling circuits while the mothers sat watching, cheering—that could get to her too, of course. Being here at night was better, all in all.

The last few nights she wasn't even alone. On the far side of the low-boarded shinny rink, a man was standing motionless under a lamppost by the icy asphalt path. He'd been standing there for three nights. His back to the rink, he was facing the twenty-five-foot-high limestone obelisk that dominated this end of the park. He was not dressed for the activity. He wore a baseball cap and a short brown leather jacket, blue jeans, construction boots. It was about fifteen degrees below zero. He'd spoken to Ellen during the first night's flooding, while she worked the northwest corner of the rink—close enough for them to talk with slightly raised voices. She'd been waving the hose head back and forth, layering water over deepening ice. Now and then he would take a step or two toward the obelisk, pause, then resume his stiff stance. He seemed to be sighting on the thing. Later, a few steps back, a step to the side. She watched out of the corner of her eye, not especially concerned. The park was known for odd spectacles. It was a sort of open-air hostel for addicts, parolees, halfway house residents, psych hospital outpatients, a shifting population of mainly harmless eccentrics.

He'd veered his head and looked at her over his shoulder, fast, a pitcher checking a runner at first base. The visor of his cap kept his face in shadow but she could see his beard, light-coloured, neatly trimmed. He had good shoulders, a nice build.

"Have you ever seen a miracle?" he asked.

Here we go, she thought tolerantly. Then, in a cordial tone, more or less the tone she used to broach any conversation: "It all depends what you mean. You warm enough out here?"

"It has to be moved," he said. His voice was mild, reasonable.

"What, the obelisk there?"

"It's a tombstone. They resent that it's here. It weighs down the dead."

"You been talking to them?"

His head tilted slyly. "Let's just say that I have heard from them. There are twenty-four thousand of them."

"It doesn't seem possible, does it?" she said. "In a space this size. Thirty thousand was the figure I heard."

"The dead are more visible than we are. They have a legal right to this ground. There are twenty-four thousand of them. They resent that tombstone. It's undemocratic."

She'd first read the plaque on the obelisk as a child, in the '60s. Parishioners had built it with local limestone in 1826 to commemorate the loss of their minister, who had died "in the thirtieth year of his age." In Ellen's girlhood and teenage years the thing had been just another neighbourhood feature, something to throw snowballs at (two points if you hit the point of the top spire, one if you hit the stone orb below it), joke about (the more or less phallic shape, the word "erected" on the plaque), or climb on (every few years somebody fell off the upper pediment and broke an arm or got a concussion). Now she guessed she could see what the man was talking about—all the headstones were long gone, pulled from the earth like broken teeth over a century ago, while this monument to one man still towered over the park and its invisibly crammed, stacked dead.

"I can move items with my mind," the man said. "I do it at the kitchen table. If I stare hard enough, I can move this tombstone. I will need to get the angle correct. It's weighing down the dead. Once I move it, I will then dissolve it. I dissolve items."

"Couldn't you dissolve something else?" She amplified her tone of banter to get through to him. "The Revenue Canada building? Kingston Pen? This park takes a lot of hits."

His face was dark under the cap. "The dead want this tombstone moved and dissolved," he said. "This is not what I would choose to do with my evening."

"Sure is a cold one," she said.

For some moments he stared at her.

"Well, good luck to you," she told him. "I mean, I can see your point. I'll have to head across now. Stay warm now." She tugged some slack into the hose and began to slide-step over to the far boards, skirting the freshly soaked places.

"And I can tell," he called out to her back, "if someone is a good person! I look at them and I know their life!"

She turned to him with a grin—who could resist such an offer? If it was an offer.

"So then, what am I?"

She met his intent, eyeless stare. She'd never, even lonely or hurt, found it hard to meet a stare. She bore no guilt.

"You are a good person."

She smiled again. "Thank you. You stay warm."

THIRD NIGHT OF FLOODING, two a.m. Plenty of work in the corners and along the boards, where the ice always grew rucked and pebbled. The middle of the shinny rink was still sunken and would take another thousand litres from the hose. But both rinks would be ready by morning.

At first tonight the man hadn't been there. Then, maybe a half-hour ago, he'd appeared. She had to guess the time because she hadn't heard or seen him arrive. If this were one of her horror novels, he would be a ghost risen out of the earth of the old graveyard. She'd been easing the hose head back and forth, adrift in her night thoughts, which moved erratically, curving, burrowing, doubling back, unlike day thoughts, which had more practical places to get to, when she looked up and there he was, confronting the obelisk, closer to it tonight…On the second night they'd exchanged hellos, nothing more. She'd sensed his deepening seriousness and concentration. Maybe he was getting frustrated, too. Or scared of failure. Did crazy men fear failure the way sane men did? Thinking of Gavin now. All his short-lived ventures. His departure had been a relief in some ways—making a driven man feel important was an unfinishable job—but she missed him, too. Nights she did. For some moments she dwelled on missing Gavin in the nights. Then she looked up: hoarse, drunken shouting. Three kids, it looked like, crossing Balaclava Street, coming up the path. She was glad the man wasn't right on the path tonight. She'd lived here long enough to know trouble at a glance. They had the Grim Reaper look—slumpy, faceless, in layers of dark, baggy hooded sweatshirts. One of them had a biker jacket over his sweatshirt. Sure enough they came to a slouching halt on the path not far behind the man, who was facing away from them, apparently unaware. One of them, tall and skinny, was holding something like a crowbar. She shuffled out from behind the boards and stood in the open between the rinks, letting the water spray onto the patch of ice connecting them, keeping an eye on developments.

The taunts began—too slurred and soft, at first, to make out. The man didn't move or glance back. Maybe he was too deep inside his meditation, or felt he was on the verge of success. The kid in the biker jacket was edging up. "Hey, man. I've been hearing about you." His voice was firmer, clearer than the others': "Hey, stare at this, man." He shoved the man in the back, not hard, and the man did turn slowly, pivoting from the waist up. After a moment his dark, visored face tilted like a puzzled dog's.

"Leave him alone," she called.

The hooded faces turned to her in cartoon unison. In other circumstances it would have been funny. The man swivelled back into his posture. The kid in the biker jacket started right toward her, hands in his jacket pockets. In her stomach a down-rush of fear. The others followed him with slack, messy movements—they would have trouble when they reached the ice. She turned to face them as they came on through the half-light between the lampposts. She gave the control ring on the hose a half turn to reduce the flow and let the stream pool outward on the ice in front of her. The hose head was a half-foot of steel tapered to a flanged hole an inch and a half in diameter.

"He a friend of yours?" the leader called to her as he approached.

Gavin had been a connoisseur of confrontations and often gave his views on the best way to manage them. *You don't get into a war of words,* he used to say, addressing her as if she cared—actually just reassuring himself. *You let your opponent work himself into a state and talk away his wind. You stay calm and quiet and hold his stare.*

"Guess you must be friends," the leader called. "Neither of yous talk."

"What's that?" the tall one said.

"They're friends," the leader said. "The statue and the human Zamboni."

The sidekicks laughed, a crude, sloppy sound. They entered the perimeter of lamplight by the rinks and they were not kids. At a distance the baggy hooded shirts had made them look slighter, younger. They were in their twenties. It wasn't a crowbar the tall one held, it was the wooden handle of a mallet or sledge. Still advancing, the leader brought his hands out of his pockets and drew back his hood, slowly, with a sort of wry formality. He was smiling, lips closed. For a moment his face took up all her view. He was shockingly handsome. A twitch of attraction plunged downward with another spasm of fear, down into her womb, twin shocks, fused and unanimous in effect. It was a cruel face, beautiful. Strong brows, high-planed cheekbones, hooded grey eyes, plump lips inside a ring of stubble. The dark hair was brush-cut, the skull knobbed as if muscled. She kept waving the hose slowly in front of her. The three stopped at the edge of the wet ice, just short of where the stream of water swept back and forth. Beads of spray sequined their trainers and lower pant legs.

"You were talking to us?" The voice was deep but nasal, grating, unsuited to that face.

"I just said leave him alone."

"It's you we want to see anyway." He looked up at her. After a moment his smooth brow crimped slightly, his eyes welled wider. He'd figured it out. He said nothing. It was the third one who said, "Is this, like, a *woman?*" He was short and concave, with a pocked face, and he seemed the drunkest or most stoned of the three.

"I don't know," the leader said. "Ask her yourself. Is there a lady in there?"

"Never fucking seen a *woman* doing a rink."

"I seen her," the tall one said. "Told me to get the fuck off the ice, last year."

"I was hardly here last year," she said.

"In that other park. Down Barrie."

"Well, I guess the ice wasn't ready," she said. She took a hopeful glance at the crazy man. He wasn't seeing any of this. She should retreat to the hut, call the police. Something stopped her. She was slow on her feet—hadn't run a step in years. At least out here there was the hose and the wet ice between her and them.

"Looks ready now," the third one said.

"What, *her?*" the tall one said with a stupid leer.

"The ice."

"Check it and see, Zach," said the leader. Zach, the short one, tried sliding onto the surface beyond the pooling water. His lead foot drove through crusted slush. He started to topple forward, waved his arms, slammed backwards onto his elbows and ass. You could hear his bones on impact. He rolled over onto all fours—hands and knees—and stayed like that, head drooped.

"Okay, you can get up now," she said. "You're wrecking my work. You should be moving on."

"We'd like to see your office first," the leader said, ignoring his hurt friend.

"You're not going to."

"We already dropped in at the hut in that other park. Up in the Heights."

"Sure," she said.

"You think I'm lying?"

His face was pale. He seemed ready to pull out a scalp as proof. Walt Unger, a small, shyly talkative chain-smoker, would be flooding the rink in Rideau Heights.

Zach was back on his feet, rubbing his wet elbows with the opposite hands—a hurt-little-boy gesture. His wince was angry, yet he glanced timidly at the ice as if it were alive and likely to buck him off his feet if he moved. "*Bitch*," he said, but it didn't seem directed at her. That was good—she didn't have to respond.

"Let's go," the leader said, and for a soaring moment she believed that he was addressing his friends, telling them they were moving on. Then she felt his cold eyes pushing deeper into her.

"Lead the way," he said.

"If I go into that office, it'll be to call the cops. And there's nothing there. You think any of us bring money out here for a graveyard shift?"

He seemed to be giving this some thought. Then he said, "Your friend at the other rink did."

"What?"

"Brought money."

"I doubt that very much."

He went even whiter. "You know what?" he said, frowning, as if he had just discovered something that surprised him very much. "You're a goof."

"What?"

"A *goof.*"

Zach let a single laugh ride the silence. *Goof.* Not the A-word, not the B-word, not the C-word. Gavin had never done time like others in his family—he'd run a series of video and corner stores, trying and failing to franchise them—but a few of his boyhood friends had done time, and so he, of course, had considered himself an expert on Inside. And goof, he'd told her, was the worst thing you could call another inmate. Fucker, loser, asshole, shithead—that whole repertoire could get you into big trouble, no question, but goof was the worst. Maybe because it felt so silly. So *dismissive.* A fucker, after all, might fuck you, or fuck you up, or fuck you over. A goof was just pathetic. Maybe handsome here had done time. Certainly he'd done time. He knew how to use the word. But the use of the word bothered, *enraged* her, for another reason altogether and now she jerked the control ring fully open and turned the hose on him, narrowing the mouth with her gloved thumb so it sprayed even harder. *Bitch* she would have preferred. A bitch at least was female. Fat bitch, even. Bull dyke. Anything in that line. This was worse than being invisible, worse than being looked through or past, which happened all the time, and so be it, she could take it, a small daily heartbreak—things could be far worse. She doused him from the knees up, briefly but thoroughly, finishing at the face—how she resented that sculpted, cocky face!—then aimed the hose over at the tall one, but he and Zach were quickly shuffling backwards off the ice.

The leader was rigid with the soaking—face twisted, shoulders hunched up, arms dangling. For a few moments his body stayed like that while his face slowly relaxed, refocused. He unzipped his jacket, reached in, pulled out a pair of red-handled ice picks, the sort snowmobilers use to pull themselves clear if they fall through the ice. One in each bare hand he came at her, his trainers stuttering over the wet ice. She turned the hose on him again. He kept coming, head lowered, squinting hard. The other two converged on her from either side with the same clumsy shuffle. She took her thumb off the outlet. The leader's face was shiny, sopping, his narrowed eyes fixed not on her eyes but lower—maybe her mouth or throat. His eyes had glazed over, unreachable. He was quivering. There was no use trying to talk. She was backing into the darker area between the lamppost and the warming hut, her heart punching at her ribs. She gripped the spouting hose head like a club. He lunged, swiping the picks in front of her face, then slipped forward, off balance. She didn't know whether to club or stab at him with the hose head but her body decided, thrusting at his face as it came up—the eyes wide—her full weight and strength behind it. Gavin's advice again. Never be tentative with a first blow. Though it hadn't helped Gavin in the end. He'd died three years back—four years after leaving her—in a confrontation on John Street, screaming in through the window of somebody's cube van until he dropped, his heart finally imploding with the decades of rage. He'd needed her after all, she realized. He relied on her outlook. To Ellen, anger was a rare detour, not a lifetime of highways.

She connected, but it was an odd feeling, blunted. Her attacker's face jerked down. The hose seemed stuck. In a panic she yanked back and he was sagging to his knees, dropping the ice picks, reaching for his face. The other two men stopped and froze.

"Shane?" the tall one said, voice shrivelling. "What'd she do to you, man?"

He was making coarse, braying sounds. She crouched down, holding the once-more-streaming hose, grabbed the ice picks, put them in her outside pocket, stood up.

"Shane?" said Zach.

"My eye," he said. The words were muffled. He lowered his hands and turned his face up toward hers, his friends still behind him. She flinched and gasped—a ladylike sound—a lady in a film, about to faint.

She dropped the hose and knelt down. "Oh my God."

"Get away," he said.

"You," she said to the tall one, who was closest to the hut, "go in, call 9-1-1."

"9-1-1? Are you fucking joking, lady?"

Now she was a lady.

"We need an ambulance," she said.

"No way, they'll take us in."

"Just ask for an ambulance!"

"He'll be OK. Come on, Shane."

"My eye!"

Zach started toward her and Shane.

"Don't move!" she told him. "You might step on it."

"You mean...?" His mouth was ajar, brows stitched together.

"We have to look for it. Call 9-1-1," she told the tall one. "Step carefully!"

He glanced over at Zach. Zach said, "We could like, call, then run for it."

"I need you both to help me look."

"They always send a cop car too," the tall one said.

"They can put it back in," she said, "the eye." She was pretty sure about this. She looked at the hut. She needed to turn off the water. It kept spewing from the hose lying at her knees, so water was lapping out around them, maybe carrying the eye further into the dark. But it couldn't have gotten far. Shane was on his side on the wet ice, curled up, rocking and grunting, one hand over the socket with its dangling nerve as she searched around him, tearing off her four gloves, peering hard, easing her hand over the ice. There were only a few spots of blood. No eye.

"Please," he whispered, "help me. I'm sorry."

"We'll find it," she said. "Tell your friend to call an ambulance! The tall guy."

"I need help, Gabe, call!"

Zach was shuffling around, hunched almost double, searching. "Pretty hard to see over this way," he said with the casual tone of a drunk looking for a dropped coin. Gabe picked his way toward the office door. Ellen was crawling over the puddled ice, tracing a circle around Shane. She would spiral outward in widening laps until she found the eye. She glanced over at the crazy man—still confronting the obelisk, oblivious. The door of the office swung open and light spilled onto the ice.

"That's good!" she called. "Leave it open."

"Hey, I think it's...shit. No." Zach was bent over, groping at something on the ice. As she watched, he toppled slowly forward.

Gabe was emerging from the office. In the doorway he stood silhouetted, panting as if he'd just run back from a distant pay phone. Her new radio/CD player was in his hand. He shrugged, sheepish.

"I did call," he said. "I've got to go. Sorry, man."

She wasn't sure who he meant by that. Pushing with one foot, sliding with the other like a curler, he skittered away to where the ice ended at the path leading onto Bay Street. As he hit the pavement he began sprinting, impressively fast for an intoxicated man with a large object in one hand.

Zach, now on his hands and knees like her, had stopped looking for the eye. He was watching Gabe disappear. She figured he would take off now too—but then he went on searching.

She said, "Zach?"

"I'm Sh-shane." A whisper through jittering teeth. The black leather of his jacket was frosting over.

"No, I mean your friend."

"Me?" said Zach. His head turned vaguely.

"Come more over this way—I doubt it could have got over to the boards."

"Be careful," Shane breathed, "they can put them back in."

She was moving away from Shane, outward in her circles. Then she thought she saw it. It had slid off a good twenty feet, to where the wet ice met the hard bank of snow shovelled to clear room for the rinks. It was in the shadow of that bank. She was sure now. She crawled toward it, trembling. The eye seemed to watch her with unnatural alertness, even a kind of indignation, as if she were too slow in coming to its aid. Closer still, it seemed to stare not at but through her, at something behind or beyond her.

"I think I see it!" Zach yelled. He must be watching where she was headed.

"Go into the hut," she called back. "There are bags in there, plastic bags in a Kleenex box, by your feet on the right as you go in. Get one and fill it with snow and bring it here. No, just bring it here. There's snow here."

"Okay! Just a minute!"

"You found it," Shane said behind her.

"You'll be all right," she said. She reached for the eye, then paused, wanting to put her rubber glove on. The glove was back on the ice beside Shane. She didn't touch the eye. She might damage it. It was hideous but riveting. Disembodied eyes made occasional appearances in horror novels, but those eyes were usually conscious, vigilant, a threat. This one was glassing over, as if losing interest in the world. Maybe starting to freeze. It didn't look real. Porcelain with an iris of grey-blue glass, and too perfectly round to be real. If this were a film she would complain about the special effects. Like when the Twin Towers fell, soon after Gavin's death—how it looked less real than the artificial disasters in films.

She wasn't sure how soft an eye was—her impression was that the main material was more or less like pudding, though held firm by a membrane. She could imagine her fingerprint remaining on the eye, a pattern he would look through for the rest of his life. She would wait for the bag of snow and ease it in with a knuckle. A far howl of sirens, the sound slowly mounting. She stayed on her knees, huddled low over the eye as if to shield it from the cold. She cupped it with her shivering hands without making contact. This way she didn't have to see it. She glanced back. Zach had paused as he reached Shane on his way to the hut. He stood wobbling above his friend.

"You're going to pull through, dude."

"The hut!" she cried. "I need that bag!"

"Okay." He staggered on, almost fell again. Then his head tilted with a drunk's abrupt, temporary alertness. He'd heard the sirens. They were closing in. He ducked into the hut and emerged briskly, as though instantly sober, and slid toward her across the ice. The whites of his eyes showed larger. She had her left hand out for the bag and he relayed it to her with his stretched right.

For a second he stood above her, captivated by the eye. He glanced back at Shane. "I got to get out of here," he whispered loudly, then stepped up on the bank and tore away across the park—the opposite direction from Gabe—his shoulders pitching and his hood peeling back. He ran past the obelisk, the man there turning his head stiffly to watch him go. As the moaning of the sirens merged into a single scream, she stuffed a handful of snow into the bag—they were kept in the hut for picking up the dog turds that cluttered the park and sometimes the ice. With the knuckle of her index finger she nudged the eye over the lip of the bag. It rolled right in. Unsure whether to seal the bag or leave it open, she turned and crawled back toward Shane. She was afraid of standing—she might slip, drop the bag, even fall on it. She crawled on her knees and right hand, her left holding the bag clear.

Shane sat up as she approached. The back of the hand covering the empty socket was blue and unbloodied. His good eye was fixed on hers. He was seeing her now, really looking. One of those rare times. Sometimes life seemed little else than a struggle to win the attention, the gaze, of others. That was what Gavin had really been doing, she supposed, screaming into that van at the end.

The ambulance and two squad cars flashed into sight, driving east on Ordnance. They would circle around and enter the park from Bay Street, by the hut. They vanished again but their sirens went on ripping the air apart.

"It's going to be all right, I think," she said, reaching him.

"If I can just keep my eye."

"You will."

"I'm sorry."

"They'll have that face of yours up and running in no time."

She wasn't sure if this was true. She'd almost said *good-looking face*.

"If I have to go back inside," he said, slurring the words through purple lips, "I can take it, but not blind. Can I see it?"

"Guess you'd better confirm we've got the right one," she said.

His torso jerked, as if shaken by a single laugh. She opened the bag. "Oh...Jesus," he said, stared back at by himself. She set her bare hand on his shoulder. His body trembled under the leather. The folds in the lap of his low-crotched jeans were frozen so it looked like he had an erection. He didn't flinch or look at her—he wouldn't now.

"Did you hurt Walt, at the other rink?"

"Not like this. Hardly at all."

"That better be true." She gripped his hood and pulled it roughly onto his head.

"And for t-t-twenty bucks. Nobody could believe my life."

With a face like that? she heard herself think. The crass assumption she now sometimes shared, that life must be a June breeze for the nice-looking. As if her life had been easy in her teen years. Shane would have been all over her then, and she would have craved him for the danger in his look. Why had nature given bad men all the attractive vitality? Like Gavin, years ago. Why did horror and romance so often overlap? She pushed her hand further, around his shoulder, feeling uncomfortably huge next to him. He seemed about to rest his head against her arm, then pulled back. A wall of hard, hot light came at them as the ambulance and squad cars shrieked up behind. To shield her eyes, she ducked her face, got a closer look at him. He seemed to be going into shock. His good eye stared off to where their twinned shadow was fast lengthening over the ice and the shrouded park. The crazy man was lit up at the edge of the headlights' fanning swath. Turned toward them at last, he seemed to be staring, his posture solemn, noncommittal, his baseball cap in his hands like a mourner. "You're going to be all right," she told Shane, though really she wanted to take him by the chin and roughly turn his face toward hers and say, "Look at me."

Noughts & Crosses

AN UNSENT REPLY

-------Original Message-----

From: <j.in.corydon@hotmail.com>

To: <nella_biagini@sympatico.ca>

Sent: April 22, 2007 1:16 AM

Subject: RE: Hello?

n,

yes yes i did get your email but needed to reflect a little. i'm sorry. and yes i do think it might be best if i pulled back a little now, i seem to need some space to hear my own breathing, my own thoughts, it is hard when we are always in dialogue. i am sorry if this feels abrupt or my reasons feel vague, they just must be. for one thing, as i guess i implied, i have been asked to keep secrets and want to keep my word. i know you understand. you, after all, are one of my secrets. and as you know yourself and even said, maybe a severing, a temporary severing is what's best now, for both of you. for everyone involved. please don't worry about me, i will be all right, i am determined to get through this time. i promise i will get in touch again when i feel i can.

love always,

j

n

As in: never again, never again. That phrase with its cardiac cadence. Slight arrhythmia. A certain tunnelled clump of muscle misbehaving, missing steps or taking clumsy extras, a drunk at the top of the stairs in the dark. When you used the abbreviation before, that n, it was an intimate act, an adoring diminutive, as though to make the beloved compact enough to carry with you secretly. You always found me tall for a woman (too tall?). Now it's as though you want to avoid repeating my full name: Arnella. Nelli. nell. n. To deduct the name down to nothing. Nobody, no one, nowhere, nothing, nought, null, nil.

yes yes

The one thing you would never say in the act was *Yes!* It was always *O no O no O no O no!* when you were getting close, and when I asked if it was because something was wrong, this "thing" was wrong, or was your pleasure (I would like to think so) intense to the point of pain, you turned shy and said it was "just what came out—you know" (your favourite lazy phrase) "like when a song shows up in your head and you just, like, let it out?" I didn't press the point. I sensed you retreating into your separate memoir of intimate events. I didn't ask if that was what *always* "came out," or only with me. Separate memoirs, former loves. How crowded our bedrooms are these days. (Or not. Not my bedroom. Not these days.) For over a century there was a tunnel extending from the crypt of the main cathedral here down to the Hôtel Dieu, the old Catholic hospital, so the nuns and priests could stay indoors in winter when they were called off to see sick parishioners or perform the last rites. A few weeks ago I read about it and for some reason kept wanting to tell you. Why not now? Forty years ago they decided the tunnel was becoming unsafe. They sealed it off at both ends, but the passageway is still there, thirty feet under Brock Street, totally dark, of course, and empty. Sometimes now when I'm alone it hits me.

reflect a little

Five days of this little reflecting. Here is what gnaws me, besides the after-effects of five days of little reflecting on your part and much waiting on mine. What gnaws and haunts me is: whatever passed through your mind in those five (plus) days, all the stuff you decided not to voice, reconsidered, revised, rejected then retrieved, reneged on again, at last deleted. I want it back, the full census of your reflections, a crammed CT-scanful, all those references to me, I can't accept that they're gone, neural flickers like email never sent or lost in transit somewhere in the digital ether we're all adrift in now. Or: whispers of a couple passing in that tunnel before it was sealed. A pair of nuns, let's say, lovers on the down low, erotically revved up by the proximity of illness, death. Death's weirdly elating ultimacy. Did they have torches? A medieval image, cinematic to the point of camp: dark figures hunched, capes wafting, torches in hand, flapping down limestone corridors propped with timber stays for safety, as in a mine shaft. Our lovers must feel unnerved, even so. They are crossing so many lines. The anxiety of the crime makes one notice other dangers everywhere. And safety measures always seem to whisper: *some day we will fail!* It feels safer where there are no measures. And either way, in their presence or absence, no safety.

i'm sorry

Sorry, maybe, because there were no reflections? You'd made up your mind? You're sorry that you stalled about breaking the news, is all? They say that from the bottom of a deep hole you can see the stars shining even at noon. I never trust those little factlets from the *Globe*; still, it's good news for the dead.

and yes i *do* think it might be best

Italics mine. But even without the italics (it's my ethnic privilege to overuse them) your implication here is that *I made the suggestion in the first place!* Actually, of course, I did: "If you need me to pull back now, I will." Naturally I didn't mean it, though. Didn't want you to *accept*. Wanted you to say *O no O no O no O no!* What's more, *you must have known I didn't mean it*—you just pretended to take the words at face value to give yourself a convenient out. Lovers are the world's only honest people, according to certain poets and sages. Ho ho ho. I'm nostalgic for the salad days, grad and postgrad in the late '70s and early '80s, York and UBC, when it was an article of faith (if not experience) in our circle that straight lovers, bourgeois lovers, were the only dishonest ones. *T[he] on/lie dys/honest ones.*

That stage of life when confidence depends on culprits.

Oh, to have both back.

i seem to need some space

But, but I thought we were bitter opponents of platitudes, you and I; we agreed that our love was *not like any other love* (italics mine, quotation yours, email 64, line 17: I am now chief archivist of your intimacies), and to consecrate and, as you would say, "honour" this singularity, we agreed that we would never speak of our love in clichés. We smogged the air with exalted vows like that. Teenage summer lovers in a song by the Boss. So, maybe a return to cliché is a neatly symmetrical way to shut things down…to *deconsecrate* our love, the way they do with those churches whose flocks have died off or moved to Palm Beach, and the buildings are converted to meeting halls or museums or daycares. Ever wondered how they deconsecrate a cathedral? I really should know, after a quarter century in my field. (A century, one learns, is a small thing.) A choir assembles for the last time, chanting in discord, an infernal chorus. At the altar a bishop exhausts the full roster of religious obscenities. The organist, wild-eyed, riffs on anthem-rock standards, Queen, Gary Glitter, The Sweet, as if playing at a hockey rink.

j, my j, you've *recanted.*

Shouldn't "recant" mean to sing again?

to hear my own breathing

If I woke in the night, the precious nights I had you here, I was always taken aback at how hard it was to detect your breaths. Even when you were deeply out (pretty much always) your breathing was delicate; once or twice I almost panicked, you know how the mind works at night, and there were always those footlights of unease around our meetings, fear of your husband interrupting our, uh, tutorial with a call, so that panic would feed on puny fears and several times I actually put the back of my hand to your open mouth to feel the breaths. Then my mouth next to yours to breathe them in. That close, I found you breathing, of course, calm and profound, with a faint sighing wheeze in your lungs, under your bare breasts, which were pillowed one over the other as you lay furled on your side. Your breath smelled fine, spicy, with a subtle finish of garlic and Syrah. Then one night it changed. That's how I knew we were coming to an end. More conventional signs had materialized as well—your canned laughter, diluted gaze, undilated pupils—but *that* was how I knew: the last two nights your breath turned unfamiliar in your sleep. Changes deep inside, where I couldn't reach. I wonder about the air in that blocked tunnel, after forty years of disuse. Is oxygen stable or does it deteriorate over time? I wouldn't know. Your husband would. Could toxic fumes have seeped in through the limestone? If the ends were unblocked tonight, could we still walk through it and breathe? How long does a closed-off tunnel remain a possible route?

always in dialogue

To you it may have felt that way. You're the one with other allegiances. (More of them, maybe, than I thought.) A day came when I abandoned my latest stalled article to check email—still dial-up then—maybe thirty times, hoping for a reply. You must have been reflecting a little. Finally I just remained online, waiting. I answered a few other "urgent" emails that I'd left to ripen for days, maybe weeks. That took some time. I've never learned, like you, to crash out a reply, in lower case, in the current electronic shorthand that I am still not used to—insulting!—though I see it all the time from my students :) Did those. Waited. Stared at the empty inbox and willed a message to appear. For quite some time I stuck it out. Funny, I've never once sat staring at the phone, though you would sometimes call me. Staring at a phone seems somehow goofier. A screen is meant to be stared at. Things are meant to appear there. Maybe I could *induce* you to write me. Eventually I took the modem cord and slunk the three flights down to the lobby and locked it in the morgue-like drawer of my mailbox. Came upstairs for a double Campari and soda. Left the cord down there for a good half-hour.

i am sorry if this feels abrupt or my reasons feel vague, they just must be

Oh and another nice thing about email: you are always sitting down to read it. No more Puccini swoons, buckling to the floor with the farewell letter clinched in one hand, the other cupping the brow. Instead, you settle deeper in your chair. The world stops entering your mind through the senses. You've been sealed off with your obsession, and shame. *my reasons... must be kept vague.* I always knew there were truths you wouldn't tell me, so I avoided entering certain corridors of inquiry; but there was also an implication, about the two of us, that we just *knew*—we UNDERSTOOD. William Burroughs said that gay love differs from straight love because a queer lover ("homosexual" was how he put it, I believe) always knows what the other is thinking and feeling, while a straight lover never does. Hmmm...better that I did my thesis on Bloomsbury and Woolf, instead of (a quip over cocktails, long ago) "Bloomsbury & the Beats: Points of Unexpected Comparison."

as i guess i implied

Didn't we make a pact never to *do* this sort of thing? To *guess* and *imply?* To become, in each other's sight, hazy at the margins by delivering half-truths? That's how people deconsecrate themselves, from human into something less. Spectres. Cyborgs. Didn't I mention this opinion? Not that you listened well, ever. Speaking of blockages. Consider the ears of the egotist...Now, as I listen, trying to peer through this blockage, I wonder if you are alone. There's your husband, of course, but he doesn't count. Two daughters. Neither do they. For the purpose of this madness only *somebody else* counts. (Especially if female.) You told me I was the first woman you had been with. Is there another now? Have I created a monster?

i have been asked to keep secrets

The cathedral's literature (I went and took one of their free tourist leaflets; lit a lampion for the hell of it) gives no clue as to how, or with what, the passageway was sealed.

i know you understand

See above under Burroughs, William.

you, after all, are one of my secrets

One of your…excuse me? I thought this was an exclusive engagement! Now I'm no longer your secret, I'm *one* of your secrets? Um, are your secrets a *clique* now? A *category?* A *women's collective?* All on the same level…Maybe your secrets should be more civil about this. Maybe they should all get *used* to one another. Your secrets are "all in this together"…no rank, no priority, no hierarchy of closeness…it's a sorority, a full *democracy* of secrets! The one exact thing that love isn't.

as you know yourself

Oh, I do. One of us had to end it. The question is: Who began it, Janet? Another reference that dates me and, by omission, you. We have all the particulars. The year (2002). The season (summer). The place (Kingston). The course (Religious Imagery in Popular Culture and Contemporary Women's Fiction), and you in semi-attendance to steal time—admit it, finally, you're a dabbler, a summer slummer—away from your aphasic husband and colicky twins. When you went back to Winnipeg in the fall, I assumed it was over, but the thing wouldn't die. Since then I've propped everything on your annual holiday here in the Thousand Islands.

maybe a severing

New word for an old context. Feels more honest than "spend a little time apart," anyway. And honesty is what we all want at such times. But *severing*—there is a hard word. I'd never noticed the "severe" in it before. Or really heard the sound of it before.

SEVering. The oiled blade sliding down to separate head from body with a blunt, chunky sound.

a temporary severing

Whew! For a minute there I thought it was permanent! As if it was in the very *nature* of severings to be that way...But a moment's reflection allows us to generate any number of counter-examples. In the fatal crash, the victim's spinal cord was *temporarily* severed. As the glaciers retreated, rising sea waters *temporarily* severed Asia from North America. Alas, it proved necessary to sever the miner's gangrenous limb *temporarily*. Somehow the bungee jumper's cord was severed in mid-leap—*but only temporarily!*

or both of you

You always wrote your emails fast, furtively, late at night or early in the morning, and there were always misspellings or little misnomers like this one. "Both of *us*," I assume you meant. You and me. Because there aren't two people hereabouts, in my world, my room. All the same...maybe you did half-mean that *I've* been as split apart as you. Between wanting to respect your family commitments and wanting you all to my lonesome? Nope: between wanting *not* to violate the current student–teacher protocol (which I always supported and still believe in and which the dying white males of the department, just them, allegedly, still flout when they can) and wanting to violate, repeatedly, you.

for everyone involved

Everyone! How did they get into this again? How I detest them! From the moment a love starts, Everyone is clamouring to get in, huffing and prodding, mobbing the door that a new couple seals fast and barricades—Everyone trying to peep through, push through, leaving messages, making demands. I should have known Everyone would get to us. They always do. Over and over I've lived my life for those days before they do.

i am determined to get through this time

The ambiguity! It makes me insane! How many times have I been over this one, trying to uncrate it? You are determined to ride out this painful, severe time in your life? Or: You are determined, *this* time, to get through? Let it be the first option! Let it be that this hurts you as much as it hurts me. Let this not be yet another unacceptable revelation—that our affair wasn't your first of the kind. You said it was. Now you might be saying that there was another time and you *didn't* get through it—never got over her. (Or him.) Other times? Who? Who? This vision of multitudes barging into your inbox, your bedroom, your body.

i will get in touch again when i feel i can

What's this if not a melodramatic way of saying, Don't call us, we'll call you? My people will call your people. My multitudes will call your solitude...but don't hold your breath. (Whatever remains in that sealed place.) Cave exploration is something you always said you wanted to try out. I can hardly bear to use the correct, ridiculous term. Spelunking. I spelunk, you spelunk. We will spelunk. She had spelunked. So we'll go no more spelunking. Partly this is why I keep bringing up that sealed tunnel—not as some elaborate genital metaphor, but because I know you would be interested and maybe want to explore it. Count me out, though. Daredevils come in aerial or subterranean form. How many folks do you know who have both skydived and spelunked? Doesn't happen. When you would talk about spelunking, I would counter with skydiving, my own potential death-wish hobby. We had to compromise on the earth's surface—on driving *really, really fast* those few times when we were far from Everyone together. Rental cars are good for that: convertibles. A *Thelma & Louise* outtake, except people probably took me for your aunt, or duenna. Remember the highway into the Cypress Hills? How amazed you were that such committed flatness could collect itself into hills—small mountains, our ears popping as we drove—the way your life seemed to be climbing up from the plains of your comfortable present onto high ridges of possibility...

love always

But there's hope here, isn't there, there's not just a name, and not just "love"—no, it's "love always," even if there is the one conspicuous, crushing change, the absence of your usual starburst of xxxxxooooo. Or xoxoxoxo. It always varied. I go back through the emails now (printed out, of course—there's a paper trail after all, sweetie, though you prudently avoided writing letters)—I pore over them again, studying, tabulating the details of the x and o firework finale of all your emails, one hundred and fifty-eight in all, but especially the last twenty or so. I am trying to track the decline. How does the end enter? Where does it get in? In your most passionate note (I won't say email), right after the Cypress Hills Escapade, there were no less than ten x's and seven o's. (Why fewer o's than x's? Why *stint* like that on the o's? And what *are* x's and o's anyway? Kisses and embraces, embraces and kisses. We argued about which were which. To both of us it seemed obvious, a matter of common sense and common knowledge, and we were stunned, in a loving way, by the other's ignorance. You said, "O is the lips open for a deep kiss, X is the arms crossed over the embraced lover's back." Touched by this effort I replied, "Ingenious but wrong. O is the circle of the embracing lover's arms, X is the eye of the lover, the eyes, closed, X-ed out in the rapture of the kiss.") Love as a game of noughts and crosses. Nine emails before the end, I find *all my love, j, xxxoooxx.* Again this marked privileging of x over o. (Five and three.) Five messages before the end, *Love forever, j, xxxxoo.* (Four and two.) Three messages before the end, o makes something of a comeback, outnumbering x for the first time in many missives, *Love, j, ooxxxooo.* In fact, the total number of signs here, eight, suggests if anything a strengthening of passion! Next, email 156, where o makes its final strong showing, *my love, j, ooxoo*—with the lone x almost lost among those still-fervent hugs (or kisses???). Number 157, the second-last, shows this tic-tac-toe showdown entering its endgame, though the salutation—*yours always, j, ox*—almost seems to cancel out that lack.

j

I'm to be spared the final humiliation. You'll remain j to me, not Janet-Marie. In signing off, you could have withdrawn that intimate, tiny link between us, that hook lodged in my heart, and keyed in your full name. You chose not to; something does remain unsevered. And after all, if the Greek in the labyrinth (you never remember the names), slowly unreeling his ball of yarn so he could find his way back, had accidentally cut the thread—maybe on a cornering wall, a knife-edge of stone—he might have sensed it break and then groped his way back in the darkness, feeling for the lost end, splicing the yarn, persevering. We're back in the tunnel, you see. Despite my fear, I think I would go down and explore it with you, if they ever opened it up again. I am drawn to a fantasy of fucking you there, maybe in a side tunnel or cul-de-sac, tugging you away from the tedious tour group with its silly costumed guide to make slow, wordless love in the kind of darkness that people never really do it in. What would that be like? To have not the faintest glimpse or inkling of the one beside you, above you, below you? So the orgasm I'd give you, the way you liked it best, would star the gloom, seeming to project on the walls a brief, grand, enveloping galaxy. There we would be our own source of light. I don't want to see anything now. Darkness is far from the worst. Your note is very short. Worst is the whiteness of most of the printout under that j. So I've filled it and other pages, your faithful annotator and emptied teacher, with these notes, endnotes, that our dialogue not die.

Nearing the Sea, Superior

THE WORLD BEING an ironist with poor taste and perfect timing, Neil Sedaka was on the oldies station crooning "Breaking Up Is Hard to Do."

"You know you don't have to do this," he said.

"You already said that, Erik."

"She was always crazy about you."

"You don't have to *say* that, Erik. I said I'd come. I just wish we could be honest with her."

His cellphone trembled in the breast pocket of his coat.

"Terminal 1, right?" the driver asked. He wore a topknot turban and had a wispy beard, no accent. He looked about sixteen. Rap or hip hop, you would guess, but he had the radio tuned to a pop oldies station.

"Terminal 1, yes."

The trembling in Erik's pocket stopped. In the overheated car his brow and freshly shaven upper lip were damp, oddly chilled.

"Jason Singer actually got married in a hospital," he said.

"Jason."

"He had dinner with us last year. He and Ginny? First weekend in June."

"I don't know how you keep track of these things," she said.

"I like people, I guess."

She let that go. Then: "But 'first weekend in June'? I mean ..."

"It was the second-last dinner we gave."

The cab started up an on-ramp leading into the airport. In his belly he felt the angle of their climb, a voluptuous sensation, cruelly out of context. The cab fishtailed on the sleety ramp and recovered. She checked her BlackBerry—it seemed their words had brought her own schedule to mind—then said, "The girlfriend was the flapper, right? Cloche hat, short curls?"

"Ginny. They were married. That's what I was saying. They got married in the hospital, in Jason's father's room. They moved the date up, so his father could be part of it."

Silence; she was back inside one of her designs. "What did her father have?"

"*Jason*'s father. aids."

You don't listen. It was one of the first things that had drawn him to her—a distractedness he'd mistaken for creative dreaminess, thus assigning soft edges to what was actually a tough, selfish trait: the quality that helped her gain a toehold in a field still vastly dominated by men. Porter—the name was her Virginian mother's maiden name—had a faculty of all-excluding focus that now struck him, at times, as inhuman. At other times he envied it. At all times it whetted his desire to possess her, which was now out of the question, and in fact, he realized, always had been.

"I don't recall much of that evening," she said shortly, as if irked at the expectation that she *should* recall it, though Erik had long since given up expecting such things.

"The conversation was scintillating," he said. "Especially yours."

She let her heavy, dark eyelids droop—her standard semaphore of warning.

"No, I mean it. You were. It amazes me you can't remember."

A few moments of silence, then she said, "It is too warm in here," and frowned, her thumb grazing his brow in an absent way, yet gently, as if she meant to taste the sweat there.

They had opposing views of social need. Neediness, in Porter's opinion, was the antithesis of charm; worse, those with needs could never be happy or free. To Erik, need was simply the adhesive that held the human world together. When especially frustrated he had thought of her, wrongly, he knew, as a sort of machine for transforming visual or verbal information into... well, all right, into truly original structures. Gorgeous structures. He was still her helpless fan.

In the terminal, on the moving sidewalk, they glided up the long concourse to the departure gates. It wasn't like her to stand behind him like this—or just to *stand,* instead of striding decisively onward. Petite, methodically put-together, she'd affixed her gaze to the bank of coffered skylights high above them, her estimation of the design unreadable. The supercilious arch of her brows, the satiric droop of her eyelids, the lines parenthesizing her mouth—all lent her a scornful look. Porter could look haughty patting a spaniel. He stared at her, rapt as always, knowing now that she was so absorbed in her study he was at low risk of receiving one of her fending glares.

Again his cellphone pulsed.

"They couldn't choose between a space pod or a greenhouse," she said.

I really should take this call, he thought.

An announcement rumbled out, slurred with echoes. It was too noisy, he told himself, to take the call.

"I think it's our flight," she said, glaring at her watch, then up at the ceiling. "There *has* to be a better way to control sound in these big volumes." She stalked past him in her long, lint-brushed coat, towing a carry-on bag in the brisk, territorial way of flight crew.

THEY HAD FINALLY separated last fall. At times it amazed him that their misalliance had survived almost a decade. Still, there had been that certain bond. It was coded, he supposed, in his genes. His parents had spent their lives and raised Erik and his two older siblings up near Thunder Bay—dairy farmers in a subarctic zone, though to Erik's Finnish grandparents, who had lost their home to the advancing Soviets in '45, that had not seemed unduly daunting. Erik's mother had only really confided one thing about her and his father's marriage, and she probably hadn't meant to. At Paavo's wake, shaken but sturdy—drinking vodka and Coke, though not conspicuously drunk—she'd told the three children, "Thirty-two years we are married and never once he walks into the kitchen without that my stomach does like this." And her large, dry hand flipped over, exposing the pink, open palm. Some years later, when Erik related that anecdote to Porter, she'd said crisply, "You could interpret that sentence in two possible ways." Yet her gaze was evasive, as if the story unsettled her, imperilled her carefully managed self-containment.

"No, you couldn't," Erik told her. "Not if you ever saw them in the same room."

What wasn't said: that he and Porter had just the same connection. Whenever they were in each other's vicinity, a vital arc would leap the synapse between them, etching the air. Some friends even confided they could feel the charge. Porter loathed such talk. And in the sweaty aftermath of sex she would act as if nothing shocking had just occurred, as if she hadn't just been far beyond herself, cursing, laughing wildly, her hard little thighs crushing his hot ears and cheeks.

THE FLIGHT HAD BEEN called but wasn't boarding. Erik kept glancing out the wall of windows at their 737 and the runway—visibility poor—and at a display panel listing several departures as delayed. On a wide plasma screen bracketed down from the ceiling, the top-of-the-hour news: a panning shot of parked cars half-buried in snow. First delays, he thought, then cancellations. It was the time of year when this part of the earth is actually turning its face back toward the sun, yet winter goes on deepening its tenancy.

Further palpitations from his phone. Around the gate, passengers, seated, standing, had a herded, nervous look. Porter calmly sat and returned to her BlackBerry, emailing a response to a colleague's question (he guessed) or, possibly, sending a note to her new man. Her expression and posture gave no hint as to which of these she might be doing.

She and this new man were engaged, waiting for both divorces to come through.

In that state of applied absorption she brought to every task, she would not notice Erik taking the call. He walked past her, toward the food court, mumbling "Coffee?" No response. He took out the cellphone. It stilled in his hand. Three messages from Thunder Bay. He punched Reply. Porter was juggling three projects these days and had made it clear, not unkindly, that if his mother died (she never used euphemisms like "passed away") before they could fly up there, she would not come along. Would not be able to. Though she might, if she could, still fly up for the day of the funeral.

The ringing was faint. Now another announcement. A pessimist would think *cancellation* but Erik was an optimist and he was finding that even divorce and grief left a basic stratum of one's character intact. The back of Porter's head—that practical pageboy cut of wondrous hair so straight and black—was still unmoving. She'd admitted, and she would never lie, especially not to be tactful or kind, that her fiancé was not the lover Erik had been. In fact he didn't seem to excite her at all. A senior partner in an architectural firm, he did command a better income than Erik, who was a high school guidance counsellor, but Erik believed the true issue here was that Porter desired to live inside her calling in every way, not just professionally but domestically, too. For some years, he saw, she had tried to slot their marriage into her life as a sort of moonlighting, or volunteer position, and she was incapable of sustaining a secondary passion. When she wanted to chat, it was about her work—her art—and "chat" was not the word.

"Rik, where have you been?" Anja's voice was panicked, chafed raw. "On the plane?"

"I'm here," he said quietly. "We're just leaving. How is she?"

"I can't hear! I've been calling and calling!"

"I'm sorry." He took a few more steps toward the food court. "How's—"

"What?"

"We're still in Toronto—we're about to board."

"We?"

"Porter's here."

"What? Porter's actually coming?"

"Yes," he whispered firmly.

Porter's demand for a divorce was a bitter blow, but Erik had been resigned to it and was even, yes, relieved, as if at last receiving a diagnosis he'd been expecting for years. Through much of the marriage he was unhappy—and yet, toward the end, it grew clearer to him that as someone of little worldly ambition he was just the sort of man cut out for happiness. It was Porter who had actually pointed this out to him—that the ambitious were never truly happy, that time terrified them, while for people like Erik time was no more than the benign, required solvent in which contentment could expand to the full. "You don't know how lucky you are," she'd told him, near the end. And while he could not yet feel it, he could sense, waiting beyond the grief he was just starting to surmount, a birthright of serenity and, in time, the large cheerful family he yearned for.

"Didn't think she'd come," Anja spat out, as if blaming Porter for something grave, their mother's condition being the obvious surrogate.

"Well, she keeps her word," he said, staring at the back of Porter's head, his heart thudding, cellphone clamped to his temple. *The longer I keep Anja from saying what I think she has to say.* Each second, for one thing, kept his mother alive a bit longer.

"I'm so angry you didn't answer. I'm alone here now!"

"We ... I'm sorry. I just couldn't. We're coming now."

"It's too late, Rik."

He opened his mouth to respond. Said nothing. Stared into the crowded food court. A beefy Native man with a grey ponytail rushed two steaming paper cups toward a cashier. His grin was wide and wincing, as if he was enjoying the discomfort of the heat searing his hands.

Erik had told Porter he didn't want his dying mother to know about the divorce. Spare her that blow. Porter considered this dishonest but chose to make a concession. His mother, Maarit, had loved Porter, admired her. Maarit had been a talented pianist who, in the manner of women of her generation, had set aside her potential career and addressed herself to home and family. Perhaps rightly, she saw Porter's aloofness and unapologetic drive as the required traits of will that she herself might have deployed. Yet she betrayed no regrets about the conventional path she'd followed; perhaps it was truer to say that Porter's establishment in the family afforded a sort of proxy completion of her own cancelled journey. And Porter, as if understanding this—accepting, cherishing the role—had answered Maarit's affection with unguarded warmth. Porter, flushed and serene of face, holding a wineglass of eggnog, her other bare arm atop the upright piano as Maarit on the bench played "O Holy Night": Maarit knew the second verse only in Finnish, not in the English she'd begun for her daughter-in-law's benefit, but now, seamlessly, Porter subbed in with the English words, singing with zest, if off-key. Erik gaped. It wasn't just that his wife was performing a song, a full *hymn,* which he had no idea she knew—she was also letting herself be seen and very much heard doing something inexpertly. She was more tenor than soprano and fell far shy of the soaring last note that Maarit herself, now singing in Finnish, easily hit, but both women seemed delighted, as if they had just performed a flawless duet on stage at Massey Hall. Erik was delighted too, clearing his eyes, clapping noisily, even as faint qualms of jealousy returned to him.

"Rikky?"

"When did it happen?"

"A few minutes ago."

"I thought we'd make it."

"Thank God you're coming! Jarmo and Gail are flying in from..." Anja's thin voice buckled. After some moments: "Vancouver. Tonight."

Erik lowered his face. His torso jerked as if he were taking punches under the heart. He had spent most of the Christmas break at his mother's side but had meant to be there at the end, too. And he saw that he'd believed Maarit would hold on until he arrived—the optimism of a youngest child who, as Porter once remarked with undisguised envy, always knew himself to be loved.

He glanced toward her now, expecting the beautiful back of her head. Her face was on him, eyes deciphering. She'd turned in her seat. People around her rising, bustling. A line was forming. He reassembled himself.

"Rik?" Anja said.

"We're boarding, An. I'll see you in two hours."

"I love you," she said, and his heart seemed to stagger.

"I love you too," he said. "I'm sorry."

He shoved the cellphone into his pocket and walked straight toward Porter, who was studying him. He supposed she was hoping her journey would not be necessary. She had no time for it, of course. The wasted airfare (he'd insisted on paying her way but she had vetoed that) would be nothing to her. She spent more on business dinners all the time. So he told himself. She stood up, her face a collage of conflicting signals, and embraced him in her new, sisterly manner, firm at the shoulders but distinct at the waist. As their torsos met, the smell of her, bitter cinnamon, clove, wafted in a warm draft from under her charcoal cowl neck. Their bodies would never divorce.

"I'm sorry, Erik."

He tightened his grip.

"I saw you crying there..."

He accepted her coming erasure from his life, but to have a few more days now—even a few more hours. If she stayed the night in his childhood home, they might make love again, a last time. There would be no stopping it. There never had been. Even now he felt the ambivalence in her embrace: her will's resistance, her body's deeper, disputing will.

He said, "It's just...Anja's in rough shape. You know how I am."

She pulled back, studied him with her interrogator's eyes: shale blue, deeply dubious. "You mean your mother's not...?"

Say it, say it.

"We might still get there in time," he said.

She held his gaze—he didn't blink either—then winced a strange smile and looked at her bag: "Well, we better get on, then."

She led him into the line. To hide his face from her, his eyes flooding, he turned to the high plasma screen. Still the news. He couldn't hear the commentary but he recognized that dark shattered coastline: a view of Superior, the inland sea they would soon be flying over, taken from an aircraft moving out from shore. Completely iced over, it looked like a polar ocean. A few times a century these total freeze-ups occurred, though at the centre of the lake, it was said, a hundred miles out from land, an ice-free inner lake always remained, churning and steaming through winter's coldest nights.

Instructions for the Drowning

RAY'S FATHER ONCE told him that if you ever jumped into the water to help a drowning man, he would try to pull you down with him and there was only one way to save yourself and him as well. Drowning men were men possessed and they were supernaturally strong. But they were also as weak as babies, seeing as they had lost all self-control.

His father shook his head, his lips clamped thin, as if such a loss were the most pitiful any man might suffer. You could neither wrestle nor reason with a man in that condition, he explained. In a sense, he was hardly human anymore.

Ray—ten or eleven years old—had pictured the victim metamorphosing into a kind of ghoul, sinewy and slippery as the Gollum he had been imagining while reading *The Lord of the Rings.*

So you would have no choice, his father concluded, his eyes narrowing and hardening behind the steel-rimmed spectacles, a gaze that always preceded a briefing on some unfortunate but unavoidable masculine duty. A drowning man would have to be knocked out cold. For his own good. A short, clean punch to the side of the jaw—that would be the preferred blow. After which you could easily complete the rescue, towing the victim in to shore. (In the boy's adaptation, the victim was tamed from raving fiend to serenely compliant human, slightly smiling, eyes closed, like those cartoon characters who always looked so gratified to have been knocked out.)

How rescuers who were not world-class water polo players were to find the leverage and stability to land a decisive blow while being dragged underwater by a panicking man was not a question the boy could have formed or would have posed. If his father said the operation worked—and he made it sound like one performed routinely in the summer lakes of Canada and the northern states—then it must.

Over the years Ray would hear other men, usually older, mention the technique often enough to gather that it had once been endorsed, if not actually practised, by a whole generation. Now it seems as dubious and dated as the quaint medical certainties of another age. Yet this afternoon, as Ray's wife, Inge, floating near the end of the dock, cries out and begins splashing and coughing, it's not the sensible modern rules of aquatic rescue that first leap to mind but his old man's advice. Then comes the thought that he's not even sure what the modern rules are. He springs up out of the fold-out recliner and pulls off his sunglasses, his latest can of IPA tipping and rolling off the dock. The blood drains from his head—he is almost drunk, he was almost asleep—and the glasses slip from his hand as he stands swaying. His sight returns. There's Inge, treading water effortfully, using just one arm. Her sunlit face is strained. Another cough hacks out of her, but then she calls hoarsely, "It's OK—OK!"

"What? You sure?"

"Just a cramp. My leg. But I think it's..."

"Inge?"

She winces, her teeth white in the sun. From the other direction, behind Ray, a jocular voice calls down, "Hey, you two lovebirds all right down there?"

"OK!" he shouts back automatically toward the cottage, where their hosts, Hugh and Alison, have retired for a little nap, as Hugh always puts it. Hugh and Alie enjoy a spirited, irreverent rapport, playfully and publicly physical. In the penumbra around them, other couples in their circle are never quite free of a sense of deficiency and demotion.

With a choked groan Inge vanishes as if something has yanked her feet from below. She flails back up, arms flapping and reaching. She could be a woman playing the victim during a lifeguard training session or someone just gauchely fooling around. No. She is a decent swimmer and she is no joker; she laughs readily enough with her friends and with Ray, even these days, but she dislikes physical comedy and April Fool's pranks of the kind that Hugh loves to devise.

Ray charges down the dock and jumps off the end where a half-empty wineglass perches as if on the edge of a bar. The water here is deep, but he dives flatly, smacking his paunch and his groin and surfacing fast. He is an ugly swimmer, a heaver and splasher, his head always turtled above the water—he hates submerging his face—but he is strong, and padded enough that he floats.

All that's visible of Inge is her face tipped sunward like a tiny, shrinking island. He calls, "Hang on!" and she stammers back, "Help, help, help me now, Ray!" It's a shock to hear *help* used right on cue and exactly as it should be. And her accent—for as long as they have known each other it has been faint, but for rare spasms of anger or passion. Now it's thickly Dutch. Her face dips under, comes back up, her mouth gawping, hands flogging the water. "I'm here," he says, and extends his left hand. "Inge?" She launches toward him. Her facial muscles flex and contort and he gets a flashback of that gurning creature conjured up by his father's words some thirty years ago. Her eyes—pure blue, no pupil—do seem half-alien, perceiving but not knowing him.

She hugs and envelops him, the way she might an exciting new man, as perhaps she already has, who can say? They've been sleeping separately for almost a year, although not on this visit, and the bed sharing up here is not merely for show or to pre-empt gossip—and Hugh and Alie are gossips—no, they really are trying to give it one more shot, and the sex last night was good, partly because it had been a while and partly because of the fresh setting and the voluptuous breezes floating in, and also, sure, because they both knew without saying a word that they would team up and show Hugh and Alie, ostentatiously coupling in the next room, that they too had a marriage.

Her skin last night was hot as always, much hotter than his. Her crushing embrace now is icy. She's all over him, clinging to him like the one thing afloat on an empty sea. *Grasping at straws.* Now he gets it. It's not about drawing lots but about grabbing handfuls of the useless stuff floating up from the hold of a sinking ship.

She's pulling him down. Grappling—*Inge, don't!*—an arm, trying to wrench free. Impossible, just like his father said. His eyes are above the water, then below: a glimpse of locked, thrashing forms, bubbles swarming, her skinny white legs hooked around his waist.

They surface. He inhales a breath, she choking and gasping. Somehow he's facing the shore. Hugh and Alie, in the matching aqua sarongs from their March holiday in Goa, are running down the flagstone steps from the cottage. Inge is climbing Ray as if he's a dockside ladder—his knees, his thighs, his shoulders the rungs. Kicking her way up, she forces him down. Water floods his yelling mouth and he gags, digs her clawing grip off his shoulder, fends her off with both hands, flattening her breasts under the one-piece she always wears up here because of Alie, who makes her untypically shy. *Nice,* she says, *I get the pot-belly but not the baby,* though it's not really much of a belly, not compared with his. She surges toward him again. He parries her arms, but her legs pincer around his hips with fantastic strength and she pulls him back down. *You're going to kill us both! Inge!* Her face underwater is deathly pale and yet frantically alive, wild eyes unseeing, hair billowing. He grabs at the surface, the light, somehow drags them both back up. He spews out water and gasps. Without thinking or revisiting his father's crazy advice, he hits her.

The blow misses the jaw—*the jaw,* as if it's any old jaw, not Inge's jaw—and grazes her cheek. Her eyes open even wider. He has never hit her—though a few times recently her charged silence made him wonder if he would have to duck a punch of hers. He has never punched anyone, not since grade school. He forgets whatever technical instruction his father once gave him. Her legs pincer tighter. Feet scrabbling for traction, he swings again. At the same time, she jerks her head sideways, toward the blow, reinforcing it. Fist and jaw meet with a crack and her eyes roll upward. Her leg-grip slackens, her whole body sags. Panting, spitting, he half turns and cradles her torso with his left arm, scooping at the water with his right. "It's OK. I'll get us back. I'm sorry. Hang on." He frog-kicks, hindered by her dragging legs, aiming for the dock where Hugh and Alie now loom, leaning forward, hollering like swim coaches exhorting their athletes on the home stretch.

Inge tenses, twitches as if snapping out of a doze. He looks at her face on his shoulder. Her reopened eyes focus. Her fist leaps out of the water like a fish and she clouts him square in the nose, slipping under after she connects. "Jesus, Inge!" His eyes, already blurred, tear up from the punch. He twists free of her. Hugh and Alie stand staring, hands lax at their sides, as if it's occurring to them that maybe no one is drowning here, maybe Ray and Inge are just having a fight—a real, physical fight, not like a professional couple on a long-weekend getaway but like a pair of locals, those trailer park townies whose bonfire parties at the public beach down the shore so obviously test Hugh and Alie's liberal tolerance...All of this he absorbs in a moment as he opens his mouth to call out—but then Inge jumps him from behind and hauls him back under. He tears at the pale, magnified hands clamping his rib cage, the rigid fingers with their bitten nails. Around them the water grows darker, colder. Bubbles boil upward in silence, lighting a route back to the surface. Suddenly, already, it looks too far. He could surrender, he could just inhale, it would be less painful, painless, he has heard, but he rips himself free as if from a jammed seat belt in a sinking car and shoots upward.

Sunlight detonates. His lungs erupt, shooting out water, blood as well, his nostrils hot with blood, his eyes half-blind. She pops up beside him, gagging and coughing. She throws another, limper punch but misses. He is breathing ammonia, briny mucus. She rears toward him again as if to attack, but no, she is churning, sputtering past him on the right, toward the dock, seemingly restored by her rage. He's furious himself now. Alie is calling in a thick and breaking voice, "It's all right, you two. Don't worry. Come on. Just come in!"

Ray keeps coughing, though weakly. He's still in trouble, in fact, and could probably do with a little help himself. Hugh is tearing off his sarong, crouching, flicking it out so that one end trails in the water like a rope, a few strokes short of Inge's reach as she labours toward the dock. Hugh should be naked now but isn't. (Is that underwear?) Beside his splayed feet, Inge's wineglass still stands. Alie is poised to dive in, but Hugh cups a hand over her kneecap; Inge is managing just enough not to need rescuing. "It's OK, girl!" Alie says, kneeling down beside Hugh, her voice throbbing. "You're there!"

Ray's legs feel heavy as anchors and his pummelling heart skips beats as he side-strokes toward the dock, toward Inge, who now grabs the floating end of the sarong with both hands. Hugh stands up—he actually is wearing underwear, baggy white boxers—and tows her in. She glances back at Ray. Her stricken gaze might be fixed on a dangerous pursuer or, yearningly, a loved one falling behind in the course of some desperate escape. One of her hands releases the taut sarong as if she means to point, wave, beckon. Alie grabs the free hand and tugs upward; Hugh reaches down as well; Inge is suspended off the end of the dock, continuing to gaze back at him.

IT OCCURRED TO HIM later that the crisis, from the moment he realized she was in trouble until he himself was dragged up onto the dock, could not have taken more than three minutes. A few hundred heartbeats. It felt interminable, of course. His memories—resolving into vivid fragments, like violent few-second cellphone videos posted on a news site—felt hyper-real and indelibly stable, as if exempt from memory's normal fading and smudging.

But he could not test their accuracy by discussing them with Inge. Her refusal to revisit the crisis—their near deaths, their mutual violence, her once-in-a-lifetime relinquishing of all self-control—was hardly surprising, especially given what they learned soon afterward. Still, in spite of everything, she surprised him the following year by wanting to return to the lake for their customary long-weekend stay. Hugh, he warned her, would certainly try to discuss the incident and his and Alie's own roles in it. But Inge was adamant. She seemed to view the return not so much as a form of trauma exorcism but rather as a way of salvaging an important tradition, in a matured, familial form. She meant to swim as much as ever (though in the end, as it turned out, she chose not to go back in at all). As for Hugh and Alie, she realized they could be annoyingly self-satisfied, but they were true friends and that mattered more than ever now.

For the first five years of their marriage, Inge and Ray had tried to have a baby, suffered miscarriages, consulted specialists, and in due course accepted that there would be no children. No way to know if children would have prevented or accelerated the fraying of their marriage over the following three years, leading up to that struggle in the lake. But a few weeks after it, trying to work out the details of a separation, they discovered Inge was pregnant. At first, pending the re-test, she was tense, touchy, guarded, as if she dreaded either outcome; with the second positive, an unqualified joy overcame her, an *exultancy* that seemed to astonish her as much as her condition. Ray, his two black eyes now faded to yellow, felt himself bumped into the role of designated worrier, the sober, tentative one, although he too felt more pleased by the surprise than he would have predicted. That the summer's lone interlude of carnality, however mutually satisfying, had resulted in conception—a result supposedly impossible—made him wonder, ever so slightly, if Hugh could have been responsible.

The boy was born in April. He could not have looked more like Ray. At the cottage in August, their first afternoon, after Hugh and Alie had retired for their nap, Inge, on the dock, unwrapped Isaac and handed him down to Ray, who was standing in the shallows by the tiny beach.

"Inge, are you sure?"

"Don't be silly, Ray. Go on, let him get the feel of it."

Ray held his naked son so that the boy faced away from him, out over the lake, Ray's hands all but encircling the rib cage and feeling the thudding of the tiny heart. He dunked him to his navel. Isaac's pale legs began frogging promisingly, his whole body writhing as if longing to be released.

Professions of Love

SOME WILL ATTEST, many, in fact, that I am one of the finest in the field. I can quote from grateful testimonials. I have received citations and awards from each of the three professional organizations to which I belong. I am surgeon of choice for many of this city's, this country's, most prominent and preferred names. I am said, actually, let me be frank, to be *the* finest in the field. Numerous colleagues have said this. Many of my patients have said this or would say this if they were asked. I could quote from some of their grateful testimonials, because, frankly, I do reread them. You may ask why I do this. I am fifty-six years old and in health and by any measure of these matters "successful." At the pinnacle of my practice: the top of my game. Well-to-do, one must add. Enveloped with honours. Or: embalmed with honours? Is that possibly the problem? That I feel I have nothing to strive for anymore? No *défi?* I prefer the French, my mother's language, my second of five tongues, a form of German being the first, *défi*, for challenge, in the sense of the World offering defiance, resistance. Which one duly tackles with zest. No, that is not the problem. No lack of zest. The ennui of arrival at the pinnacle is not the problem. A trite malaise of middle age. "Is that all there is" and so forth. No. Forget this. I like being here at the pinnacle. At the pinnacle it is thrilling and the thrill does not jade. Nor am I a man for whom self-assurance, like a slowly accrued encrustation of diplomas and titles and press clippings and social compliments and admiring looks and so forth, is a superficial phenomenon. Thin gauze, let us say, in constant need of reapplication, laid over a wound leading inward to a profound abscess of uncertainty. I do have uncertainties, but they are peripheral. Or, to rephrase the fact, not of my very essence. Always I have had this self-assurance. Just why, you may ask, I do not know. Even in childhood, yes, this superior assurance, albeit I was not especially large or powerful or fast, those boyhood prerequisites of status.

Never mind boyhood and its tedious clichés. This is about recent events. I have uncertainties, as I have said, but at the marrow of my character, no. My wife is leaving me. You are familiar with the adage that no man is a hero to his wife. I believe that the phrase actually runs: No man is a hero to his valet. The point is identical. I wonder if my wife has been the reason I have felt compelled, now and then, to reread public testimonials on my work, press clippings, even the private letters I occasionally receive from patients. To be sure, these have lent comfort when, now and then, I felt insufficiently appreciated, as everybody, of course, occasionally must. What I feel now, however, is a species of "grief": a process, one reads, with many steps, "anger" being a station of the cross on that Calvary, though I seem not to have reached it, or to be in the vicinity. I never have been the sort to bear malice or make a long-term patient of my grievances, doctoring them along to sturdier strength, I am not obsessive in that way. I have always been an untroubled sleeper: though not at this moment particularly. Bafflement, I believe, trudges up that path alongside grief. In a sense I did act contrary to her wishes, but my motives were benign. I went against her wishes in the way that a man may go against a wife's wishes in arranging, say, a surprise party on her behalf when what she wants for her birthday, she has said, is to go out with him to their favourite, say, Greek seafood restaurant. Duly promising to take her to Molivos, secretly he ploys to "deny" her wish. The party is a gift that supersedes his promise while *surpassing* her wish! His motives are the motives of generosity, love! If he is especially thoughtful, he will have the party catered by Molivos.

She is four years older than I. A beautiful woman aging, on the whole, less well than she might be aging, and in that expedited fashion of a woman after her change of life. We have been married for twenty-nine years. Two sons, twenty-two and twenty, grown and now departed, attending the same university, Duke, in the United States of America. So mostly we have had each other to ourselves for the last two years. This has gone less well than one might have foreseen. For the first time we have been obliged to rehearse a long future conducted with no one for company but each other. She said, at first, that she was content, happy at the prospect. The prospect troubled me! For the first time in many years, it seemed, with the haze of harried parenthood cleared away, I was able to look at her seriously. It seemed that she, or someone, something, had applied to her face the pancake makeup of mortality. I would have liked to suggest, diplomatically, that things might be done. How odd if the wife of a dentist should sport disintegrating incisors! Absurd for the mate of a fashion designer to attend social functions in a fretworn housedress redolent of naphtha! And so forth. Nothing would have been easier than to perform some simple work. I had been dropping, let me speak frankly, mild hints, from time to time, for a number of years, hints that she seemed not to detect, or decipher: or which possibly she chose to suppress. I stopped doing it. Listen. For a number of reasons that do not matter here, reasons of ethical principle mainly, albeit also, to be frank, of personal biography, having to do with my extremely divorced parents (both now happily buried), I would like very much to stay married to my wife. To use the common phrase, she has been a lover and a friend. Or the common terminology: supportive, loyal. If consistency and discipline have helped gain me success in my professional life, I try also to be consistent in my personal life. And I love Fidelia. There has been no other woman save Fidelia since my twenties. Surely I have looked at other women, you think, you ask, in my mind disrobed and dishevelled other women, since my marriage in April of 1980, pleasantly dishevelled them, yes, to be sure I have, on the street and in restaurants and galleries and at social functions I have spied them and, of course, in my operating theatre, there above all, I have scrutinized women with an intensity of focus which most men, I think, could barely conceive of. It is my *job!*

Too many of my colleagues call themselves, in private or, sometimes, in public, Artists. I refuse to do this. It is pretentious, in many ways. In certain ways. At least, many feel it is pretentious. Then again, does it simply, I wonder, restate the obvious, the *actual,* as a vulgar boast? For there is, come to that, a trace of truth to the claim. The canvas on which one works, the clay in which one works, is the face of the patient, of the women (and, increasingly, men) who come to one, many of them aging, of course, but some of them young and lovely, many in the performing arts, of course, others who are merely, who can blame them, vain, and wish to anticipate the attritions of time and one's many cares and that unacknowledged devil, gravity. Others are merely neurotic. These patients have been under my power, not to mention, often enough, a thorough anaesthetic, and I have never once, what is the phrase, "abused power." The profession is not without temptations and this one most evidently. *To exploit the patient's potential obsession with her doctor.* This is common wisdom. Psychoanalysis provides a word, not to mention a vast literature, on the subject. And it should know! To the patient, however, I am no mere psychoanalyst-father-figure, and certainly no ordinary doctor. An ordinary doctor can, with luck, by forestalling death, slow time. *I reverse it!* The effects of a skilfully conducted, successful operation can seem, frankly, almost preternatural, even to the surgeon himself: and after the fact, I have never once taken advantage of any patient's unconscious perception of me as, how shall I put the notion, more than merely human.

Of course, I was lucky enough to *love* my wife through all those years, not merely to be attached to her in the dry canons of the law. So the temptations of beauty, whether intact among my secretaries and assistants, or revised upon my table (these latter, of course, being the most tempting, for readily imaginable reasons well-explored by myth and classic literature!), were resistible. But in the two years since our younger son left home, my resistance has weakened. Finding myself day by day less drawn to my wife, who appeared to be drying up before my eyes, as if, almost, my eyes themselves were inducing these changes, I began to suggest more frequently and firmly that she should allow me to help her in the way that I had helped so many strangers before. Such a procedure would of course be "unofficial": the profession naturally "discourages" practitioners from performing on spouses, which is not to say that such things do not occur, they DO, and no doubt more commonly than I, who can cite several collegial instances, can attest.

Exactly what needed to be done was obvious. Nothing especially drastic. There was nothing specially unique about the ways in which age was affecting her, there never is. Around the eyes, the lips, the jowls, that horribly graphic noun, and the delicate skin of the throat. What concerned me was my own growing sense of, yes, almost, sometimes, *revulsion,* when, all right, *whenever* I would sit down to dinner across from this rumpled imposter, or wake in the morning beside her. I never had been able to persuade her to train herself to sleep on her back, to prevent pillow wrinkling around the eyes. A practice on which I had instructed countless patients. *Lie like a corpse to avoid looking like one.* I never used, of course, this dire motto by way of explanation: a quip of the profession, there are many such. In fact, I knew enough of my wife's character, how could I not after so many years, to realize that she was disturbed by my suggestions, and so I abstained from further such, albeit with an accruing sense of concern.

For my desire to help her was a matter of loving pragmatism, yes, as opposed to reckless idealism (I wonder if there is any other kind?). I could not *prevent* myself from feeling unattracted to this increasingly unrecognizable flatmate; I *did not want* to abandon her; I had the *means* and the *expertise* to remedy the trouble. Yet I knew she would be resistant. After all, her utter lack of vanity was one of the things that had drawn me to her years before and had kept us together since! In my profession, I am of course constantly exposed to vain characters, persons truly steeped and mulled in their vanity, mobilized by vanity, fully *indentured* to vanity. How refreshing, for all those years, to come home to a woman who was naturally beautiful and hardly seemed to know it or to care! She wrote about food for various prominent publications and I happen to know that when speaking to the editors of certain of those women's journals, she could be rather evasive about my profession. *I hated that!* She herself often voiced certain cavils and caveats about the profession, especially as the nature of my work changed over time. Yes, changed. In the early years, I worked mainly to rectify congenital defects, such as cleft palates, or to help recast the faces of burn victims. In time my reputation grew. Times were changing, as they always are, and increasingly patients approached me for "merely" cosmetic procedures, and this came to seem my métier. I had a capacity in that line, perhaps because, as I used to compliment Fidelia, I had the model, the matrix-plate, the Ur-mould, the form and very armature of natural beauty at home to work from.

My wife was not pleased by the direction my career took or by the new constituency of my clientele, which, admittedly, included certain unsound persons, like the lady who always petitioned me to give her toy terrier, too, "a little nose job," so that owner and pet should more perfectly resemble each other, but I believe that Fidelia, like me, is conjugally stubborn, determined to "hold things together" both for the benefit of our sons and out of regard for the life we have had together, the past, the present, the future. (In our favourite Greek restaurant, on the menu among other charming illiteracies, appears THE FUTURE OF THE DAY: one of our favourite shared jokes. Squid, typically.)

We love each other even more than we did at the start. Yes, despite my occasional, perhaps I put it too strongly, revulsion. Yes, and yet in certain lights. The light of breakfast assuredly. I will prepare the coffee with a traditional hand grinder while she sits at the table, the tabby, Familiar, in her lap. I love her inextricably. But a disjunction has entered, had entered, my regard. I yearned to correct it. My physical attraction to her, my lack of it, had fallen out of proportion to the love I felt. For if she had changed with age, so had I! Professions amend one. *Mine had made an invidious critic of my gaze.* My heart embraced her; my eyes poked and prodded. I felt cloven against myself. It made me think too much. Too much thinking is the death of marriage. I would end up leaving her, sleeping with other women, as other Swiss-German fathers, let us say a Certain Swiss-German Father and leave it at that, have done, for they, these women, are so readily available, avid for the deft, silver-haired Inverter of Time, and I knew that, should nothing change, *I would leave my Fidelia*.

Increasingly these were my thoughts in the weeks before the incident and its aftermath. Fidelia had seemed troubled, preoccupied for some time, she has always been prone to seasonal depression, and our annual holiday, this year in Belize, had helped little, perhaps because I was helplessly, visibly attracted to the mermaidenly younger women around us. Mentally disrobing them was of course unnecessary. I tried to disguise my ogling. This never succeeds. She tried to disguise her distress. Nor does this. I tried harder. I knew that I was causing my Fidelia pain. Near the end of the holiday, slowly wandering the beach alone, having left her napping, I saw an attractive woman, her back turned, rise out of the water in a corona of spray, hair fetchingly disturbed by the sea, and as I waded into the shallows to draw closer, a helpless satellite, the woman turned toward me and the jarringly aged face, framed, I now saw, with greying hair made darker by drenching, was *Fidelia's:* a face that did not belong on that body, which of course is exactly the case with her, she is naturally slim, stays fit with little regimentary exercise, has the legs of a woman twenty years younger. I believe that as I recognized her, she saw the enchantment die on my face, and in that instant of several linked deaths she saw everything.

In March, amid mild depression, Fidelia suffered a minor cerebral ischemic event. Initially it appeared to be a stroke of greater seriousness, but her condition stabilized within hours. A very minor stroke, the doctor, the medical doctor, diagnosed: more a warning than an actual stroke. He predicted that the minor lateral numbness that she continued to suffer at unpredictable times would diminish, and it did, that her right hand would soon recoup its full and considerable strength of grip, and it did, that the slight but discernible downsag at the outer corner of her right eye and her lips would correct itself within a few weeks, and it did not. By August he had revised his prognosis in regard to these latter asymmetries. They would likely be permanent. *She could have them surgically corrected, however.* Life, of course, is more or less a textile of such ironies. I have often wondered, why? I now believe that it must be owing to the quality of our attention, how our fears and fascinations (every fear is a fascination!) seek to materialize, the Unmanifest willing its own manifestation. How everything longs to come to life.

After waiting for another month to see if there would be any detectable improvement, during which time the asymmetries seemed, if anything, to grow more distinct, Fidelia, to my surprise, chose to have something done. Once she had made the decision, her attitude vis-à-vis the procedure was uncharacteristically impatient. The minor cerebral ischemic event had made her rethink many things. She was exercising more conscientiously. In every way she had grown more prudent about her health. I believe she was coming to regard Time, as I have come to regard Time, as I have perhaps always regarded Time, as the ENEMY it is. Not that I believe it to be defeatable! Only neurotic fools and faddists believe as much, or pretend to believe so, and I am neither neurotic nor faddist: nonetheless I feel that a certain, what, a certain *honour* lies in fighting a losing battle with courage and resolution, undertaking a *défi,* for what is life, after a certain point, but a rearguard action, a tactical withdrawal, for that matter what is every face I freshen but another recruit in this campaign against a predatory, insatiable opponent that seeks to strip us all of our dignity and our future, our grip on consciousness, our creaturely delight! Perhaps, then, I am more soldier than artist. Or: I am both at once. Or, in Fidelia's case, a suitor, one whose rival is mortality itself, and who will not simply step aside as his rival marks her as his own.

In the week before I operated, in September, I made no suggestions that, while she was under the anaesthetic, I could do *more* of the work that I had, in my mind, been rehearsing, revising, rethinking, *perfecting* now for some years. I kept waiting for her to ask me to undertake this, what, this "supplementary work." She said nothing! Of course she would say nothing: having declared herself contrary to the enterprise for so long, what could she have said but nothing, albeit certainly, knowing my feelings on the matter, she might have been expected to speak out *against* such work! Her silence, then, led me to suspect *that secretly she might well want something done,* but did not know how to ask! Pride would prevent it. Or call it, paradoxically, "vanity"!

I made love to her the night before the procedure, of course. "Of course," I add, albeit the act had occurred rarely enough over the preceding two years, especially over the preceding months. I was gentle and I comforted her, I was capable, in the darkness, of feeling the old familiar passions, *ja,* in the darkness where her body felt much the same as it had always, while her face in the dark was simply a face in the dark. Some married people, we are told, make service of the darkness as an aid to fantasy, so as to pretend that the husband or wife in their arms is not their spouse. *I used the dark so as to pretend that she was!* This poignantly evolved preference, for darkness over the light, for blindness over vision, what was this if not another loss of dignity for us both, the latest reverse in the unwinnable battle against Time, a dry run for that eventual, conclusive darkness and terminal anaesthesia. Nevertheless on that night my desire was immense, the blind orgasm coldly numbing my scalp, like, yes, a local anaesthetic, clawing a cry from me that scarcely sounded like my own. Hers was quieter, yet she clenched me with all her limbs as if to grip the life out of me.

Afterward, I told her not to worry. She was not worried at all. Her breath smelled of hunger as she said the words, she had had to fast since noon, of course, because of the coming anaesthetic, and yet, despite the presumed discomforts of this fast (Fidelia being a woman who loves to eat), she fell asleep long before I. As I lay there, I remembered a particular occasion from years before, when our younger boy, Oskar, either hearing our sounds or seeking some nocturnal comfort, perhaps a glass of water, entered the master bedroom. Finding Fidelia aboard me, sitting up, her hands gripping my head, fingers in my hair, which was then longer in the style of the time, while I groaned as if being injured, he called out with a truly heartrending sincerity: Mama, please, he didn't mean it! He didn't mean it, Mama, please...! When I did eventually sleep, I dreamt of a cat, bony, starved, not our pampered Familiar, lying on its side on the bed mewling with some grief it was of course helpless to articulate. In the dream, nonetheless, I felt this grief as my own.

The work on her right eye and the right side of her mouth proceeded quickly and with no complications. Amina, my anaesthetist, who had never actually met Fidelia before, as she, Fidelia, never came to the office, asked, at one point, I do not recall exactly when, if there was another patient booked in before noon. She had thought, she said, that I had cancelled the other pre-noon surgery. (I had.) She was puzzled, I think, because I was working quite fast, as if we were short of time, whereas in fact I was merely eager to get through the preliminaries on Fidelia, albeit I was of course working carefully and was only able to finish the work rapidly because my concentration was so acute, so engaged, so *instigated*, almost as if I feared Fidelia might regain consciousness too soon (impossible), or was it simply my excitement at being embarked on a task for which I had so long prepared myself in imagination, in phantasy? Then again, I always have felt hurried, feel that time is so short, a fact which, I believe, any truly vital being must believe: an eighty-year lifespan is a mockery of human dignity and potential, an "intelligent" and "curious" person could live three times that length without ennui or loss of direction. I believe this although Fidelia, strangely, never has, or had, agreed with me, she has made a separate peace with Time and thinks, as did a certain philosopher I read when young, in my father's library in Rorschach, that "what is, is right." However, as I said before, her minor cerebral ischemic event had clearly brought her over to my way of thinking.

Amina gave small indications of surprise as I began to work on Fidelia's uncompromised left eye. This, although she must have realized by now that I was planning to do further work, for she had already commented, with slight concern, on the amount of anaesthetic I had asked her to administer. Again I was working swiftly and efficiently, as if my decades of experience had all been in preface of this morning's procedure. Still not perfectly sure that Fidelia would not feel, if she knew, some vestigial resistance to my plans, I wanted to make certain my revision of her would be as perfect as attainable, a cause for eventual delight, not shock and distress. I spare you the more esoteric clinical details. My procedures comprised various small incisions, tightenings, liftings, buttressings, injections of filler, in short, nothing you could not glean or deduce from the pages of some of the very magazines that Fidelia, which is not her real name, has written for on countless occasions. Amina interrupted me once, while I was working on Fidelia's left jowl, yes, that vile, vivid noun must be applied, to ask if I was all right and would like to sit down for a moment, would like a glass of water: apparently I looked unwell, my forehead was damp, she said, and I explained that I had never before laboured on a loved one (a "sister-in-law," I had given her to think), implying, of course, that I was nervous, albeit nervousness was not what I felt. *I felt, if anything, elated!* The sculptor is said to discern and exhume a Form dormant in his medium: I was effecting changes that would disinter the face, the long-beloved face, that mortality had sought first to blur and next, at its leisure, to obliterate! My wife did not understand that such a gift could be, that it was possible to appeal and overturn the "kangaroo court" verdict of Time, to find the external and internal facets of one's being re-harmonized, to feel whole again, returned to oneself, and she herself would be elated in time, albeit initially, of course, she would feel slightly unwell after the anaesthetic, and her face would appear, in places, somewhat bruised and red, even if my methods are "of the best," and full recovery is now a matter of days, not weeks or months.

I will not try to describe more of the procedure save to say that a point came, around noon, while I worked on the incipient wattles of my wife's beautiful throat, when my excitement was replaced by a feeling I have never before experienced: a sense of full mastery, gratifying to the ego, of course, and yet indivisibly fused with a selfless access of love. My whole Being, its "selfish" and selfless parts, was integrated in this instant that felt like a sort of culmination, or consummation, professional and personal. I had practised all these years in order to learn what I must learn so as to restore my wife to herself, her self entire.

Fidelia, slumping and only semi-conscious, we helped from the table into the dimly lit, womblike cubicle where heavily anaesthetized patients are left to recover until they are ready to be taken home. I asked Amina, which is not her real name, to leave us and to close the office for the day, and to allow the secretary too to leave early. This notice of a surprise half holiday visibly pleased my pretty young assistant, albeit she gave me, I felt, an oddly scrutinous glance. The cubicle resonated with soft baroque and classical music that played in an hour-long loop. Occasionally I would come in here on my own and sit or lie quietly while ruminating on matters which have no bearing on this account. Albinoni's lachrymose adagio was playing. Soon, of course, Pachelbel's canon would ensue, and then other pacifying standards. Seated on the side of the daybed, I held my wife in my arms, *Pietà*-wise. Finally she opened her eyes, partly opened her eyes, and said, softly, that she felt nauseous, nauseated, I mentally corrected her, and she added:

—My eyes feel tight, Rudi. And my mouth.

Mouf, she pronounced the word, in her grogginess, as the boys had done when they were small. She was in fact quite childlike at this moment, something I have noted often in patients recovering from anaesthesia. I was moved. I said:

—I know, darling.

—Did it go all right, everything?

—Yes, perfectly.

—Feels like I've been asleep for so long.

—It always does. It's like a … now what is the term?

—Why's everything so sore?

—A beauty sleep. That is what it was.

—The problems are fixed?

—They are. Rest now, close your eyes again.

—Why does it hurt everywhere, why's it starting to hurt?

I kissed her delicately in the middle of her forehead, her lips would be too tender as yet, albeit they would soon be fine. Everything, I thought, would soon be fine: and, purely in terms of the procedure's aesthetic success, they did turn out perfectly.

—I hope you'll be happier now, Rudi, I know you didn't like what the stroke did.

—But this was for you, darling.

Her smile here was ambiguous, as if pained. Of course, it would be pained. To smile is somewhat painful after such procedures. She said:

—I hope you'll be happy now.

—You've always made me happy.

—And now I'll be like before, won't I?

—You will.

—I'm so sleepy, though.

—Go back to sleep for a while, *mi Schatz*. We'll go home when you're ready.

She stretched her lips: another brave smile.

—More beauty sleep? she asked.

—Exactly.

—I shouldn't look in a mirror yet, I guess?

—Not yet.

—I don't mind.

—No, darling, I said, thinking of her modesty, of how agreeable she had been, about most things in our life: you have never minded.

Expecting

THE CALENDAR INDICATED spring, but the weather was equivocal and kept the city on hold. Steep sunlight, as yet unfiltered by any leaves, dazzled the eyes and burned the skin, but the winds were icy. A month of recidivist weather: tomorrow it might easily snow. Leonard and Halli Losco were driving home after their Sunday brunch in the Market—a ritual that had been central to their life together since they'd met four years ago, but which Losco suspected might soon be subject to suspension, or worse. Halli was due in two weeks and last night had experienced some preliminary cramping, a benchmark they'd learned about in the prenatal classes that had recently concluded.

"So here we go," Losco had said.

"Not yet, silly," she'd told him, curled on her side, her head on his shoulder while his eyes probed the ceiling, as if for hairline cracks. "I mean, it could be a couple more weeks, even more."

Losco as a child had been so anxious that, had he grown up three decades later, he'd have been well acquainted with therapists and would have swallowed medication with his morning juice. Instead, he'd painstakingly coached himself beyond his phobias and become—as his business partner, Vance, put it—cowboy calm. He was a bulky, plodding kid with black-frame spectacles and curiously abbreviated legs. Sitting very upright at his school desk, he seemed of average height, even a bit above, but when he stood up, his large head remained more or less at the same level and his true stature was revealed. This anomaly generated both merriment and creativity among his schoolmates, who called him Tiny Lessco, Lost-legs, and Legs-low, as well as Colossco, Moscow, and Loser Losco. More laconic peers skipped the preliminaries and simply shoved or struck him, though seldom with any committed hostility. Allusions to his ethnicity—he'd inherited the swarthiness and vaguely Semitic features of the Maltese parents who insisted on ferrying him to and from school each day—were less frequent and, when they came, oddly tentative. Possibly his schoolmates considered ethnic slurs superfluous given his physique, or else they didn't know how to go about disparaging the Maltese, who were not quite Wops, or Kikes, or Greasy Greeks, or Pakis, or anything else, and came from an island no one had heard of or could find on a map.

Then Losco chose Stendhal's *Le rouge et le noir* for his grade ten French project and was struck by its little hero's Napoleonic willpower. It hadn't occurred to him that you could so fully and plausibly concoct a new character for yourself, thus tightly regulating how others viewed you. Invisibility was not the answer after all. Nor was a class clown's ingratiating hijinks. Image management was the key. So Losco—constantly goading and grading himself—worked to perfect a quiet, wry, never-ruffled persona that his peers began to notice. At university he was widely admired and even imitated by men who, a decade earlier, would have despised or overlooked him, or noticed *only* his lower half, a condition he had not grown out of and continued to regret. Still, he was rarely anxious now about his physique or any other thing. His years of disciplined shamming had convinced his very core.

Halli was the sort of woman whose every step or gesture is a small calamity for any watching male—so Losco told himself, with pride. Slim and tall, she moved with effortless grace. Yet she seemed unaware of, or indifferent to, her charms. Her large brown eyes appeared wholly uncalculating—instead sympathetic and gently amused. She laughed often, though rarely at jokes. She lapsed easily into reveries or trances but in a moment could bear down and focus with tenacious practicality.

He had never been with a woman of such varied enticements and hardly a day passed when he didn't shake his head and marvel at this outcome. As for Halli, like women before her, she was drawn to his calmness, which read as uncomplicated male confidence and which he knew must seem all the more remarkable given his size and appearance. His one good feature, he believed, was the firm, stoical jaw he'd sprouted in his teens. With a replica straight razor he groomed it each morning, weekends included.

The irony was that once Halli entered his life, his boyhood anxiety began to creep back. The sensations: motion sickness without the motion; a slight but chronic tightness under the sternum; the unsettled pulse of a man constantly expecting final notice from a loan shark. In the bedroom there had been a few close calls and Losco, aiming to pre-empt serious trouble, had supplied himself with pharmaceutical fail-safes that in the end proved unnecessary.

Still, they'd been happy, often deliriously so—or so he believed, much of the time, when the anxiety was more or less in abeyance. But with the pregnancy it became worse, a flutter felt not just internally but around him, somehow, in the spaces of their house, like a faint tremor from a construction site. When he finally told her, she said in her sensibly upbeat way, "If you didn't feel even a tad nervous, *I'd* be nervous, love. It shows you're taking this seriously." He joked that he was just worried that their son—he'd insisted on the ultrasound—would inherit his stature instead of hers.

Odd how the return of unpleasant symptoms—so familiar despite their long absence—could also bring a trace of relief.

Driving them home now, Losco gripped the wheel of the car with hands at ten and two o'clock. The traffic was light, but his eyes flicked mirror to mirror, as if they were on the 417 at rush hour. He'd drunk too much of the restaurant's potent coffee and he could feel the pulse under his chin. A glossy metallic-blue SUV loomed alongside, swung closer and then, as Losco tensed, veered away. Without signalling, it steered into a turning lane and then, too fast, onto an off-ramp.

Halli said, "What's that?"

From the corner of his eye he glimpsed something detach itself from the roof of the SUV and fly off.

"What was it?" he said. "They hit a bird?"

She was looking back. "Pull over, Leo."

"What, here?"

"We have to stop, love."

"What *is* it?"

"I think a wallet. It's on the shoulder of the road."

"Or maybe a learner's manual. That idiot can't drive to save his—"

"Just pull over, Leo, OK? I think it's—"

"OK, OK, I'm pulling over!"

"I think it was on the roof."

He brought the car to a stop and reversed along the shoulder. The Audi A4 was a standard and he had driven it for eight years, tall in the seat, jaw heroically firm, eyes fixed coolly on the road in a way that several women before Halli had admitted they liked, trusted. He was backing up quickly, nearing the off-ramp.

"Oh, a car just drove over it! No, it's OK—they didn't hit it."

"Guy must have been filling up," he said.

She looked at him.

"In the SUV," he said. "Must have left his wallet on the roof. This is as far as we can go."

"OK—I'll go get it."

"What, are you kidding?"

"Love, I'm fine, I'm not in a wheelchair!"

"Let me go for it, Hal, OK? Please?"

He leapt out before she could argue. He walked back along the shoulder and looked both ways up and down the off-ramp—it was only one way, of course—then stepped into the lane to retrieve the wallet. He made himself move casually, transparently, nothing to hide from the few passing cars. Security cameras must be observing him too. For a moment he saw himself on video, a small, blurry figure stooping and reaching for some object. Maybe he should have let Halli get it after all? No one would ever suspect her of a nefarious deed—Halli, pregnant and with her usual bright aura of blamelessness, of exemption from the usual human failings.

He gave her the fat wallet and pulled back onto the parkway. She told him she would find some ID, a number to call. Her cellphone lay in her lap, inches from her distended belly (lately he'd been pestering her to keep it out of her lap and away from the baby). Looking through the wallet, she said, "We'll call him as soon as I find a number. If he lives nearby, we could take it right to him!"

The prospect of this little expedition—its novelty, its helpfulness—clearly pleased her. Something he'd noticed about his revived anxiety was that it pre-empted such generosities (not that they'd ever been his strong suit) by making him warily weigh every action, and by tilting him even further toward cynical suppositions. He was thinking now that the wallet was likely stolen, then gutted and left on a stranger's car roof, a clever way to dispose of it randomly.

"Any credit cards?" he asked.

"Three different ones. And a driver's licence, health card, sin card—Jean-Denis Beaulieu, that's his name. Even his passport."

"His *passport?*"

"It's in the—oh, what do you call it—in the cash slot, with the cash."

"How much?"

"A twenty and a five. I'm still looking for a number. Wait, here...I'll call him, this must be his card. It's a video arcade in Gatineau."

"Really? I didn't think there were any of those left."

Peripherally he saw her lift the phone to her far ear, then cover the ear closest to him with her free hand, a natural enough manoeuvre, yet it set off a thrill of pain under his heart, as if she were trying to exclude him from some private exchange. Silence. Then she was speaking, apparently leaving a message in her flawless Parisian French. He knew many of the words and heard her leave her cellphone number and their home number, but, oddly, he couldn't make out the message's full import, though in context it should have been easy.

"I was hoping it was a cell number," she said, setting the phone back down in her lap, on top of the open wallet, "but I guess it's a land line. But he might check for messages once he figures out he's lost his wallet and passport."

"I would."

"I know you would, sweetheart." She said the words fondly enough, but then again, the line between settled affection and love's erosion in habit and predictability—was it not a fine one?

He pulled into their flat driveway, needlessly setting the parking brake, and turned to her. "Home."

She sat unmoving. These days, when the fatigue hit her, it was abrupt and flattening. For the last five weeks or so she'd been taking a long nap after their brunches. Gently, briskly, he relieved her of the wallet, then jumped out of the car and came around to her side.

As he unlocked the front door of the house, he glanced back across Cedar Street, which was cedarless, wide, no sidewalks. Murray Olson—a perpetually tanned, lanky widower in his seventies—raised a hand and left it aloft almost in the manner of a blessing. In his other hand Olson held the tall rake with which he'd been turning the earth, readying his garden. Halli irradiated him with a broad, spontaneous smile. No one besides Losco could have guessed that she was desperate to climb upstairs and collapse into bed for the rest of the day.

He disliked bringing the wallet over the threshold into their home, as if this step transformed a commendable act into a de facto theft. After tucking Halli into bed—promising her he wouldn't spend his whole afternoon trying to return the wallet—he went straight to his office, eased shut the door, and checked the home phone for messages. Nothing. He called one of the man's credit card companies. To his surprise he found that they would do nothing to help either him or Jean-Denis Beaulieu. The man on the line, Pardeep—strong Indian accent but flowing English—seemed astonished that Losco expected him to give out a customer's contact details. "But he's lost his *wallet*," Losco protested. "We have his card—he'll want it back, right? Can't you at least reach him and give him our number?" The wallet—square, black, metallically shiny—sat on his desk as it had on the road. He eyed it as if it were some improvised explosive device. "I mean, I really want to get this thing back to him."

The man said the company could do nothing until the customer contacted them.

"And *has* he?" Losco demanded.

"I cannot answer this question, sir."

Next he tried the police. They were no more helpful. They suggested he consider contacting them after twenty-four hours if he still hadn't heard from the owner of the wallet. He left a message at Beaulieu's work number, as Halli had done, though Losco recorded his in English. He keyed in the web address of the video arcade and crashed out a wordy email, more detailed than necessary, his fingers snapping over the keyboard. He flagged it urgent. Then he rifled through the wallet again—careful to replace everything exactly—but found no other contact number, though he did notice something that both Halli and he had missed so far. Several items were out of date: a debit card, one of the credit cards, also Beaulieu's driver's licence and Quebec health card. But the sin card and passport were current. He rubbed his eyes, blinked moisture onto his contact lenses, and looked again at the passport photo: a man with the neck of a rugby tackle, a stubble beard, thick black hair that seemed to erupt from his scalp just an inch or two above the eyebrows. What no such image could indicate—and who understood this better than Losco?—was the person's size. Beaulieu might be anything from a giant to a burly dwarf. (Losco glanced again at the driver's licence, where an actual height was listed: 180 cm.)

An internet search turned up little information, just a few hits linking the man to the video arcade and citing that same phone number. Two other men shared his name, one of them deceased, the other a notary in Laval with a busy Facebook page.

Halli slept for three full hours. Since long before the pregnancy she'd enjoyed this happy capacity to sleep at any time. Losco saw this knack, which he mostly regarded with affection but at times also envy—even a trace of puritanical censure—as another sign of her healthy, feline nature. She did not live to one side of herself but wholly within her own being, her own instinctive life.

He was in his office, checking email again, when she came in.

"Leo—honey—I told you I'd deal with it. I *knew* you'd…"

"What?"

"Nothing, love. It's OK. So he hasn't called back?"

"Must be nuts. Hasn't he noticed his wallet is missing?"

"It's Sunday, Leo—some people don't check things as often."

He studied her face, half expecting something new to appear there, some expression he'd never seen before. He said, "It's just—I hate having this thing hang over us."

"Then we won't let it! Would just soup be OK for dinner? Maybe Thai?"

"Let me do it, Hal, I said I would."

"I've had a long rest, love. Let me, I want to."

And she withdrew before he could object. For a moment he felt he might lower his brow to his desk and weep. She loves me, she loves me, she loves me as much as I love her—and how can that be? And yet it seems she really does, still.

He turned to some of the work he'd meant to catch up on during her nap. He and his partner had an investment consulting firm and for a year Halli had handled the communications side of certain portfolios (she could calm and conciliate the prickliest clients), but lately, of course, she was falling behind.

The telephone on his desk detonated. "Hello?" he said in the cool, noncommittal bass he affected whenever answering.

Through a heavy accent—not French—a loud voice pushed out a word and repeated it. At first he thought it was a garbled *hello,* then he thought it was *Halli,* then, perhaps, *Ali.*

Losco said his own name, then, "Who am I speaking to here?"

"This is *Halli?*"

"Losco, Leonard Losco. Who is this?"

"She leaved me a message."

"Today?" The tweak of jealous suspicion came with a sense of familiarity, as if he felt it all the time or had long been expecting it; this could not be Beaulieu, surely; this was the eventual interloper who had always been destined to call.

"Of course, yes, today!" said the voice.

"What is this about?"

"What? You have my wallet, yes?"

Losco glanced at call display and scribbled down the number. "Please tell me your name."

"Jean-Denis Beaulieu."

Losco's own French accent was mediocre, he knew, but he himself could have pronounced the name more correctly.

"Would you rather speak French?" Losco asked. "I think I can manage. My wife's is better, but, uh, she's—"

"Halli?"

"Yes, Halli, my wife!"

"No, my French is no better than English."

"But—"

"My mother was not Québécoise," he said brusquely, as if he'd had to explain too many times. "I grow up elsewhere, Albania."

After a moment Losco said, "OK, well—so can you come pick this thing up? No, hang on," he said, hesitating to give their address. "I can bring it to you. Where are you?"

"No, I am not," the man said confusingly. "I pick it after dinner. Where is your house?"

It hit Losco that he couldn't be out delivering lost items this evening, he had to stay with Halli. "What time would after dinner be?"

"What? I am not sure. Maybe eight."

"Why don't we say eight p.m., then. I'll be waiting."

"Maybe I be a bit later."

"Please don't. My wife...she's not feeling well."

"Ah yes, I see," the man said, now sounding amenable, even sympathetic.

With a spasm of dread that Losco recognized as irrational, he gave their address and simple directions.

In the kitchen he found her seated on one of the shining stools by the new black marble island. She was hunched over, a hand spread over her belly, the other splayed on the marble. On a cutting board lay the chrome-bright Japanese chopping knife, tiny cubes of sweet potato, strips of bell pepper, veiny leaves of chard.

"Hal?"

"Don't worry. I'm fine. Just a little cramping. The soup's"—he finally took in the delicious aromas of chicken stock, coconut milk, lemongrass—"almost done."

"Let me take over. I knew you shouldn't be doing this."

"Oh, Leo, enough—I told you, I'm not a patient."

Firmly, but with a complete lack of vehemence—trusting as always that the world would listen to her with respect and, sooner or later, agreement—she'd maintained that the medical establishment had pathologized the natural process of pregnancy. Gradually she'd overcome his resistance to a midwife, though she had then compromised as well and agreed to have the midwife attend her not at home but in the obstetrics ward of the nearest hospital.

He wondered if he should be taking her there now.

She agreed to lie down in the living room and watch a little TV while he finished the soup and steamed some rice. She couldn't see him from the couch where she lay. He poured himself a Scotch from the supply he kept in the cupboard, for guests. She, of course, was not drinking while pregnant, and he had insisted that he would teetotal as well, in solidarity. He very much missed wine at dinner—and contrary to the forecasts of acquaintances, the craving did not fade. Most evenings now, after she turned in, he would serve himself a double, afterward carefully washing the glass and observing his hand—a stranger's, small and hairy—replace it in the cupboard.

Over their supper, after he'd filled her in on the phone conversation, she said she was curious to meet the elusive Monsieur Beaulieu, but by eight thirty he still hadn't arrived and she said she couldn't wait up any longer. Losco kissed her at the foot of the stairs, then loaded the dishwasher very quietly, not wanting to miss the sound of the doorbell.

He went out onto the front porch and looked up and down the empty street. It was almost dark, but there was still a glow to the west above Olson's roof—a surface decidedly in need of repair.

"Where the fuck *is* this guy," Losco said in a gangsterly undertone that he was pretty sure would have shocked Halli.

At 8:55 he took a second Balvenie up to his office and called the number he'd jotted down. Two rings, then an answer, *"Allô?"* A background of white noise, the hum of a highway or busy street.

"Jean-Denis?" He hoped his gruffness would convey his feelings and spare him elaboration.

"Oui, c'est moi."

The tone was blunt and cold, acknowledging nothing.

"Leonard Losco here... Hello?"

"Yes, I am here."

"But you're not *here*."

"Pardon?"

"You said you'd be here at eight!"

"At eight, yes. It was impossible."

"You're on your way now?"

"I think so."

"You *think* so?"

No answer.

Losco tried to fill his lungs, his chest suddenly tight. He said, "I'll see you shortly, then," and added, as if Beaulieu might have forgotten, "I have your *wallet* here." Silence. *"Hello?"*

The man had hung up.

By nine thirty Losco was in a full-blooded fury. What if he too had needed to turn in early? He snapped the laptop shut, having cleared out his inbox—a feat he tried to accomplish at least twice a month and which usually left him feeling cleansed and in command. He closed his office door, slipped downstairs, let out Halli's old cat, Mitch, then fiercely emptied and cleaned the litter box. Down in the finished basement he changed into his gym gear, switched the widescreen TV to a documentary channel and boarded the treadmill. His short, hairy legs chugged beneath him, adrenalin overriding the whisky. He felt he could easily run for an hour, and maybe he would—though surely Beaulieu would appear in the driveway before then? Losco would see him coming: the basement was dark except for the TV, while a grated window high in the wall gave a ground-level view of the lawn, the driveway, and Olson's house across the street.

Olson's upstairs light winked out. It was after ten. *Blameless Bastards,* Losco was joining the documentary a bit late, followed an Irishman's search for his elder half-brother, taken as a baby by the Church from its unwed mother a few years before she married and went on to have a "legitimate" son. On her deathbed, she'd told this son that his half-brother had been raised by nuns in a special home. The son's search had revealed that thousands of children like his brother had died in these homes, often of minor ailments—"an outcome bespeaking neglect"—and that while death certificates had been issued, few graves could be found.

Programs of this sort could be counted on to sharpen a workout. The angrier Losco became, the more he took it out on the machine, pounding the conveyor belt with his shoes while panting retorts and epithets at the TV. He'd rarely gone to church as a child. His parents had been conservative and traditional in most ways, but for reasons that Losco never managed to learn, they attended mass only at Christmas and Easter.

At 10:50 he stepped off the treadmill, towelling sweat from his sheared, balding head, and stood watching the screen as a voice-over described the discovery of some thirty tiny skeletons in an old septic tank behind a nunnery west of Dublin. Across the screen flashed images, thankfully low-res, of the grisly excavation—or was it Losco's sudden tears that made them look indistinct? "Sooner or later all buried wrongs must face the light of justice," the narrator intoned, and Losco in a thickened voice snapped back, "Yeah, right, tell me another good one!"

At 11 p.m. sharp—a touch calmer after the exercise—Losco called the number again. After four rings a recorded voice mumbled something about not being available...*pas disponible.* He called back and listened more closely to the recording. No invitation to leave a message or call-back number.

He showered quickly in the basement washroom, so as not to bother Halli, then dressed and ran back up the two flights of stairs on his toes, silent. In his office he checked the phone for voice mail. Nothing. His email inbox was already clogging up again—spam, a few auto-replies, social media site invitations—but nothing from Beaulieu. He slid the bedroom door open and peered in. She was sleeping quietly. He ran downstairs and stepped out the front door in his slippers, then walked to the end of the driveway and looked up and down the street. The wind had died; the air felt milder than out in the harsh sunlight this morning. He looked back at the house to confirm that the street number was visible under the carriage lamp, as if the pruned juniper by the door could have sprouted a few feet higher since dusk. His eye was drawn up to their bedroom window and a memory seized him, not of real life but of a film he had seen years ago. An old farmhouse is turning on its occupants, a family. The father is outside at night, doing something—patrolling the grounds? No—there's an axe in his hands—he's chopping wood. He looks back at the house. In the high window of the room where his children lie sleeping, the face of some monstrous creature glows, staring out at him.

He went inside and phoned again and this time left something after the beep, a gruff repetition of their address. Haltingly he added, *"Je vous attends avec impatience,"* though as he hung up it came to him that the phrase actually meant something quite affable, "I look forward to seeing you," or even, "I can't wait to see you."

He took the wallet downstairs and sat on the couch in the front room, facing the street, curtains open. On a table beside him were a telephone, his glass of mineral water and another Balvenie, just a taste. The wallet's contents he emptied onto his lap. This time he noticed that Beaulieu was smiling slightly in his passport photo, one corner of his mouth curled up, which was odd, in fact astonishing—the bureaucrats at Citizenship were notorious for rejecting photos betraying even a flicker of a smile. Born Montreal, 1975. Customs stamps indicated that he'd visited Albania several times in the past few years.

The telephone rang and he swept it up.

"Yes?"

A phrase in that surly, Slavic-sounding French.

"Could you repeat that in English? Is this Beaulieu?"

"Are you still waiting me?"

"Of course I am! Do you want your wallet tonight or not?"

"What?"

"It's past eleven now. It's eleven thirty-*five*. Do you want your—"

"I cannot come there yet. I am very busy. I will come there soon."

"You're not serious."

"I am not…what? I will be there no later than one."

"One in the *morning?*"

"What…? Of course."

Losco heard himself babbling into the mouthpiece. "Forget it. OK? I'm going to bed now. I've got to be up first thing tomorrow. It's almost *midnight*. I'll stick your fucking…I'll leave your property in the mailbox and if it's still there tomorrow I'll be leaving it with the cops. The police—you understand?"

"You cannot do that."

"Oh, I can't? What can't I do?"

"You are meaning, the box for mail, outside?"

"Where else?"

"But you have my passport."

"I don't *want* to have your passport, OK? I want to give it *back* to you!"

"But, maybe someone steals."

"From my mailbox in the middle of the night?"

I should never have given him our address, Losco thought. Should have taken the thing straight to the cops.

"I tell you, I come there soon. Maybe before one."

"Look in the mailbox, then. I'll be asleep." Hardly. Losco knew his own nervous system—he would be alert for hours unless he took a sleeping pill, a practice he was resisting lately, since at any time he might have to drive Halli to the hospital. "Don't mind the barking of our dog," he heard himself add, conjuring a second, more formidable pet. "He can't get out at you."

"You cannot do this—I tell you this."

"Oh, you *tell* me this? I'm waiting ten fucking hours here and you tell me what I can or can't do?"

"Honey?"

"Just a minute," he said, and covered the mouthpiece. "Halli? Darling?"

"What's going on down there, Leo?"

"Nothing, Hal." She must be at the top of the stairs—yes, there. "Go back to bed, Hal, I'll be right up."

"I'm cramping again. I think maybe it's happening! I'm really wet."

"What, you mean your water broke?"

"I don't know, maybe. I just woke up. Oh...I've got to sit down."

"I'm coming, Hal!" He unblocked the mouthpiece and said softly, like a philanderer ringing off in a rush, "I've got to go." The line was dead. Onto the table beside his unfinished drink he tossed the gutted wallet and the various cards and passport, then leapt up and ran to the stairs. She was sitting at the top in the white linen slip she'd been wearing to bed this third trimester. In the half-light her eyes looked small and red, her lips tight.

"I'm phoning the midwife," he called up firmly, as if expecting opposition. "She'll meet us there."

"Wait…it might be easing off."

He took the stairs two at a time and sat beside her, put his hand at the base of her spine, kissed her clammy cheek.

"Come on, beautiful. I'll help you get changed."

The phone rang. He swore, startling her, and she flinched as if at another contraction. He leapt up and made for his office, calling back, "Sorry—just a sec!" He closed the door behind him and swept up the receiver. "What?"

"You hang up on me."

"You hung up on *me*. Now leave us alone, I've got to take…" He caught himself; he'd almost revealed that the premises might soon be empty. "I've got to get some sleep. I'll put your wallet outside now. Don't ring the bell when you come—I won't answer the door."

"But I come *now* to the door!"

"You've been saying that all fucking day! And I've let the cops…I've told them I've been trying to reach you—to return your property."

"Leo!" he heard.

He rammed down the receiver. "Just a second!" he cried, then plucked the receiver back up and called the midwife, Simone—he'd put her number on speed-dial—and asked her to meet them at the hospital. Then he grabbed his car key and his own wallet and strode out of the office.

He held her small suitcase as he opened the front door for her. She was supporting her belly with both hands, hunching over enough that she and he were almost the same height. Her eyebrows were crimped as if from the pains—or maybe fear, though she showed no other sign of it. As he locked the door, the land line rang from both his office and the living room. "Forget it," he said roughly, as if to Beaulieu.

He helped her into the front seat of the Audi.

"Leo? It's OK. We're going to make it just fine."

"I know that! Do you have everything?" It hit him that he was forgetting something himself. His cellphone? Yes. It didn't matter, she had hers.

"Honey," she said, "you want *me* to drive?"

As he neared the end of their street, trying to accelerate smoothly, reasonably, a white cargo van sped past them in the other direction. A street lamp's glare on the van's windowless side briefly showed the ghost of some painted-over name and logo.

"God damn it! I knew there was something."

"What?"

"Nothing," he said through his teeth.

"Leo, I need you to be calm now, for me."

"I know. You're right."

There was little traffic on Carling, and the lights, to his surprise, favoured them. He'd looked forward to this trip, brief though it would be; he'd planned to shine as her imperturbable pilot, guide and guardian. Now it seemed almost too easy. Something must be wrong, or about to go wrong. Some of the signage in this familiar strip now seemed charged with ominous significance, EMERGENCY STAIN REMOVAL, while ahead in the night the hospital's glowing H reared like a prophetic initial.

"Almost there," he said.

A red light finally stopped them. Her cellphone rang in her purse.

"Leave it," he said.

"Could be Simone," she said in a pain-flattened little voice. "Wait—this number. I think it's the wallet guy. I forgot about him. He didn't come for it?"

Losco stared ahead at the light. "Never showed."

"They're getting really close, the pains."

"We're there, Hal. There it is. Look."

"Oh!" she said. "Did you remember to bring Mitch in?"

"Damn it!" He slammed the base of his palm on the wheel as the light changed. "I forgot—I forgot the cat too!" They lurched forward with a roar. Among all the apprehensions bearing in on him now, worst was the old assumption that at some point, under some unforeseeable, fatal pressure, the elaborate device of his persona would crack.

IN THIS PART of the city, moving up meant moving down the slope, toward the Ottawa River, Westboro Beach and the "village." Two years after Oliver was born, they found a larger, slightly older house, a close stroller-push from the shops and the shore. If they were going to have a second child, they would be needing more space, they'd agreed, though for him there was another, more visceral reason he kept to himself: the first house had never felt fully secure after the night of his son's birth.

In the second house one night—Halli lazing on her side, her head on his shoulder, her mouth by his ear (she disdained the protocol confining women to certain awkward post-coital postures while trying to conceive)—she said, "You never did hear back about that wallet, did you?" It seemed this latest try had reminded her of the day leading up to Oliver's birth.

When Losco had driven back from the hospital at six the next morning, to let in the cat and feed it, he had found neither voice mail nor email from Jean-Denis Beaulieu. The wallet and its contents lay on the side table beside his unfinished Scotch and the lamp left on, forgotten in the scramble of their leaving. Curtains wide open. In his relief that no disaster had come to pass—the thug-faced Beaulieu smashing a window, breaking in, trashing the place, maybe finding and hurting Mitch; above all, Halli coming to some harm in childbirth—he'd sunk into the couch and plunged his head into his hands, shaken by sobs that were both violent and soundless.

On his way back to the hospital, from which he would bring his family home that afternoon, he'd dropped off the wallet at the police station.

"No," he says now in a tone of mildly intrigued surprise, as if the oddness has only just struck him. "I never heard anything more from the cops or that guy."

Their marriage is young enough that he can still remember every lie he has told her, and this is one of them. The truth: A few days after their return from the hospital, groping in the mailbox, irritably trying to dig out a flyer clinging to the inside, he found something he must have missed for several days—an old parking ticket, not his. On the back, someone had written a line with a failing ballpoint pen, the strokes almost slicing through the paper so that even where no ink had flowed, the message could be read:

YOU FORGET ME BUT NEVER I FORGET YOU

The words froze his nape and scalp and made him look up and around the quiet neighbourhood, as if someone must be watching the house, had been stalking them for days. Murray Olson waved from the garden where he was digging. Losco calmed himself. Nothing had happened, nothing was going to happen; Beaulieu had his effects back by now; he must have hacked out this note in a moment of balked fury. Losco crushed the note in his fist and buried it in his pocket, though that evening he removed it, flattened it carefully, reread it several times, then tucked it in a fold of his wallet, where it would remain secretly, dangerously, like an adulterous note he couldn't bear to destroy.

Everything Turns Away

About suffering they were never wrong,
The Old Masters: how well they understood
Its human position; how it takes place
While someone else is eating or opening a window
or just walking dully along
—W.H. Auden, "Musée des Beaux Arts"

1

IT WAS NOT yet summer, it was summer as it should be, hot but not sticky, the grass and new leaves as green as they would go, the verges of lilac along the railway line in exuberant flush. With your wife and fifteen-year-old daughter you drove west into the franchise fringes of town in a small silver car that had rolled off the assembly line near the end of the previous century. You meant to test drive several less-used cars at a dealership overlooking a postcard marina on a Lake Ontario bay.

A salesman named Walter—heavy, bespectacled, delivering his pitches in the laconic monotone of a man who has learned not to get his hopes up—introduced you to the three prospects you and your wife had found online. One was a new-looking black hybrid model that cost about five thousand more than you'd agreed to pay. You'd thought you might be able to bargain, but Walter in his anaesthetized drawl apologized that in this case the price was final. Still, the crimson compact was promising—the paint looked fresh, the odometer reading was modest, and the price was in your range. Walter handed you the key, slapped a magnetic test-drive licence plate into the slot above the rear fender, and off you drove. He sat beside you, raking his hand through an auburn comb-over that the wind kept compromising, while your wife, Lise, and daughter, Emma, sat in the back.

"Lovely day for a drive, isn't it, Nick," drawled Walter. Maybe in some retail circles they still train salesmen to punctuate every utterance with the target customer's name, a gambit that seems almost touchingly antique. Aren't folks these days too savvy for such obvious cons? But also lonelier, needier, so charades of kindness and kinship still trip a gratified response.

Walter went on personalizing his sales script as he directed you along what he called test-drive route numero uno. The route included urban and rural stretches and a drag strip of vacant highway where you could assess a vehicle's acceleration. A rush of boyish delight surprised you as the car lunged forward, sweet-scented air buffeting in through the window. You'd woken too early to that familiar mid-life torpor; you're barely awake and already the day has routed you: lie very still, don't get swept into its current, for now let's call it a draw. Then, like almost everyone else, you get on with it.

You were retracing your route to the dealership via a busy road that ran past the backyards of modest suburban houses from the sixties or seventies, their patios and a few swimming pools visible through the trees. It was on this stretch that you became aware, in spite of Walter's autopilot patter, that Lise and Emma were whispering about something.

One of them tapped you on the shoulder. You heard Lise's voice. "Excuse me"—this more to Walter, who was talking—"I think we should pull over for a second."

"What's going on?" you asked.

"We need to back up. Em thinks something's wrong back there."

"With the car?" asked Walter with a resigned sigh.

"Someone might be hurt."

You pulled over onto the gravel. As you turned to look back, Emma leaned forward, her mouth clamped as if she wished her fixed gaze alone could speak and spare her words. "I saw something the first time we went by, but that was from the other lane. I just saw again, closer. I think a guy is hurt, maybe unconscious."

You started to back up along the shoulder.

"She had to point him out to me," Lise said. "Maybe he was drunk and fell. He's lying on his deck. She says he hasn't moved since the first time we passed."

"I think he might be bleeding."

"She thought he might be wearing a red cap…"

"He's there, Dad!"

You stopped again. For the first time, silence from Walter.

"His face is still upside down. His head's back over the edge."

"Probably sleeping one off," Walter now spoke. "Me, I can't see anything, but I'm due for new specs."

"It's not a red cap," Emma said quietly.

You looked hard but couldn't find the man, though you could see the deck, the patio doors, a white-brick bungalow. From your position the branch of a large tree beside the road was hiding part of the deck.

"Could be drugs, too," Walter said. "He'll probably be OK, though."

"He's not OK," Emma said.

You pulled back onto the road, U-turned, accelerated and veered left on a yellow light as it turned red. Silence in the car—Walter rigid, his arms straight out, his ruddy chapped hands braced on the dashboard. You drove a block west and turned south onto a quiet residential street.

"Here?"

"I think so," Emma said.

You pulled in at the curb in front of a landscaped front yard: groomed flower beds, hedges, a blue spruce symmetrical as an artificial Christmas tree. Beyond it, a white bungalow. Picture window, drapes drawn. The vacant driveway recently paved. As you jumped out, Lise said, "Don't go behind the house yet—knock on the door."

"Why?"

"Could be a drug thing—there might be someone back there."

Walter was staring ahead through the windshield, eyes unblinking.

"Be careful, Dad!"

Her concern was touching, then disturbing as it hit you that she, with her sharp vision, had seen something you all couldn't. You approached the house, legs weightless, anaesthetized; as always in situations of potential emergency you were excited, also worried about the fallen man, also leery of playing the busybody, puncturing a stranger's privacy, maybe pissing off some hostile type whose friend or customer had passed out on the back deck.

You rapped on the solid door. From the other side, a detonation of high-pitched barks and yips. The outburst subsided until you knocked again. You looked back at the car. Lise and Emma—faces side by side—watched you through the open back window. Walter too had now turned his pale, despairing face in your direction. You walked past the garage, rounded the corner and ran along the concrete walk leading to the backyard.

Emerging into the yard, you froze. Ten feet away, a man lay face up on the sunlit pine of the deck, head lolling back over the edge as if craning to look across the yard toward the road. The deck was the height of your chest, so he lay directly in front of you. Grey-green face under streaks and spatters of dried blood. The sealed eyelids flecked as well. On his emaciated torso, lengthwise, a length of polished mahogany. A cane? Emaciated, old or ailing—he has slipped, fallen, smacked his head. Unconscious? No, it's too late. He is gone. You have never seen a body so conclusively vacated.

These impressions occupy just seconds. You are caught inside a coroner's forensic snapshot. No, it's not a finished image, it's a fresh print, still developing, the mahogany cane transforming into the stock of a rifle, no, something shorter, thicker—a shotgun lapsed onto the man's torso. Barrel toward the face. The blood there not from facial wounds but spattered up from below. You can't see the wound, or somehow don't see it, in fact you're already turning away, fleeing toward the car. The passengers gape as you run toward them. You leap in, slam the door, start the car and babble words at them, old man, shotgun, suicide, dead.

AS LUCK WOULD have it, both you and Emma left your phones in the car in the dealership parking lot. Walter says he has always seen these drives as a chance to leave his phone *behind* and get *away* from life—and now he adds softly, hopelessly, as if assuming you'll ignore him, "Best not to speed, Nick…We're almost there…If he passed a while ago, a minute won't matter."

Silence from the back seat. You look in the rear-view mirror: Emma staring fixedly out her window. You reach the dealership a few minutes later. Lise and Emma decide to wait outside while Walter leads you in through the showroom to his open-concept cubicle. It's like the mock-up of an office on a stage: three walls that go halfway to the ceiling, no front wall. He gestures toward his chair, his desk, an office phone. You sit and key in 911. You try to speak calmly, quickly. A burning current crawls under your scalp. The pulse in your jaw is like a second heartbeat. The dispatcher, as if new to the job or too sensitive for it, sounds genuinely shaken. You wonder if you do too. Your friends and even Lise tell you you're skilled at hiding panic, sadness, but maybe you simply numb up and freeze.

"I wonder if I should have stayed with him," you say, feeling queasier as it hits you: by leaving the scene, you may have done something unconscionable. The body is alone, as it must have been for who knows how long before you arrived, and this condition—a kind of exoplanetary solitude—now seems a terrible indignity.

"No," the dispatcher says. "There was a gun there, you had to leave."

She gets you to repeat the address, sends two police cars and an ambulance, then keeps you on the line to get your details—address, telephone number—as well as Walter's. He's leaning on the hatch of a gleaming coal-grey SUV, polishing the lenses of his glasses with a square of toilet paper, as you recite coordinates into the phone.

You hang up and stare at your hand, still gripping the receiver. It looks artificial, or like an uncanny motion-capture version of yours. The veins appear green. Your watch says 12:20. You half see Walter approaching his desk, approaching you, this stranger in his chair. He leans down and—as if gently reminding you of the masculine duty to push on with life's errands in the face of misfortune—murmurs, "Dare I ask, Nick, if you've made a decision about the Camry?"

TWO HOURS LATER, a cop parked his motorcycle in front of your house. You led him through the house and into the backyard, where you'd been sitting, a little chilled, in the shade, awaiting him, sipping a beer you wanted to guzzle.

The cop was tall, had an action-figure physique, and wore motorcycle boots and aviator shades. He sat across a patio table from you. With a pencil on a yellow foolscap pad he hastily, messily wrote up your accounting of events. It seemed an oddly informal, unofficial practice, prone to inaccuracies. He sipped strong-smelling coffee out of his stainless steel travel mug. You craved something stiffer than your beer but wondered if you were already flouting some statute by drinking while providing a sworn statement. You tried to describe exactly what you'd seen and done—usually a challenge for a fiction writer, but not in this case, not for you. The event seemed to deny any licence to the part of you that compulsively mines and mutates experience.

After finishing, you added, vapidly, "Such a beautiful day, too."

"They tend to be worse," he said, removing his sunglasses, exposing thoughtful, long-lashed blue eyes. "It's a myth that Christmas is worst."

Maybe, you suggested, the first true summer day feels like a leering Fuck You to someone whose inner world is gripped in winter. The cop inclined his head noncommittally. The ensuing silence—in fact brimming with sound, manic, almost deranged birdsong, cars hurrying past to somewhere—you broke with a question about the man, and a little to your surprise the cop related as much as he knew—not much, but more than enough to implode your initial assumptions. The victim was not old, just in his fifties. He didn't live alone, although he was alone this morning, except for the dog you'd heard barking.

"We're trying to track down his wife. Looks like she went out of town for the weekend."

"So he planned this—waited for her to leave," you said, instantly replacing your first assumptions with new ones. *She was with another man and didn't realize he knew.* Or, *There was no other man, but she was leaving him anyway.*

"And he recently retired from the military," the cop said.

"Could he have been over in Afghanistan?" you asked, then added, "No. Probably too old."

Were you making the cop uneasy? Likely he was unused to such dogged curiosity and reflex deduction—the professional habits of fiction writers and investigative journalists, along with private detectives, gossips, conspiracy theorists.

You told the cop how surprised you were that no one had seen or heard a thing. He explained that one neighbour did hear something, around 10 a.m., but figured it was a big firecracker.

"Ten a.m. So he'd been like that for two hours."

"I'm afraid so."

The cop gave you contact details for professionals that any of you might want to consult, he said. Especially the young one. He put on his aviator shades and pushed back from the table. "You should be proud of her. Good eyes. And she chose to speak up."

2

FOR TEN MORNINGS afterward you checked the obituaries on the website of the local newspaper until you found him. You didn't recognize the face in the overexposed black-and-white photo—it looked much fuller and younger than the blood-streaked face you had glimpsed. But other details made you all but certain: the date of death, the code phrase "died suddenly," a reference to retirement from a logistical job in the military. An online check to link the surname to the house address came up positive: a paving company listed his driveway as a recent contract.

You made a note of the memorial service date.

From the beginning you'd felt that if there was a service, and if you found the information in time, you should try to attend. Forming another assumption out of skimpy evidence and ready stereotypes, you'd decided few mourners would be present. A final existential affront. The military, you guessed, might dispatch a small delegation of some kind, but who could say? You meant to enter quietly, sit at the back, then slip away before any next of kin could approach and ask about your connection to the man.

On the morning of the memorial service, you put on a suit and black tie but then, agonizing, changed back into your summer writing gear—cargo shorts and a T-shirt—before deciding last minute you had to go after all. You dressed again and ran out the front door, re-knotting your tie as you jogged the six blocks to the funeral home chapel.

Sitting at the back was the only option. Maybe two hundred people, dozens of them in military dress uniform, packed the room. There were confused or curious-looking children, there were teenagers who seemed genuinely stricken, not simply dragooned into the pews. This was a relief—people had come to mourn the man after all—as was knowing you could come and go anonymously.

The too-thin widow, barely able to walk, was helped up the aisle by bulky men from beyond the city—hands huge, rough and red—in ill-fitting suits and loose-knotted ties. She remained seated and sobbing at the front while other mourners went up and spoke at the lectern. Then a priest with a bald head, boyish face, and irrepressibly sunny demeanour read a eulogy the widow had written. Its content, despite his breezy delivery, made it clear the manner of death was no secret. The man had slid into depression in his late forties and then, developing unspecified ailments and daily pain, was forced to drop the physical outlets that had helped him cope: beer-league baseball, fly-fishing, and, more recently and devotedly, gardening.

Now you recalled the landscaped front yard, the trimmed hedges, the parterred and graded flower beds that—come to think of it—had been sparsely flowered despite the season. Maybe just perennials, the stubborn aftermath of his endeavour.

Peering down at the tightly rolled program batonned in your fist, you're struck again by how the hand seems a stranger's.

FROM A SHELF over the desk you reach down a chunky, important-looking anthology and turn to the poem "Musée des Beaux Arts," the one where W.H. Auden laconically reflects on Pieter Brueghel the Elder's painting *Landscape with the Fall of Icarus:*

> *how everything turns away*
> *Quite leisurely from the disaster; the ploughman may*
> *Have heard the splash, the forsaken cry,*
> *But for him it was not an important failure; the sun shone*
> *As it had to on the white legs disappearing into the green*
> *Water...*

In a footnote, the anthologists observe that the figures in Brueghel's composition have failed to notice not only Icarus plunging out of the sky but also "a dead body in the woods." In next to no time you find an online image of the painting, though finding the overlooked corpse is harder. But a few minutes later, using the magnifying tool to search the woods beyond a field that a farmer and his horse are ploughing, you spot him. Only his face shows clearly, inverted, staring upward, white against the dark forest floor. You recoil from the screen; his positioning and pallor graphically recall the face of the man on the deck.

Could Auden have missed the figure? He wrote his poem after examining the painting in the Musées royaux des Beaux-Arts in Brussels. He would have studied it closely. He must have noticed that secondary, nameless casualty but chose to focus on Icarus alone. Adding a stanza about the dead stranger, after all, would have herniated the poem, introducing a distracting sidebar, like cramming a second protagonist into a short story.

But visual art works differently—more or less instantaneously, not in time sequence—and the face in the woods is integral to the painting. Partly, you guess, it's a memento mori, one of those small skulls that Renaissance artists planted in the margins of their works as quiet, pious reminders of mortality. And because of the head's placement on the left side of the canvas, it's a compositional counterweight to Icarus, who's plunging into the sea on the lower right. The balancing works anatomically too. The dead man's face, along with a bit of his dark-clad torso blending into the undergrowth, physically completes Icarus, of whom you see only a pair of white legs.

Each one's unwitnessed fate echoes the other's, yet the hidden victim seems more forlorn. Icarus, after all, is the namesake and protagonist of the painting. Its title directs you to find his submerging form. Nor is it hard to locate; his flesh, unlike the dim face in that Dantean forest, is spotlit by the sun. Above all, he's an illustrious figure—a sort of misbehaving celebrity, a universal metaphor, a byword to the point of cliché.

AT THE CHAPEL the priest, still failing to funeralize his demeanour, read from Psalm 34: *The Lord is close to the brokenhearted. He rescues those whose spirits are crushed.*

A sense of being unseen, alone and spectral, must be a root sorrow for many of the broken. Yet there's more than one way of not being seen. You can feel insignificant to the point of invisibility or—while living an outwardly successful, publicly visible life—sink under the weight of a pain unapparent to the world.

Maybe Icarus, that golden boy, was a suicide too.

BACK AT YOUR DESK, still in your suit, tie loose, collar open, you studied the program from the service. The photo on the front showed a man in his late twenties or early thirties, lanky, fit in the understated way of people who labour physically but don't frequent gyms. His stance: confident but not cocky. Relaxed grin. He's wearing a white T-shirt half-tucked into faded jeans and, improbably, a red baseball cap, like the one Emma first thought he might have had on. Behind him, a chain-link backstop and beyond that a ball diamond out in the country somewhere. To judge by the light and the freshness of the outfield grass, it's late spring. His apparent age, and the birth year cited below the photo, date it to the late seventies or early eighties.

You set him in motion again (isn't that the point, isn't that what fiction is meant to do, and shouldn't this be fiction?) on the young grass, loping and tossing the ball to friends, fielding grounders with that unruffled grin or wincing into the sun as he tracks a pop fly that somebody, maybe you, why not, you then in your mid-teens like your daughter now, have hit out to him from home plate…You all return to the bleachers and gather around a Styrofoam ice cooler packed with squat, iodine-brown bottles that he and his friends snap open with their plastic lighters. You barely say a word, shyly thrilled to be present, happily swigging the bitter lager, included or at least humoured by men who are solidly lodged in their adult lives.

A SCREAM SPLINTERS the wall between the child's room and the master bedroom, Lise shooting up out of the sheets and slurring, "Em…? Go to her! Help her!" Beyond the wall more screaming, then breathless, unintelligible gibbering. You stagger, heart punching, out the door, up the hallway, through the child's slightly open door, reach down to a gasping, humid form in the dark. You stop short of touch for fear of re-terrifying her. You murmur the words we all say in such crises, not always factually. "It's OK…"

"No."

"It's all right. I'm here."

"He was there—right there."

"Who?" you ask as if you don't know. "No one's here, love. Just me."

You sit carefully on the edge of the bed. If there were light, your pulse might be visible in your throat like a lizard's.

"Sweetie? It was a bad dream. Should I turn on the lamp?"

"No, I can see. He was at the foot of the bed."

"The man we found."

A retinal flash of that coroner's snapshot.

"No, someone younger. There was no blood."

You cup your hand over her forehead, not feverish but clammy.

"He was scared," she whispers.

"*He* was scared? You mean—"

"He. He didn't say anything."

The pulse in her temple is slowing.

"Oh my *God*"—abruptly she sounds like herself again, returned to her body—"I *hate* these dreams."

"They'll stop, my love. I had them too, till I was about sixteen."

You've told her this often. In fact, you had a few more night terrors at seventeen, eighteen, even older. And maybe they don't so much cease with age as shift over into daytime, subliminal, deniable.

"I got them from you?"

Another fixture of the debriefing ritual.

"Afraid so. Along with all the excellent traits."

"Ha ha."

"Maybe worse than yours. Once my voice changed, I'd bellow. Neighbours would hear. Awkward questions were asked."

"I shut my window when I think it might happen."

"One of them said it was like living next to an abattoir."

Nice. A slaughterhouse reference, tonight of all nights.

You tried to save him, love, and you might have.

"Think you can go back to sleep now?"

"I'll try."

If the dead man had had children, might they, their existence, have saved him? Ostensibly you are your child's life guide and guardian, but at times she protects you, inconspicuously, in the way of a guy wire, keel and ballast, a parking brake on a steep hill.

MONTHS LATER, trying to set down words and pin down, after your various misconstructions, whatever could be firmly known, you decide to compare your recall of the man's house to the reality. But you can't drive out there. The car you were trying to replace is back in the shop, and an unforeseen shortfall has forced you to put the search for another on hold. You turn to the internet to visit the place virtually.

In that eerily paused, preserved little world the sun is high, the trees in bud but not yet in leaf—that equivocal pre-season in your city when the light, as yet unfiltered by greenery, is glaring yet the winds off the lake remain wintry. A state akin to adulthood, when you seldom entirely, naively inhabit any one mood, good or bad. You click on a link and find a date for the images: mid-April, just over a year before the suicide.

You begin on the main road from which Emma first glimpsed him, but you can't tell which backyard is his. You navigate round to his own street. Again, nothing looks right. You check your notes for his address, then left-click back up the street in blurring little surges.

Finally you recognize the house. The blue spruce looks more familiar by the moment, as does the fieldstone half fence you only now recall, and those terraced garden beds raked and ready for the spring flowers. You think of the farmer and horse in the painting, ploughing human order into the soil. In the foreground of the frame, at the end of the driveway, sits a phalanx of paper yard-waste bags, evenly packed to the top, and behind them a bundle of neatly tied deadfall and branches. Ghost-gliding back down the street, you see that no one else has left anything out for collection. Do the neighbours not bother with their yards, or has the dead man always tidied up and set out his refuse early in the season, ahead of collection day?

Gardening, like farming, is a promissory act. To sow is to project, to cast your faith forward into the next season or the following spring. Stumbling on this evidence of his diligence and care—this generative intention still active just a few hundred days before he blew out his heart—leaves you moved, body motionless, hunched over the screen as if the weight of gravity has tripled. We forget how much energy it takes to move a body across a room, let alone from one end of a life to the other.

Now imagine the Street View vehicle, with its mounted camera, passing along the main road not when it did but some thirteen months later, the beautiful morning of his death. If you and Walter, among hundreds or thousands of others, missed his face amid the branches and shadows of his backyard, then the Street View curators who vet the panoramas for legal reasons might have missed him too. Certainly they'd have missed him. The image would remain online, his face waiting to be realized in the landscape.

Notes Toward a New Theory of Tears

SEEKING LETHE

A SATELLITE VIEW of Cyprus, the island olive green and cracked copper, its outline the shape of Aladdin's lamp. The Mediterranean is turquoise as absinthe. From this remove, no sign of the island's divisions, though from lower down—the cruising altitude of a Turkish F-16—segments of the Green Line are visible.

Day by day, nuance by nuance, the colours of the seas around Cyprus change as they cool with autumn, although for now—early November—the shallows still look and feel tropical. On the beach beside the abandoned city of Varosha they feel warmest after dark. This evening as usual the beach is empty except for the latest sea turtle hatchlings, a few laggards or adventurers not yet in the water. A few days' perilous swim to the southeast, along the channel of light the rising moon will soon cast, lie the coasts of Israel and Gaza.

By the standards of the region it's early for sleep, but some on the island, mainly the very young and the very old, are already unconscious. Across the island, in a Paphos hotel suite, a trauma therapist with the Canadian Forces is in a sort of chemical coma, having self-administered Apo-Lunaquil (29 × 7.5 mgs) washed down with a triple shot of Finnish vodka. A few days ago this doctor—who tends to the needs of traumatized soldiers airlifted back from Afghanistan for "decompression" on Cyprus before their return to Canada—was suspended for erratic conduct. Should he die, the suspension will look like the deciding factor in his suicide. In fact, he simply could not face another night of re-dreaming one of his patients' PTSD visions—one that seems to have driven the patient to drown himself off that empty beach at Varosha. At any rate, the patient is missing and Dr Simon Boudreau is in a dreamless stupor from which, by his own pre-estimate, he is unlikely to surface. (He'd have taken fifty pills, to make certain, if he'd had them on hand.)

If sleep is designed not just for rest but also as a restorative break from pain—a sanctuary from suffering—it's pitifully ineffective. The doctor's theme, the subject of the book now hibernating in his hard drive, is that human history can be viewed as one long, ever-evolving quest for anaesthesia. *Ultimately all of our activities, from falling in love, to praying in church, to going to war, are actuated by personal suffering and our wish to avoid or transcend it.* Civilization, then, is the epic story not of our striving toward higher consciousness but of our efforts to *escape* it—into sedation, oblivion, the waters of Lethe. Various herbs, mushrooms, wormwood, alcohol, hashish, opiates natural and synthetic, ketamine, ayahuasca and mescaline, barbiturates, benzodiazepines, SSRIs, the endorphins of exercise, the oxytocin of sex, ad hoc agents such as Lysol, Listerine, Sterno, glue, lighter fluid, rubbing alcohol and aftershave... *Humanity has never stopped seeking quick chemical escapes from sadness, from stress, from insecurity and from pain, which is to say from* HISTORY, *our own personal history or the larger one around us.*

TEARS FOR MARSHAL NEY

THE DOCTOR ASSUMED he would lose consciousness too quickly and irreversibly to re-dream his patient's dream, or flashback, which—put briefly and mercifully—involves the killing of villagers in an olive grove in Kandahar. (Army sappers were chainsawing the trees to eliminate an alleged al Qaeda hideout.) As usual, alas, he seems to wake up in the very midst of the grove, except now abruptly it's an *orchard,* apples, pears, his grandparents' cider orchard in the Richelieu Valley where he spent summers as a boy. He wanders the long corridors of the orchard amid graphic carnage, yearning for the quietus of a single headshot, like the vanquished Marshal Ney after Waterloo, spurring his horse around the field in search of death: *Is there not a single bullet anywhere for me?* A series of explosions like mortar rounds and the doctor is awake, his mouth parched, his head sawed open, the sheets sodden and cold at his groin. The explosions go on: a violent rapping at a door.

He looks at the wristwatch on the nightstand, precisely propped up and angled in his own ritual manner, like a tiny alarm clock. Four in the afternoon. The date is nonsensical. Then it comes to him, who he is, where he is. His eyes are full of tears, his face drenched, as if he has been crying for the last forty hours here in bed. Tears for Grand-papa and Grand-maman and the cider orchard—nowadays a trailer park on the outskirts of St-Valentin—tears for his drowned young patient, tears even for Marshal Ney, whom he briefly *became* in his search for a single euthanizing bullet, tears for the adolescent children and the wife he deserted years ago, tears at his recent suspension and disgrace. *Tears are the clear blood that flows after a breaching of the heart.* He mistrusts that phrase, his own, as too metaphorical, too *lyrical,* although in essence he believes it. It's from a later chapter in *À la recherche du Léthé,* his abandoned study of the human quest for oblivion. *Science does not yet fully understand human tears.* In his view, science spends far too much time analyzing the chemical makeup of the actual secretion, trying to grasp how so many different, seemingly unrelated, triggers can produce the same chemical phenomenon. Science would like to explain the evolutionary advantage of tears, all those different sorts of tears...

The doctor believes that tears of sorrow are roughly equivalent to the blood that flows from damaged tissue—blood that then clots and closes the wound. As for the wound itself: In aging we build around ourselves a protective hull, but even the hardest of these can be breached. A sharp word, a jilting or rejection, pierces the shell from the *outside;* at other times, an impulse flies from within oneself toward another, in sympathy, or pity, or profound admiration, piercing the shell from *inside.* Either way, the protective field is compromised and tears are the blood that ensues, first marking the hole's presence, then cleansing it, clotting it, sealing it. Children cry constantly because they have not yet grown a shell; a man grieving his mother weeps often because his adult carapace has been so shattered that for now he is little more than a child. And now the doctor himself, emerging from chemical coma, defenceless, hauled back onto life's stony shores—he is his own body of evidence.

SO MANY SLEEPERS

AMONG THE fifty-eight messages flickering in his inbox when he comes to, Dr Boudreau—now an afterimage of himself, shuffling in flip-flops and a coffee-stained amber kimono—finds one from a Montreal colleague to whom he has confided his nocturnal difficulties. Boudreau skims the message and clicks on a link: an article published in 2003 in a learned journal focusing on the history of the Middle East.

Boudreau notices a sidebar link, "Settlers in Occupied Territories Cut Down Olive Grove," and clicks on it, a *Guardian Weekly* report on a similar event in 2010—hardline settlers, allegedly in retaliation for something, eradicating a Palestinian olive grove—and along with this item a link to a story about a stand of oil palms in the Congo, hacked down by torchlight to deprive the locals of food, palm wine, and oil to sell, and *this* article was accompanied by no fewer than half a dozen links to "related items," including one from Vietnam and another concerning frontier hero Kit Carson and his US troops clear-cutting three thousand peach trees in Canyon de Chelly in 1864, to shatter the will and the hearts of the Navajo, and Boudreau, now exhausted, can only assume that his colleague hoped this chain of links, this tour of atrocities, might dilute the power of the one atrocity rerunning nightly in his dreams. *You see, Simon... there was nothing unique about it... At least they were mostly trees, not people!*

In early December the doctor—reinstalled in his two-and-a-half in Montreal, pensioned for disability by the DND, and still having access to a couple of scrip-writing colleagues—begins to stockpile tablets for a second attempt. He is practically insane with insomnia, beleaguered by dreams, an internet eidolon who in the deeps of the night might be glimpsed from down on frozen Rue Octave, up in his dark kitchen, face ghoul-lit by the glow of his laptop screen. Except nobody walks past.

In mid-February he tries again to subtract himself from the world, and fails.

Doctor-assisted euthanasia, he reflects, has just been legalized. How can it be so hard for a doctor to figure out how to assist himself?

READING ONESELF TO ONESELF

SEEMS BOUDREAU has eradicated all ability to sleep in the wake of his latest self-induced siege of hypnotics. Once again he's conscious and pondering in the small hours, listening to Strauss's *Last Songs* and rereading aloud a passage from *À la recherche du Léthé.*

No study of our quest for oblivion would be complete without a discussion of the lies we tell ourselves, which, like drugs, allow us not to know what we wish not to know. Every person has a staple lie, so has each nation. The lie is the face, the interface that we pose between ourselves and a world that we fear to face naked. As for nations, are not most of their wars fought to uphold the flattering lies they tell about themselves? An anthem is a lie we sing together, about ourselves, and to ourselves, like a lullaby.

A small, soft dog in booties and a Montreal Canadiens sweater trots past on the icy street below, and what in God's name is it *doing* out there alone? God, so lonely, these nights, but Dr Boudreau seems to be unkillable, and not just by Big Pharma; he has considered defenestrating himself, but the early March snowdrifts, three storeys down, are colossal and would buffer any fall.

Somehow he can still derive faint pleasure from the sonic splendour of this music, even as it soundtracks his pain. *Was* the doctor a little in love with his patient? Perhaps—and had he been born just a decade later, after the collapse of church power in Quebec, who knows how different his life might have been? The lie is the face, the interface, we fight to maintain. *The Church's lies; his own lies.* Oh, probably, yes, he did love Corporal Trifannis, but not in that sense—more like a son, the son he once had and more or less deserted. And perhaps he first began dreaming Trif's dream not so much to understand it better, and not just out of professional curiosity, but *to take it fully upon himself,* yes, just so, to relieve his young patient of its unbearable weight. He can see that that's probably the case but is too depressed, hence self-despising, to acknowledge what a profoundly kind act that was—an act whose very existence confirms that this is a world worth living in and for.

Boudreau, unsleeping conscience of a comatose city.

UNSIGNED VALENTINE

SPRING! THE SCREEN before him glows with a *Le Devoir* follow-up on Elias Trifannis, *soldat canadien de Montréal disparu en Chypre.* Trif is still assumed drowned, and now the Canadian authorities—no doubt much to their relief—are closing the case. The article re-quotes Boudreau himself. After his medical discharge and return from Cyprus last year, he was asked whether his former patient really might have murdered civilians and then committed suicide. To the first part of the question he replied, "Not a chance." To the second, "Why not? We know other personnel are doing so, plenty of them." Beside the text is an army ID photo of a young man, hairline receding, the haunted softness of his large brown eyes countered by an athlete's neck and a heavy jaw showing cocktail-hour shadow.

The doctor opens a new file, meaning to compose a suicide note, but then—agonizing as always over the minutiae of diction and grammar—he gives up, deletes, and passes out with his brow on the keyboard. A spate of lower-case gibberish appears on the screen like an electroencephalographic printout of his garbled last thoughts.

He wakes in a hospital bed, body bristling with tubes and wires. A double room, but he is alone. The life-signs monitor shows medically acceptable numbers. To deduce by the date and time displays on his watch—set on the bedside table, though not in the ritually precise manner he himself would use—some seventy-five hours have passed since he washed down the pills with the apple brandy. His thoughts now leap to his youngest child. His son, a toddler, barely two years old, is back in the locked apartment, alone and forgotten—somehow the paramedics missed him when they came for Boudreau! But wait—how did anyone even know about Boudreau himself? The child could not have called for help! The doctor's mind now unclouds just enough for him to recall that René—the least estranged of his children—is in fact a grown man, married and living in Paris, who has never set foot in the apartment. But *now* it becomes urgently clear that a dog, of all creatures, is locked in there instead! Extraordinary—Boudreau has forgotten that he owns a dog! He dislikes dogs, after all, prefers cats, although come to think of it he doesn't care much for cats either, the stink of their litter, their tails exclamatorily raised above their anuses...All the same, with schizophrenic certainty Boudreau now KNOWS he does in fact own and adore a small dog and that this terrier, in its goose-down booties and Canadiens sweater, is waiting pathetically by his desk, *has been awaiting him for over seventy-five hours!* Its name returns to him—Trif. Its kibble dish is long empty, licked to a mirror shine. The water bowl is empty too and there can be no recourse to the toilet: not only does Boudreau lower the seat (as if this lonesome little courtesy might magically lure another woman, or even a man, into his life) but he also closes the lid.

The doctor *must* save the dog if he can. What a fate, to be locked up, alone, forgotten, terrified! Pity and love swell through him. He knows he must act now, but he's unspeakably weary. He's slipping under again. Footsteps in the corridor jolt him back. Somebody enters. He keeps his eyes closed and breathes audibly. There's a scratching of pen on paper, then footsteps receding. His eyes shoot open. He sits up, morbidly sore, faint, queasy—yet for the first time in months he is not dwelling on his own pain. Squeamishly but efficiently he detaches tubes and wires and the catheter, then teeters to his feet and limps around, searching for his effects. He finds nothing. He'll have to flee in this invalid's smock, flapping open behind, but here, look, a pair of institutional slippers, a bathrobe hooked on the back of the door—the robe he was wearing when he collapsed at his desk.

He gets past the nurses' station, 4:20 a.m., nobody there. He's keeling like a drunk. On his tongue a bitter, bituminous paste. His guts feel stricken as if he has been retching violently, of course, yes, they will have pumped him out. He shuffles on, as if trying to mop the floors with his too-big slippers. His little feet, how his ex-wife detested his dainty little feet! He nods to two orderlies, one sallow and unshaven, one pink and pimpled, who wheel a gurney on which a sheeted body lies. Onward he goes through the sliding main doors, in his ghostly robe, while the Haitian woman at the desk calls, *Arrêtez, monsieur! Monsieur, arrêtez-vous!* He calls back to her, *Do not trouble yourself, madam, I am a doctor!*

His apartment is a few blocks from the hospital. A warm night for early May. He would run if he were able. In the tiny park off Rue Octave, the blooms of the crabapple trees are starting to open. A detail returns to him from deep in the past and the kitchen of his doting grandmother, how you can make a delicious jelly from those apples...

His body has reached the building, his brain forgets the entry code. He shuts his eyes and his fingers find the pattern. In the elevator, rocketing up, he grows dizzy and his knees buckle. When the thing stops and opens, he crawls out into the hallway, then onward to his door, barefoot, the slippers somehow lost. *I am coming, little one, ne t'inquiète pas! I will save you.* He has forgotten his door key code. Again his fingers cogitate for him. But wait—how did the paramedics get in without smashing the lock? The concierge, of course—she let them in. The real question is, who called 911 in the first place?

The doctor is baffled and will remain so in the weeks to come. Seeking an object for his growing gratitude, he will investigate the question, but in vain. The paramedics refer him to the hospital, the hospital to the police, the police back to the paramedics. Was it the concierge, who has never once met his gaze? "No, monsieur," she will tell him nervously (still not meeting his gaze—especially not now!), "I knew nothing until the men arrived." Was it someone who called him repeatedly that night and could not get through? René, or Boudreau's happily remarried ex? And what about the doctor himself? Out of the chasm of a drugged coma is it possible that he remembered his Hippocratic oath, or simply realized he was worth saving in the end? Quantum odds, at best. In due course, Dr Boudreau will stop seeking an answer and do what he has never once done in his life: accept a mystery on its own terms. An unsigned valentine from the Void. Somebody rescued him somehow, and he, when he wakened, thought only of saving somebody else.

He opens the door and enters. As if crossing a threshold in the mind, he is once more fully rational. Naturally there is no pet, either to rescue or to find dead. He breaks down and sobs, first with joyous relief, then with a renewed and crushing loneliness.

THE LATE HARVEST OF DR SIMON BOUDREAU

WITHIN A WEEK of his third and last failed suicide attempt, the doctor visits the local animal shelter and adopts a balding, cadaverous Persian cat. This animal, subjected to his obsessive attentions, soon fattens up and re-furs. She curls at his feet in a collegial if somewhat entitled silence while he returns to work on the final section of *Seeking Lethe.* Quite often he writes through tears. But sad as he is—seemingly at a molecular, mitochondrial level—he is no longer suicidal. The Void has issued its verdict. Unlike his young patient, the doctor must live.

His armed forces disability pension lends him a certain modest freedom. His conscience heckles him in this regard. The government is not taking such good care of the several thousand maimed or traumatized soldiers who by now have all returned from the war, or mission, or whatever it was.

The aftermath of war is like the hangover of a failed love affair, on a national scale. We look back and recall an initial fever of certainty, then the thrilled, giddy plunge, and then, when it's over—as we survey the ruins and see through the lies—we can't imagine what we were thinking.

Where, in the end, are all the adults?

Boudreau has been reading up on orchards. At night now he dreams not of that olive grove in Kandahar but of his long-dead grandparents' orchard in the Richelieu—sun-steeped, photographic dreams of those phantom fruit trees, row on row. Which means that those trees are not lost after all, because whatever exists in the neurons *still exists on the level of raw matter,* molecular, mitochondrial, an orchard in the mind and heart.

In June the doctor, gaining strength, begins to venture out for lengthening strolls. He notices just how many flowering, fruiting trees—not to mention sprouting greens—flourish wild here in the metropolis, just blocks from his building. He conducts a little research. Turns out that there *are* people who collect urban apples for the local homeless shelters. But who collects all the other wild food? By July, he is busily harvesting and delivering to the shelters scads of the touchingly outcast edibles thriving in the parks, in schoolyards, on domestic lawns, on the flanks and double summit of Mount Royal. Volunteers at the shelters—mostly women his own age or pierced and tattooed kids—humour this sunburnt, bespectacled eccentric as he lugs in bags of saskatoon and service berries, mulberries, thimbleberries, highbush cranberries, currants, rosehips, a few pears and plums—yes, firm, succulent plums, falling on the lawn of an apartment complex and left to rot!—and certain kinds of rowanberry (beautiful and edible, folks eat them in Estonia, though to the doctor's annoyance the older volunteers warily decline them). The dandelions, mint, wood sorrel, garlic mustard, lamb's quarters, purslane and wild chives he presents as a *fait accompli:* a large plastic bowl of salad dressed with a simple vinaigrette.

Purslane, he pedantically informs the anarchist helpers at an anglophone shelter, was Gandhi's favourite green. ("For real?" says one of them, while another, with a bull ring in his nose, holds the door open for the doctor like a dutiful son.)

In September he's collecting ornamental crabapples—he intends to make jelly, so as to offer the fruit in disguise—when the news breaks. His young patient has been found alive, having survived all this time in the ruins of Varosha, that sprawling necropolis on the east coast of Cyprus. An hour later—after reading every online version of this report he can find, in English, French, and Greek—the doctor writes to his son René for the first time in over a year and asks him, among other things, to put him in touch with his younger son and his daughter, who are both living in Canada somewhere, last time the doctor heard.

Remarkably, the world seems to be refilling with children, his children.

A few days later he receives a terse email from his younger son asking him not to contact him ever again, and also—a mere ten days after submission!—his first rejection for *À la recherche du Léthé*. You have to hand it to the gods. Their timing is as infallible as that of Hollywood filmmakers, who ensure (so the doctor has read somewhere) that precisely 65 percent of the way through a film, just when the hero is transcending his or her trials, some fresh misfortune hurls the outcome into doubt. Of course, in a film this setback is merely a set-up for the hero's eventual, climactic triumph. Real life follows a more random script, if you can call it a script at all.

Dr Boudreau pours himself an ouzo with two ice cubes and sits staring at the screen while the liquor louches like absinthe. After a while he clicks over to the file containing his jilted book and starts reading. A little to his surprise (and even while peering through the bifocals of fresh rejection) he finds himself not wholly horrified. So he continues to dip into the book and read with increasing relief, even pleasure, as if perusing the fine and honest work of a stranger—yes, dense with cruel truths but not devoid of all hope. *To conclude, any person's quest for oblivion is of course doomed to succeed: in death. How much better is the utter* failure *of the quest that occurs when one actually wakes from the coma of quotidian life!* Etcetera. He knows the final lines by heart.

He opens a new document. With painful slowness he begins another letter to his lost son. There is no reason why he should think just now of the baby sea turtles who, every year at this time on Cyprus, begin hatching and scuttling down the beaches to the sea, a curious and affecting spectacle the doctor witnessed last autumn near Paphos. In fact he's not thinking of the turtles at all. Still, as he laboriously keys in words, a lone laggard—the final of many thousands—is flopping into moonlit shallows that instantly transform its awkward crawl into watery flight. It soars outward, the bottom sheering away beneath it, as if in a dream where you've been lumbering over the ground working your arms, trying to lift off, then suddenly you're weightless, airborne, the earth falling away...This last swimmer must be enjoying his own wordless versions of relief, elation, even a sense of nascent mastery, as he finds himself in his element for the first time.

As If in Prayer

THE NIGHT SHIFT at the camp had been quiet enough for sleep and the day broke mild and windless. I borrowed Tariq's scooter and rode ten minutes down the cliffside highway before turning inland onto a nameless, unnumbered road. I'd wanted a route that would avoid the larger towns while also taking me past a now-notorious landfill site; online images showed a pyramid of discarded life jackets whose immensity could be gauged only by the trucks parked at its base dumping fresh loads.

I rounded a bend and it loomed ahead, less impressive in reality even with sunrise lighting its thousands of orange-and-red facets like live coals. It was just a heap of garbage, after all. Many of the life vests were useless fakes, nylon shells that the human traffickers had stuffed with bubble wrap, boxboard, sawdust or rags. The fakes sold for ten euros in the markets of İzmir—six for the children's vests. I paused on the side of the road. After a minute I held up my phone, turned it for the wider view and fiddled with the zoom. I shoved it back in my parka without pressing the shutter button.

I rode on into mountains that were green with olive trees below the snow line and the bare summits. The road was empty. Looping upward, it gave views back toward the Aegean, tropically turquoise this morning and yet, as we all knew by now, cold enough to kill.

The first village I rode through was still shuttered and silent, as I'd hoped. I rode like a novice anyhow, stiffly upright, one hand shadowing the brake. My caution would have tickled any old men sitting out in front of the cafés, had the cafés been open. I'd driven no vehicle of any kind in just under two years.

The second village's main street—only street—was likewise deserted, though a fragrance of warm bread was wafting from somewhere and, when I stopped to check the map Tariq had drawn for me, I heard the chugging of an olive press.

At first the authorities were burying the drowned in an old cemetery on a hill above the island's main port. By October they'd run out of room. They chose a new site, exclusively for refugees, near a remote mountain village where no tour bus ever ventured. It was this village I entered next. In the little gorge of the street, the Vespa's two-stroke engine made a nerve-shredding din. There was a time in my life when that amplified snarling would have excited me, made me open the throttle and delight in the speed-surge dragging me back on the seat.

Most hand-drawn maps are confusing and useless, but not Tariq's. As indicated, just beyond the village a dirt track veered left off the road. I took the turn, then bumped along through an olive grove, the old trees' bottom-heavy torsos fantastically burled. Their willowy leaves absorbed and deadened the scooter's chainsaw howl. The heavy black fruit was still unharvested.

I emerged into a clearing the size of a baseball field. Olive-treed slopes rose amphitheatrically around it. The clearing was studded with gravestones and there were open graves with little dunes of dirt beside them. A small car and an even smaller back-hoe were parked on the edge of the clearing. Near them a man, his face and chest visible, stood in a grave.

He was watching me, the blade of his shovel frozen mid-air.

I cut the engine. The turned earth was too loose to support the kickstand, so I walked the scooter back and leaned it against a tree. One of the olives hanging in front of my eyes was so ripe that the skin had burst, revealing white pulp streaked with mauve. As I touched the olive, it fell into my hand. I put it in my mouth and tasted the bitterness of fresh-crushed oil and something harsher that seared and furred my palate.

I approached the gravedigger, crossing the morning shadows of a row of headstones. They were thin tablets of white marble, like the stones in war cemeteries—in fact, like the ones just across the straits from here at Gallipoli. Inscriptions in Greek with Arabic below. unknown man, aged 30?, # 791, 19/11/2015. The care and expense that the bankrupt authorities had put into the stones was a heartening surprise. Only the number signs, like Twitter hashtags, seemed to fall short on decorum.

I stopped in front of the small grave. Maybe the man still needed to enlarge it? He'd put the shovel down so that the shaft bridged the hole. In this mountain air and direct light, things leapt into clarity with surreal resolution. There were tiny nicks in the cutting edge of his otherwise new shovel. His broad-boned face, looking up, was sallow and freckled. Sun-marbled eyes behind steel-rimmed spectacles, the round lenses too small for his head. Trimmed black beard, no moustache. A black keffiyeh around his neck and, over the stubble of a buzz cut, a white skullcap.

I wished him good day and peace, thus all but exhausting my Arabic. When he replied in Greek, "*Kalimera,*" I automatically answered, "*Ti yineis*"—How's it going?—as if I couldn't see.

"*Mia chara kai dyo tromares,*" he said, the *ch* sound rasping low and throaty, as in Arabic. *For every joy, two troubles*—a standard Greek response. He went on in Greek, "You're bringing news about more bodies on the way?"

"It was calm last night," I said. "Just five or six boats, maybe three hundred people. They landed wet and cold but all right. Not like last week, thank God."

"Sure, why don't we thank God? He has come to expect it."

I never said things like "thank God" anymore. I must have been trying to connect with the man; despite his track suit top, khakis and construction boots, I'd assumed he was a young Muslim priest or lay cleric. Probably, too, I'd meant to reassure him that I wasn't one of those hostile islanders who had lost jobs to the crisis.

I said, "I think your Greek is better than mine."

"Well, I've been here long enough." He explained that his name was Ibrahim, he was from Egypt, he had arrived in Greece ten years ago on a work permit. He'd stayed on as a labourer in Piraeus and eventually came to Lesvos for a construction job. In September—laid off like everyone else—he approached the authorities and volunteered to wash, shroud and bury the bodies of the Muslims drowning nightly in the seas between Turkey and Lesvos. "October was a very busy time, as you probably know," he said. "You are a foreign volunteer?"

"Yes, from America. It's Peter."

"Are you ill? You look as if you need to be sick."

The astringency of the olive was intensifying as it dissolved. I'd been wanting to spit, but I wasn't about to do it while he stood chest-deep in an unfinished grave, telling me about his life.

I talked around the stone, my mouth puckering: "I ate an olive. Off the tree there."

"Ah!" His white incisors shone cleanly, though the eye teeth were yellow. "You thought you could eat them right off the tree! Many volunteers make this mistake."

"No, no, I knew. I was here as a child, a number of times. We—my Greek cousins and I—we used to pick and chew olives, on a..." *On a dare,* I wanted to say but couldn't remember the Greek phrase. "It was a game. We'd see who could last longest before spitting."

"Please, friend, spit now."

I took a few steps toward the dusty, dented car, hawked a few times, then toed dirt over the spatter of violet pulp. The car's hatch was half-open. An old Fiat Panda. As I walked back, the man lifted his hands and gazed around us: "A fine spot here, isn't it? As far from the sea as you can get on this island, or so the villagers tell me. For the sake of the people I'm burying, I'm relieved."

My lapsed Greek, along with his accent, created a kind of satellite delay; I was always a few words behind, and even when I caught up, I wasn't sure I understood.

"They're letting me stay in an abandoned house in the village," he said.

After a moment I said, "Yes, they told me in the camp, but I came straight out here to find you. I figured that after this last week, you'd still be busy."

Eight nights before, a rubber dinghy crammed with Syrian families had capsized a half-hour off Efthalou Beach. The people whose life jackets were genuine were pulled, alive or dead, out of the sea that night or the next morning. The ones wearing fakes had vanished, and then, after bloating and resurfacing, washed ashore.

But some of their belongings had washed up only yesterday.

"I did actually bring you something."

"Foreigners have never lived here before," he said quickly, "let alone a Muslim. Not since the time of the Ottomans. Two nights ago, we had snow."

I unslung my day pack and set it down by my boots. There was a splash of olive pulp on one toe.

"My little house feels a bit empty in the evenings," he pushed on, "especially now with the sun setting so early. Still, it's the first house I've ever had. You have a family, children?"

"Maybe someday," I lied. "I guess you don't, yet?"

"Now more than ever I'd like to. But what woman will have her children with a man whose hands have buried so many...?"

No display of hands to emphasize the point. They hung slack at his sides. I crouched down and unzipped the day pack.

"I do wish they'd chosen a slope," he said. "A slope would be better at this time of year. Drier. I hate seeing water in the graves! Of course, trying to operate the digger on a slope..." He kept speeding up. I was straining to follow. "I use life vests as pillows for them, between the sheet and the earth. For pillows, it doesn't matter if the vests are real or not, so long as they're soft."

Our faces were closer now that I was hunkered down. Faint acne scars on his cheeks above his beard. Behind his lenses, the eyes were intently fixed: the desperate gaze of a castaway.

I reached into the pack. The little rosewood box I'd brought here was swaddled in a toque and a hoodie. "Last week," I said, "we actually found a vest stuffed with..." I didn't know the Greek for bubble wrap. He wasn't listening anyway.

"It's remarkable how efficiently the sea strips them," he said. "It wastes no time at all—and still it is not satisfied! Given a few extra days it removes arms, legs, more."

From the slopes behind him a voice, probably a goatherd's, was calling.

"This one I'm burying, her life vest was filled with ——" (a word I didn't know—possibly bubble wrap?), "which of course is useless for anything *but* a pillow. Still, I won't be using it. Her body needs no pillow."

I was holding the box with two hands, watching his lips move above his beard, waiting for the words to resolve into sense. Resisting the sense. Grateful I was no longer fluent. "I'm sorry to bring you this," I cut in. "I don't even know what you should do with it." I snapped open the box. It might once have held earrings. The burgundy felt lining was stained darker where sea water had leaked in. Nestled on the felt, like pearls, lay three baby teeth that someone had kept—maybe the parents of a child who had died back in Syria, maybe a living child who had saved them and carried them aboard the raft.

"Bury it on its own, maybe?" I suggested.

"God, I suppose, is the only one."

I looked at him.

"Without a broken heart," he said.

I tried to ease the box shut, but the hasp caught with a click.

"I guess this must be a child's grave," I said.

"Of course, yes, I said so! An unknown child."

Ena agnosto paidi. I'd missed that whole phrase. I said, "And I guess it would be wrong to assume that these—that the box—is this child's?"

"Had she been the only one, maybe we could." He took the box from me. Held above the grave, it looked even smaller, the sort of thing in which a child might ceremonially inter the husk of a cicada, or a dead mouse pup found curled in a field. "Still, we should put it somewhere. And it might be hers. Thank you for bringing it all this way."

"It's little enough."

"Yes, tiny, it weighs nothing."

"No—I meant it wasn't much to do. Not a long ride. Let me help you finish here. I've been digging a lot at the camp."

"What—graves at the camp?"

"No." Extra latrines, I'd meant.

"This one is already bigger than it needs to be," he said.

They lay on a northwest-to-southeast axis, the graves, bearing toward Mecca and the morning sun, the heads of the deceased oriented as if in prayer.

"I can help you carry and put the body in," I said.

"Everything is being performed in accordance with the tradition," he said. "So, 'by Muslim hands alone.' I am even reciting the funeral prayer. To me, these things matter little now, but to them, I think..."

He put the box in his track suit pocket. I got up.

"I understand," I said, relieved.

If I'd meant my little courier run as another crumb of expiation, I'd failed. If I'd meant my service here on the island as a larger penance, that too had fallen short. As had "community service" back home, as had my suspended sentence. I told him nothing about the accident, of course, the details no more pressing for being mine. Maybe there is no penance, only time passing. A child's death is a tragedy back home, but a thousand deaths—if they happen here—are just data for a churning news engine. Even the drowned boy in that famous photo: not a person but a figure surfacing, briefly triaged from the unnumbered and unnamed.

"Did you know that in certain places they bury people standing up, just as I am now? Of course, this hole"—he used the Greek for hole, not grave—"would need to be deeper."

The music of December in the islands was drifting down from the slopes: a melody of goat bells, a backbeat of oak switches slapped against branches to bring down the fruit. He was speaking to me again, more slowly. As if understanding, I nodded.

Wash her.

Water and... snow?

Home. Her home.

I bent down to shake his cool, dirt-seamed hand and wished him well.

As I gripped the scooter handlebars, I glanced back. He was holding the shovel, standing in the grave. I walked the machine out through the grove and by the time I reached the road, his last phrases—a prayer, one he would now recite in Arabic?—had settled into sense.

Wash her with water and snow and hail...
Give her a home better than her home.

Acknowledgements

"Five Paintings of the New Japan," "The Beautiful Tennessee Waltz," and "'A Man with No Master...'" were originally published in *Flight Paths of the Emperor* (The Porcupine's Quill, 1992).

"Townsmen of a Stiller Town" was originally published in *On earth as it is* (The Porcupine's Quill, 1995).

"Shared Room on Union," "Those Who Would Be More," "The Dead Are More Visible," "Noughts & Crosses," and "Nearing the Sea, Superior" were originally published in *The Dead Are More Visible* (Knopf Canada, 2012).

"Instructions for the Drowning," "Professions of Love," "Expecting," "Everything Turns Away," "Notes Toward a New Theory of Tears," and "As If in Prayer" were originally published in *Instructions for the Drowning* (Biblioasis, 2023).

STEVEN HEIGHTON (1961–2022) was a writer and musician. His twenty previous books include the novels *Afterlands*, a *New York Times Book Review* Editor's Choice, and the bestselling *The Shadow Boxer*; the Writers' Trust Hilary Weston Prize finalist memoir *Reaching Mithymna: Among the Volunteers and Refugees on Lesvos*; and *The Waking Comes Late*, winner of the Governor General's Award for Poetry.